THE YEAR OF UH
by Jud Widing

Chelsie,

  Thank you so much! I hope you like the rest of the book as much as the "jealosy" line!

copyright © 2017 by Jud Widing
All rights reserved.

designed by Boy Bison
boybisonzines@gmail.com / instagram @boybisonzines

This book or any portion thereof may not be reproduced or used in any manner whatsoever without the express written permission of Jud Widing except for the use of brief quotations in a book review.

Chelsie,

Thank you so much! I hope you like the rest of the book as much as the 'jealosy' line!

PROLOGUE
ARRIVAL

Twenty-eight hours after Nur bade Africa farewell, here came America, rushing up to say 'howdy' at 200 kilometers an hour. The landing was a bit rough – not that she had much to compare it to, this being her second-ever flight. A laconic voice flopped from the speakers, the classic American airline pilot's drawl that set one wondering if perhaps he wouldn't have preferred they crashed after all. The other passengers laughed, so the message was probably something to do with the graceless conclusion to an otherwise smooth journey – not that Nur had understood a word of it, English being her second-ever language.

Or at least it *will* be, once she learns it.

As the Boeing 777 whined and whistled its way to the gate, Nur took a trip down memory lane, to her first-ever flight. Was it really twenty-eight hours ago that she waved goodbye to her parents, boarded an Airbus to Paris, and left Seychelles for the very first time?

Sure. Twenty-eight hours ago, she was in Africa,

halfway around the world. Twenty-eight hours, objectively. *Subjectively*, though, the journey lasted more in the ballpark of a million billion hours. She was well educated, and knew all about time zones. But she'd never *experienced* them before. Education is fine and good and necessary, but there's a stark difference between learning all about voltages and conduction, and sticking a fork in an electrical socket.

Witness: she left Seychelles at 10 pm. Ten hours later, she arrived in Paris at 6 am. Ten hours after *that*, she departed Paris at 4 pm and, after another seven hours, arrived in Boston at 6 pm.

Perhaps it wouldn't have been so bad had she been able to sleep. But she hadn't, so it was. This was hardly surprising; she was a naturally anxious person, and it wasn't as though she'd expected her neuroses to lighten up at 30,000 feet. But she was also a naturally sleepy person, and had made a point of abstaining from caffeine and all its works (its glorious, glorious works) in the day prior to her departure. What this decision failed to yield in slumber, it more than made up for in irritability and headache.

Speaking of irritability and headache, Nur felt a finger jabbing at her upper arm. "We're here," hissed the finger, in Seychellois Creole. "Nur. We're here."

Nur De Dernberg suddenly felt as if she could sleep forever. She found that her sister Deirdre had that effect on her.

"I know we are," Nur replied as patiently as she could.

Jab. "Hey." Jab. "Nur." Jab. "Hey." Jab.

"What is it?"

"We made it."

Nur flopped her head forward, turning skeptical eyes towards her fifteen-year-old sister. Sincerity and emotion weren't Deirdre's style, and yet there was quite a bit of both swirling around those three words. Nur was familiar with this game, though: now it was a simple matter of teasing out the tiring irony of a setup, or waiting for the snarky punchline...but neither came. They'd talked about America plenty in their younger years, and now that they were here, Nur saw nothing but dewy earnestness in her sister's eyes. It was catching.

"We made it," Nur confirmed warmly. With some effort, she peeled a white-knuckled claw from the armrest and patted Deirdre's smaller, softer paw.

They both slept soundly the rest of the way to the gate.

The pale-faced boy in the too-tight jacket told them to have a nice night. Something to that effect. Nur wasn't *completely* clueless when it came to English. It was, after all, an official language of Seychelles. She'd picked up key phrases here and there, bits and pieces, but she'd never studied it. Which was just as well, because if she *had* studied it in Seychelles, maybe her parents wouldn't have been as inclined to let her study it in America for a year.

Thanks to some helpfully pictographic signage, the De Dernberg sisters staggered their way down fluorescent-lit hallways to reach the baggage claim. From there it was a matter of looking at the flight number (trusty numbers, the universal language!) and tracking down the carousel displaying three matching figures.

It was a no go on the matching numbers, but Deirdre spotted a young woman with a bright blue Mohawk who had been on their flight, standing purposefully in front of a stationary belt. As they fell in behind her, Nur reflected that there's more than one way to sheer a sheep.

As they sat on a chilly mesh bench, waiting for the carousel to groan to life, Nur tried to listen in on neighboring conversations. Not being *completely* clueless regarding English, she figured she'd be able to make out some snippets of the overheard exchanges. Best as she could tell, the primary thrust of the chatter was 'blarb blarb blarb blarb'.

So while not *completely* clueless, she quickly came to learn that she was *almost entirely, to such an extent that perhaps rounding up to 'completely' would not be unreasonable*…clueless.

Fortunately, there is a second universal language, and it is industrial sounds.

BBBBBRRRRRRZZZZZZ, the baggage carousel informed the assembled. It thoughtfully accommodated the hearing impaired by spinning a little red light, such as might be found on an ambulance for clowns. Nur retired her voyeuristic ambitions and rose to her feet, gesturing to the bulky backpacks they'd lugged onto (and, more importantly, off of) the plane with them.

"Stay here and watch our stuff?" It was an order, but the only way to prevent Deidre's out-of-hand dismissal of these injunctions was to end the sentence an octave higher than where it began.

"M*hmmmmm*," the younger replied, her typical truculence having returned with a vengeance. Nur started to roll her eyes, but wound up double taking as Deidre pulled a pack of gum from her bag and plucked out one minty-fresh stick. It was an American brand, and they hadn't stopped to buy anything since debarking.

They had walked past a few cart vendors, though.

They had all but *brushed* past them.

Nur finished rolling her eyes, but with an extra

oomph the first go-round had been lacking. She couldn't well snatch the gum from her sister, march back and return it to whatever vendor she'd stolen it from. For one, she wouldn't know which vendor it was. For two, she wouldn't be able to communicate the concept *my troublemaking sister stole this gum from you, she does this a lot and I apologize that I was not vigilant enough to have stopped her from doing it in the first place, please forgive both of us, I would pay you for it but I only have enough for a taxi cab and I need that taxi cab.*

She did know how to say "We're very sorry, your room will be ready shortly" in English, but she wasn't sure which sounds corresponded to which semantic concepts. Getting it wrong back in the De Dernberg Towers was no biggie, as context clues filled in the blanks. The airport was a setting less conducive to self-correcting mistranslations.

Anyway, there was a third reason; the big angry red signs that, even in their incomprehensibility, signaled that going back the way they'd just come was no longer a viable option. And, finally, reason the fourth: here came the checked bags, somersaulting down onto the carousel.

Nur watched as travelers to her left and right rushed forward to yank their bags from the scuffed merry-go-round. The woman with the bright blue Mohawk grabbed a bag covered in patches and buckles and zippers, a minority of which appeared to serve any practical function.

The perennial fear of fliers made Nur's acquaintance then; she imagined their bags being left at the layover, sagging on the Parisian tarmac, under the weight of a torrential downpour as the lights of her 777 shrank into the dark of the night (she departed on a clear afternoon, but nevermind that). Wild coyotes came then (not zoologically accurate, but nevermind that either), to tear open the luggage by the light of the full moon (visible despite the swollen rainclouds, but this too should never be minded) and make a nest of the priceless valuables inside (she didn't have any valuables, and what she did have was all easily priced, but minding of this detail, as with the others, should happen never).

At last, Deirdre's bag emerged from the mysterious netherworld beneath the belt. It Plinko'd off a few other bags before *thunk*ing onto the silver lip of the carousel.

Nur knew "excuse me", and used it liberally as she slunk her way between her fellow travelers to meet the valise. The throng had thinned since that red light started spinning, but those remaining graciously gave Nur room to maneuver.

She picked a spot a few feet in front of Deirdre's case and waited a few seconds with her hand outstretched. Letting the belt do most of the work, she slipped her fingers through the handle and pulled.

After about five clumsy steps backward, she managed to extricate her fingers from the handle. Walking alongside the bag, which as far as she could ascertain was full of anvils and bowling balls, she reassessed her approach. She paused a moment, falling behind the bag a step, then clutched the handle with both hands and yanked. The idea was to use its forward motion in her favor, to inch it up and over the side of the lip. The practice was to hurt her back.

She paced the bag all the way around the carousel, until Deirdre was back in sight, chewing her gum with her mouth open, as she did when she wanted to be annoying, which was just about always. Mercifully, Nur was too far away to hear that moist, breathy *aaal aaal aaal* sound her sister made a point of making. Nur hoped that as Deirdre grew up, they could share more moments like the one that passed between them just after they touched down. But until that time, she would continue to indulge that fantasy in which she woke up one inverted summer's dawn, being, and having always been, an only child.

Hobbling after the bag, one hand wrapped impotently around the handle, Nur called to Deirdre at the apotheosis of her orbit. "Why is your luggage so heavy?!"

aaal aaal, now Nur could hear it. Ugh.

"It's not!" Deirdre called back.

"It is!"

"No, you're just weak!"

Nur straightened up, and let the luggage get away from her. "Then why don't you come and lift it, with those big heroic muscles of yours!"

Deirdre shrugged. "You told me to stay here and watch the stuff!" *aaal aaal aaal.* "Ask for help!"

Ah, that's what it was. Nur didn't know *how* to ask for help, and Deirdre *knew* that Nur didn't know how. She just wanted to make her big sister feel a fool. Well, she'd just see about that!

Nur dashed after the bag, clutched the top handle in one hand and the side handle in the other, and lifted from the legs. Groaning a bit despite herself, she managed to conscript her entire body into the effort of hoisting the bag over the silver rim and onto the buffed linoleum.

It fell with a satisfying *thud*, and she managed to keep herself from doing the same. She wiped a hand across her brow and it came back sweaty, which tempered her pride. But still, she'd manag-

"Blarb blarb *blarb*," said a tall, muscular man next to her.

He sounded friendly enough, but Nur wasn't about to venture one of her very limited responses without knowing what the prompt was. She settled on "hm?"

The flurry of blarbs coalesced into words. Unfortunately, the words still didn't make any sense.

"Sath bym gat, am," he repeated. Nur despaired of ever learning such a strange and garbled language.

The man pointed to Deirdre's bag.

No thanks, I've got it, is what Nur wanted to say. But she couldn't. So she settled on a negatory "m-mm".

The man pointed again, with slightly more insistence, as though that would clear up the confusion. And, as it happened, it did.

Nur took another look at the impedimenta that had claimed the sweat of her brow, and despaired once again. It was very nearly the same as Deirdre's, but…

She slipped back into the comfortable blanket of Seychellois Creole. "Oh hell, this isn't even the right one!"

As the big man took his bag and strode easily through the automatic glass doors, Nur turned back to Deirdre, whose sticky, mint-green grin communicated knowledge that it had been the wrong bag all along. Nur wondered how hard it was to make somebody disappear in Boston (if American movies were to be believed, the answer was *not very*).

The De Dernberg Sisters, in America at last. They made it.

CHAPTER 1

Their first real glimpse of the city was by the peeled citrus glow of the setting sun. Most of the eventide fireworks had gone up while the cab was whisking them through a long tunnel, and they emerged just in time to see the show.

Zipping through the narrow streets of a low, Italian-looking district, they rounded a corner and came out at an open, paved park. The view wasn't anything special in and of itself: a smattering of skyscrapers (nothing of a scale that couldn't be seen in Seychelles; one might get closer to the mark by calling them 'skyticklers'), vibrant verdure in tight patches, strolling couples snuggling against the first cool sighs of an outbound August. But the whole was greater than the sum of its parts; this was a vista to bridge that pesky divide between education and experience. She'd read all about Boston in the weeks (oh who was she kidding, *months*) prior to their visit. Now, in this long-shadowed glimpse, she was finally getting to meet the object of her fascination.

She liked what she saw. It felt...cozy. Not the way

she'd expected to be describing an American city, but there it was. Warmth flooded her weary mind. She didn't even notice she was smiling until her cheeks started to hurt. Her spirits were high, so it was with great trepidation that she turned towards her sister.

Deirdre was staring out the window, elbow propped against the glass and the beveled edge just below it, head hanging limply in her palm. Whether she was bored or angry or what, Nur could never guess, and she wasn't about to try. Deirdre'd be in the same mood later. For now, Nur just wanted to enjoy the ride. And she did.

The cabbie parked at the curb and turned back to the sisters. "Sill ihp heysh ahl ni repop," he said in what Nur could only assume from her reading was a pronounced New Englander accent.

"We…don't speak English." She knew *that* in English, but hated to use it. American cities were dangerous places, from what she'd read, especially for girls aged nineteen and fifteen. Highlighting one's inability to make sense of the city was one step removed from bunching one's crisp cash into balls, throwing it at people's heads and shouting "Here, *you* take it."

Then again, if the cabbie hadn't guessed they didn't speak English when they mutely tumbled into the backseat and handed him a well-thumbed piece of paper with nothing but an address and the words "PLEASE THANK YOU" on it, the thought of perfidy would probably never occur to him without a full-color diagram showing him the steps. If he were going to take advantage of them, he'd have done it already.

And as the squat, two-story pastel-yellow shingled edifice outside the window looked an awful lot like the pictures Nur had seen of her uncle's house, the cabbie appeared to be honest.

Honest and bright aren't the same thing, though. The cabbie pondered "we don't speak English" for a moment, before replying by repeating himself, but louder and slower.

"SILL IHP HEYSH...AHL NI REPOP."

Deirdre sprang back to life, whirling on the well-meaning cabbie with loud, slow Seychellois Creole. "WE DON'T SPEAK ENGLISH, SHE SAID."

Nur grimaced. The cabbie shrugged, popped the trunk, and got out of the cab. Nur followed suit before Deirdre had a chance to explain herself. She wasn't interested in hearing it.

After a mercifully brief round of 'cabbie tries to call their bluff on not speaking English', Nur paid and sent the kindly buffoon on his way. They schlepped their luggage up the steps to the front door. Deirdre lunged forward and rang the doorbell, then fell back in with a surprised Nur.

Nur was a surprised Nur because that's how Deirdre *used* to be - she *used* to be downright effusive, bubbly and giggly and fired up about life. The type to rush forward and press buttons, just to see what they did – whether they lit up or beeped or bingle-jingled – that was who Deirdre *used* to be. Curious, excited to learn. Post-puberty Deirdre was gloomy, and Nur couldn't understand why. It was exhausting, being around her. She still loved her sister, but that love was slowly morphing into the instrumental 'yes I will pick you up when you fall but I don't actually want to talk to you about it' love found only amongst blood relatives who would never be a part of each other's lives were it not for the accident of birth.

Perhaps a year abroad will bring back the old Deirdre, Nur thought to herself. The thought was equal parts meditation and incantation.

The windowed door in front of them swung open on the whitest woman on the planet. "WELCOME TO AMERICA!" their Aunt Amy screamed in clunky but functional Seychellois Creole. Their little ginger aunt (aunt by marriage, naturally; Nur and her family had dark, smooth skin) snapped her arms out, grabbed each sister by the shoulder and yanked them inside.

The prevailing sensibility of the house was an uneasy rapprochement between traditional Seychellois (which is itself an even uneasier compromise between African and Colonial styles) and classic New England. This is to say, it was a mess. Palm fronds cast long, lazy shadows on bescribbled baseball memorabilia, buttoned leather and wicker stood arm-to-arm like reluctant buddy cops on the case, and most explosively, the current flag of Seychelles (adopted in 1996, a mere 20 years after the country attained Independence) hung next to gilt-framed oil paintings of the sorts of men who were all about Independence, albeit for people who looked more like Amy and less like Nur and her family.

It was a collision of cultures, on the intersection of national pride and interior design. There were no survivors.

"Ah, what a lovely home you have," Nur bluffed like a champ.

Amy beamed proudly at this. Her glee was infectious, to such an extent that Nur began to believe her pro-forma compliment. Come to think of it, it was, in its own peculiar way, a very lovely home. Amy absolutely owned the space and all its idiosyncrasies, and that confidence bled into the walls.

That was Aunt Amy, anyway. None of this tracked with what she'd heard of her Uncle…

"Why thank you!" Amy bellowed in her charmingly labored Creole, learned at a late age for love.

Deirdre gestured back towards the door. "Should we leave our suitcases on the front step?" she mumbled.

"Anywhere you like!" Amy opened a drawer on a decidedly Colonial side table and fussed around for a moment. "You two must be tired! Jetlag? There's a coffee maker in the kitchen." She pointed. "There's the kitchen! There's also food upstairs."

Amy ran into the kitchen. Leapt back out. "Sorry, scratch that, the food is also in the kitchen! Your *beds* are upstairs. You'll be sharing a room, your Uncle may have mentioned that. But not beds! He's not here right now, your Uncle. Nor am I. He'll be back soon. As will I. I have to go."

Amy hustled over to the coatrack by the door, and swung a heavy trench coat on. "I don't need this," she announced as she removed the coat and put it back on the hook.

"You two can entertain yourselves for a few hours, right? Or go to sleep? If you want to walk around I put T cards on the kitchen. The T is the public transit system here. It closes a little after midnight, so don't stay out too late! Also the cards are *in* the kitchen, not *on*. With the food. The kitchen. The cards. In my hands." And there they were, two tap-cards in her hands. Nur didn't see Amy pick them up, and in all probability, neither did Amy.

"You'll figure it out," their Aunt smiled brightly. It was a smile that said yes, they *would* figure it out, if for no other reason than to not cause such a lovely smile to have been in vain. "I have to go now. Sorry I can't stay longer. Bye bye!"

Amy swung open the door again, and gasped. "Girls, I've found your missing luggage! It's on the porch! Goodbye!" She leapt over the luggage and bounced down the walkway towards the well-lit street.

Nur and Deirdre silently pulled their not-so-missing luggage inside, making a point of locking the door. Deirdre staggered over to the couch and zonked out halfway between the vertical and the horizontal, quite literally falling (while) asleep. Nur made a cursory effort to pick her sister up, that she might take her upstairs and get her into bed, but hoisting somebody else's luggage off the carousel had sapped her strength. The joke was on Deirdre after all. So satisfied, she settled for taking off Deirdre's shoes. Nur went upstairs by herself and slept in a foam bed that changed itself to support her.

CHAPTER 2

Jab. "Hey."
Jab. "Nur."
Jab. "Wake up."
Ja-
"Whu?" Nur inquired.

Deirdre stood beside the bed, a pouty crescent frown plastered on her face. "Wake up," she repeated.

Nur turned over. "I'm sleeping!"

"I know. That's why I want you to wake up."

A dry moan crawled up from deep within Nur. Finding the time disagreeable, it tried to scramble back down. The resultant noise was half air raid siren, half duck.

"There's a no-Creole zone down there. They won't let me talk to them."

Nur rolled onto her back. She slapped her right hand over her eyes. "Can you ask them to cut me in on that?"

"No, because they won't let me talk to them. Dummy." With an unbecoming note of desperation, she tacked on "please come downstairs."

Sigh. "Alright, alright, give me a minute. I'll be right there."

Deirdre nodded, which was as close to a 'thank you' as Nur had expected, and left the room – but not before throwing open the curtains of the *east-facing window.*

"Aaargh!" Nur cried as the sunlight punched her right in the photoreceptors. She threw her other arm up to shield herself like a vampire in a silent movie.

As her pupils shrank to pinpoints, she shimmied up onto her elbows and got her first good look at her room for the next year. In contrast to the rest of the house, it was tastefully Spartan. Two twin beds with a varnished wooden sidetable between them, a bookcase bearing weathered paperbacks and hearty succulents. It was a room unfinished, a room that demanded spare personality from whoever might be occupying it.

She beat a hasty retreat from the room, because that was a demand to which she wasn't sure she could accede.

Nur descended the creaking wooden staircase with the side-to-side swagger of the sleepy. She wrapped a hand around the curling banister and let inertia spin her around 180 degrees towards the kitchen.

The table was small and bright, *bright* orange. Deirdre sat at the end furthest from Nur, facing her. Aunt Amy sat on the right side, attacking a bowl of oatmeal with far too much relish (far too much peanut butter, actually). And at the nearest head of the table, back to Nur, sat Uncle Dr. Bernard De Dernberg. De Dernberg lore spoke of Uncle Dr. Bernard in hushed tones, because it didn't have very many nice things to say about him. He was a man whose reputation preceded him, mostly so it could shake people by the shoulders and say "we've gotta get the hell out of here, *he's right behind me.*" Nur found herself trembling slightly. Her extreme case of the tummy-grumbles played its part, but mostly it was nerves set to rattling at the *thought* of falling under her Uncle's gaze.

Slowly, his head began to turn, exposing the salt-and-pepper temples where color was sacrificed to keep the rest of his slick mane jet-black.

Turning, turning, slowly turning, she saw his clean-shaven cheek, his wide crag of a nose, his downturned lips, still turning, turning, and given those sparkless owl eyes of his, she'd hardly be surprised if his head *kept* turning without his shoulders as chaperone.

Mercifully, he did stop turning, with one arm draped over the back of his chair. Uncle Bernard stared into her eyes and out the other side, and didn't seem overly impressed with what he saw. Sensing a challenge, Nur locked on to his gaze. The floor was a handsome hardwood pa-

She had averted her eyes downward. When had that happened? She wasn't aware of doing so. With great effort, she dragged her eyes up up up to meet Uncle Bernard's.

"Good morning," she ventured in Creole, "thank you so much for allowing us to st-"

"NO," he thundered. Deirdre flinched. Aunt Amy gave a half-apologetic 'that's my Bernard!' shrug and kept on eating. "I am going to say this once, in Creole, so you understand me. You are here to learn English. You're not here to enjoy yourself. You may, but that's incidental. Your parents paid for you to come here, to *learn English.* So from the moment I conclude this sentence, we will *only* speak English in this household."

Uncle Bernard held his stare for a few more

moments. Nur sought desperately for some humanizing imperfection in that thunder-cleft visage. A bit of egg on his chin, or some pink eye, or perhaps it would be too much to hope for a runny nose…still, she checked. Negatory across the board. Uncle Bernard's face was too perfectly *itself* for human flesh, and perhaps that look of eternal frustration was at the injustice of not being born as a slab of marble.

Slowly turning, turning, turning back to his meal, Uncle Bernard quietly resumed eating. Nur looked up to Deirdre, who was trying her best to make an "I told you so" face. Smug satisfaction didn't quite gibe with such fearfully slanted eyebrows.

Nur fixed herself some toast and fruit and sat down. The four ate in silence.

"RAAAAAAAAAAAAOOOOOOOOOOHHHHH!" Deirdre mentioned halfway to the nearest T stop. "I can't take the silence! *'You're not here to enjoy yourself.'* Why is Uncle Bernard being such a butt?"

Nur walked alongside her sister, hands stuffed in her pockets. She too was less than thrilled at the 'English only' edict; the likelihood of meeting anybody else who spoke Seychellois Creole in this city was slim, which meant that until she learned English, the only person Nur would be speaking to *for the next year of her life* would be Deirdre. She wasn't expecting to get on especially well with her uncle, but at least he'd be… well, not Deirdre.

Off to explore the city full of conversations in which they could take no part, they got on the inbound C line at Summit Ave with an absolute minimum of hijinks. They tapped the T card on the T card tapper, the tapper said *beep* and in they went. After ten-odd minutes of jostling, they emerged from the underground Copley

Station as planned. It was a journey completely without incident and therefore not worth mentioning, except to say that it was completely without incident, which for two young people in a strange land utilizing a public transportation system for the first time *is* worth mentioning.

Of all the sights Deirdre had expected to see while climbing the stairs into the sunlight, a giant Romanesque stone church was low down the list. Behind the autumn-tinted leaves of two haphazardly placed trees (urban beautification on a budget), a boxy bell tower stretched upwards from the low, earthy edifice spread along the whole block. Somewhat undercutting the majesty was a shirtless guy with drumsticks banging on an overturned bucket, but Deirdre supposed there was no *right* way to practice one's faith.

Nur, meanwhile, was hardly surprised at the sight of the church. She had done her research, after all. She nudged Deirdre with her elbow and pointed up towards the bell tower. "That's the Old South Church, I'm pretty sure. Built in…1873? It was o-"

"Why do you know that?" Deirdre signaled her level of interest in the answer by pulling out her phone and staring at like it had just insulted her.

"I know because 1873 was also the year Napoleon III died, wh-"

"Not how. *Why.*"

Nur ignored that and turned around, pointing to the structure directly behind them. It was nearly the same height and length as the Old South Church, but sans tower or dome or compensatory adornments of any sort; it was a building with the self-confidence to eschew make-up on a hot date. "That's the Boston Public Library. Look at the size of it! There are over 23 *million* things in there, books and maps and manuscripts and-"

"And we can't read any of them."

"*Yet*," Nur corrected, though she privately wondered if she'd ever be able to do so. "Come on over here…" She guided her screen-gazing sister towards Copley Square, a charming little oasis of green amongst the architectural hodgepodge.

A lifetime of hospitality training made Nur a natural tour guide. She pointed through the patchy copse of well-trimmed trees to another long, squat stone building, this one shaped a bit like a dumbbell with a stomach tumor, its seven stories looking especially unhealthy in the shadow of the only true skyscraper in sight.

"That," Nur chirped, "is the Fairmont-Copley Plaza. Very famous hotel, in this city."

Deirdre darted her eyes up to it for a moment, which on the sliding scale of teenaged millenials was akin to a ten-second *ooooooooooohhhhhhhh!* "So maybe we can work there when our hotel goes down the tubes."

Rather than encourage her sister with the reaction she so clearly wanted, Nur just plowed ahead: "Built in 1912, the F-"

"Again, *why do you know this*?"

There is a time for letting things slide, and a time for trapping sliding things under the heel of your boot and doing the twist.

Nur wheeled around and slapped half-heartedly at Deirdre's phone.

"Hey!" Deirdre cried as she protected her precious smartphone by punching herself in the stomach with it.

"I know these things because I thought it might be a good idea to learn *something* about the city we'll be living in for the next year. Don't you? Can you *try* being open to a different culture?"

"What do you think I'm doing?" Deirdre asked her phone, and then provided the answer: "I'm trying all the Wi-Fi networks without passwords."

"Why do you need Wi-Fi?"

"Because we don't have data here, so we can't do anything witho-"

"No, why do you need Wi-Fi *now*?"

"Got one. Hang on...culture!" Deirdre pointed to the glass-paned skyscraper looming over Nur's precious Fairmont-Copley. "That's the John Hancock Building. Windows used to fall off of that and kill pedestrians."

"What website are you on?"

"Culture.com. Does it matter?"

"That's not culture."

"Fine. It was built in 1976..." Deirdre mockingly pushed an invisible pair of glasses up the bridge of her nose. "...same year as *Rocky* was made."

Nur threw her hands up. "Or how about the same year as Seychelles achieved independence?!"

"Because we're in the *Rocky* city!"

"No we're not! That was Philadelphia!"

"Then what city are we in?"

"Gah! You see? Culture isn't just factoids! It's-"

"You were just spewing a bunch of factoids at m-"

"Yes, I realized immediately after saying that that I contradicted myself. *BUT*, that doesn't make me wrong!"

"Just inconsistent."

Nur walked away. She had to. Had her sister *ever* been this bad? She couldn't recall. The prospect of a year of this, no reprieve, no conversational pallet cleansers...she had to walk away.

"Let's go find the school," she called over her shoulder. The Big Sister instinct told her to follow her voice with a glance to make sure Deirdre was behind her, but at that moment in time she felt quite certain there were worse things than losing her little sister in a strange city. Most of them involved *not* losing her.

CHAPTER 3

Green streaks under golden trees between earth-tone buildings. That, based on Nur's limited wanderings thus far, was Boston in a nutshell. Commonwealth Avenue was no different, save a considerable width that made room for a generous, well-groomed walking path between the two lanes of traffic.

Nur and Deirdre kept to the sidewalk on the side closest to Copley Square.

Trusty numbers ticked higher and higher as they rolled along the gentle southwestern slant of the avenue. The less trustworthy numbers deigned not to show their faces – 160 Commonwealth was easy enough to find, but, just for instance, 168 was nowhere to be found. Presumably it *existed*, and presumably it was this here four-story brownstone – so like the other four-story brownstones that shaded them from the rising sun – but you wouldn't know it without spotting 160 and working from there. *A shoddy job of ordinance enforcement*, Nur decided, because she knew from her reading that American cities had a lot of *ordinances*.

Case in point: The Crabshoe School For The Language of English was 264 Commonwealth. Here were three four-story brownstones, each a slightly different shade of red clay. 262 Commonwealth, its three golden digits gleaming on the glass over the door, was a punchy tennis-court-red. 266 Comm Ave, taking a similar auric pride in its numeric placement, was a purple-tinted burgundy.

And what of the unnumbered, hueless sandpaper-tan intermediary?

A mumbling clutch of young adults loitered on the steps. Their *blarbs* had a warbling, staccato apprehension that Nur understood perfectly. They were saying *this is the place.*

"This is the place," Nur relayed to Deirdre. The younger sister nodded silently, though with a look of attentive engagement she'd heretofore managed to suppress.

"Are you sure?" came her reply, though there was an unmistakable sincerity to the question.

"Yeah. Look." Nur strolled up to the nearest throng of almost-definitely-students, only realizing too late that these were probably not the best people to be talking to. Not just because some of them were standing around puffing on cigarettes (a habit Nur found repulsive even *before* losing a beloved cousin to lung cancer). It was mainly because they were chatting in a language that wasn't English.

Perhaps they were all more comfortable speaking a native tongue, but given the building before which they were sucking tar, more likely was that none of them *could* speak English yet. Nur had a scant few phrases memorized for English, but she had approximately zero for…well, everything other than Seychellois Creole.

Too late to turn back now. She was within chit-chat

distance of the group, which was also second-hand smoking distance. Suppressing a cough, she raked her eyes over them and deployed one of the English phrases she had learned, knowing full well it would come in handy.

"This is...the English Language School?" she inquired. The pronunciation sounded on point to her, but judging by her audience's faces perhaps left something to be desired.

Perhaps that something was an audience that spoke English.

Nur reverted to the old standby of universal conversation. She pointed to the numberless brownstone behind the smokers, coughed slightly, and reiterated her question at three-quarters speed. She was once again met with perplexity, now in double-time.

Oh, wait a second.

She pointed once again, and came at her question from a more direct angle. "Crabshoe?"

"Aaaaaah," the group all said as one. They closed in to a loose huddle, nodded silently for a moment, then turned back to Nur. "Crabshoe," the nearest one repeated with a smile.

Returning his smile, Nur turned back to Deirdre, certain she could feel her brain relaxing as she reracked the groaning weight of *SPEAKING ENGLISH* and flopped into the cozy beanbag of Seychellois Creole (a metaphor that didn't *quite* work, but worked well enough for her taxed, jetlagged mind, thanks very much).

Her brain went *boi-oi-oi-oingggg* as it snapped back to attention. Deirdre was gone.

Nur glanced left, right, and for some reason, up. No Deirdre.

"Did you see where my sister went?" she asked

her new indeterminately Asian friends (she'd really have to get a more specific lock on their provenance *butnotrightnow*) in Seychellois Creole. She knew they wouldn't understand, but, hell, she hadn't thought to work that one out in English. Upon reflection this was a rather grievous and fundamental oversight.

The guy who had parroted "Crabshoe" back to Nur looked genuinely concerned. "Dangsin-eun hangug-eo malhabnikka?" he asked. "O Italiano? Oder Deutsch? Yàome zhōngwén? O Español?"

"Français?" Nur prompted hopefully. She didn't know much of any French, but she could potentially struggle her way through.

The guy shrugged.

Five languages this guy knows, and none of them are useful! Which was a casually chauvinistic thing to think, but now was hardly the time to be confronting personal demons: a sisterly demon was putting more and more distance between them with each passing moment.

Nur pointed to where Deirdre had been standing, made a little walking gesture with her first and second fingers, and shrugged.

"Ili Rossii?" the polyglot dumb-dumb continued. "Of Afrikaans?"

SEVEN LANGUAGES! One of them being Afrikaans, which Nur *didn't* know. This was humiliating.

Nur pointed more forcefully to where Deirdre had been standing, made a very stern little walking gesture with her first and second fingers, and shrugged violently.

Comprehension lit the guy's face. *Finally!* He pointed back up the street, to the northeast, and arced his hand hard to the right. *Around the corner.*

See? Was that so hard? was what she thought. What

she said was "thanks", in English, because she knew that one. She took off at a sprint before the guy had time to reply.

The street down which Deirdre had wandered was called Fairfield. Nur dashed along this glorified alley, emerging onto Newbury. This was smaller than Comm Ave, packed with people wandering amongst the boutique-y storefronts running the length of the street.

Left, right, but this time not up. Still no Deirdre.

Nur imagined returning back to Uncle Dr. Bernard alone, having to look into those frozen eyes and tell him that she lost Deirdre on their first ramble through the city...

Imagination shrank from the task. It was too much. She just wouldn't return home until she found her sister, and that was that.

Ah! She has her phone! I'll just call her and oh curses. With the 'plan' they had, which wasn't much of a plan at all, the De Dernberg's phones were little more than rectangular flashlights without a Wi-Fi network. Even then, calls were out of the question – all they could do was text. To communicate, they'd *both* have to be on a-

"Stupid!" she shouted at her sister, who she spotted halfway up the block, just wandering. Gratifyingly, her sister turned and looked – with mischief on her face. Nur stormed over to her, which took longer than she'd have liked, as she tried to storm politely around strolling couples. She had a lot she wanted to say, but it turned out she was in a non-verbal mood, because when she finally reached Deirdre she slapped her hard on the cheek.

Neither said anything as they walked back to the T. As the train rocketed through the underground portion of their journey, Nur sat in a chair, while Deirdre stood with her back to her sister, facing the window.

The train being lit and the tunnel being not-so-lit, Nur spotted her sister's face in reflection against the window. It was a soft face, slouched and wrinkled. An old, sad face.

Anger, Nur would have expected. But the depth of agony in those eyes, translucent against the rushing dark of the tunnel, unnerved her. Her sister was a mystery, one she wasn't entirely sure she wanted to solve.

The train emerged from the tunnel, and sunlight obliterated the reflection. Now Nur could only see the back of her sister's head. So she thought about other things.

CHAPTER 4

Class began the next day. Nur had pushed for a few days of acclimation, to settle their jetlag and collect their bearings. It wasn't as though staying with their Uncle for a few extra days would cost their parents anything, right?

Probably right, but parental injunction trumped youthful common sense, and so they flew in the day before classes began. Which, thanks to Crabshoe's *very* open enrollment, was a Wednesday.

Nur and Deirdre hadn't exchanged a single word since the slap the day before, and they saw no reason to break their streak of silence. They quietly sauntered up the steps of the ever-coy 264 Comm Ave, continued up a creaking wooden staircase to the second floor, and broke off to enter their respective classrooms (helpfully identified by pieces of primary color construction paper tacked to the doorframes; a great system for everyone who wasn't colorblind). Green for Deirdre, red for Nur. It was with great frustration that Nur realized her class was the beginner's course; Deirdre had placed into one class higher. She must have been studying English back in Seychelles, damnit!

That's cheating, Nur thought, heedless of that thought's absurdity.

The classroom beyond the red paper was small, with twenty-some chairs pressed against the walls, forming a long, hooking horseshoe, with all eyes pointed towards the open center. Nur stepped in and turned to see a well-smudged whiteboard taking up nearly every inch of the fourth wall that wasn't absent, i.e. a door.

"WELCOME" was scrawled across the top of the white board. She knew that word in English, at least.

Turning back to the room, she scanned the motley crew of aspirant English-speakers. Perhaps the class hadn't yet filled out, though the analog clock on the wall insisted that it was 8:58 AM, and class began at 9:00. So, then, maybe the only other people in this class were: a short little blonde woman who was probably from Eastern Europe; a tall, bureaucrat-looking guy with even darker skin than Nur; an older Indian woman who Nur slightly resented straight away because she looked *amazing*, and it was early on a Wednesday so she had no call for looking that good; a youngish guy with greasy hair who was such an Italian stereotype Nur suspected he might have been exiled for crimes against national pride; and the…uh…indeterminately Asian guy Nur had…erm…"spoken to" yesterday.

He looked up, this Asian guy, and smiled. Nur smiled back.

His smile only growing wider, he pointed to his side. Made a little walking gesture with his fingers. Shrugged.

Nur choked back a chuckle. There wasn't really any reason to, other than the room was dead silent, and for some reason the prospect of slicing the quiet with a giggle had *faux-pas* written all over it (though perhaps not in those words).

How best to signal to this guy that she found Deirdre? She considered the 'thumbs up' approach, which she knew was highly American, but she also knew that 'thumbs up' was an offensive gesture in some cultures. She just didn't know *which* cultures. Not that it would have helped if she had; she didn't know which was this guy's culture.

Baffled, Nur settled for raising her arms above her head and touching the tips of her fingers together, making a wide-based pyramid. She wasn't sure what this was supposed to mean, and fortunately, neither did this guy. They *both* chuckled at this. Without thinking about it, Nur walked over to the guy and sat down right next to him.

After a brief moment, the laughter passed, but their eyes lingered.

SLAM.

All eyes snapped to the door, so recently slammed. An egg of a woman with a blonde bob and blobby body surveyed the scant faces in the classroom with legs wide and arms akimbo. She looked like a fairy-tale witch who had been run ragged by round-the-clock gingerbread oven flashbacks, and yet…Nur *immediately* admired her. She was possessed of an undeniable confidence that shouted to the world, *I'm going my way, and you're welcome to tag along, but you're just as welcome to go fly a kite.*

The woman looked directly at Nur and rapped herself hard on sternum with a gnarled, ringed pointer finger. *Bmp bmp.* "My name is Tuppence Crabshoe," she over-enunciated. "Welcome."

And then Tuppence said something else that Nur

couldn't understand. She cocked her eyebrow as hard as she could, because somehow she hadn't thought to learn "I'm sorry, I don't understand" in English either. Yet she had "I'm sorry, breakfast ends at 10:00AM" down cold. Hindsight!

The guy turned to her and pointed to Tuppence. Stating the obvious, he said "Tuppence." He pointed to himself and *ooooh I get it*. "Hyun-Woo," he purred through a knowing smile. Rather than point at Nur, Hyun-Woo let his hand flop backwards, so his fingers (*tiny* fingers, Nur couldn't help but notice) curled gently from his upturned palm, a cross between clutching an invisible apple and baby's first *come hither*. It was a charmingly idiotic gesture.

"Nur," she told him, and *only* him. Whoops. "Ah, Nur," she repeated for the rest of the room.

A wicked grin slice across Tuppence's face. *Now* she was a fairy-tale witch, for certain. "Welcome, Ahnur!" she bellowed with good cheer.

"Welcome, Ahnur!" the rest of the class repeated.

Nur shook her head. "Ah…no." *What is the English word for 'only', or 'just'?* She didn't know it. Instead, she straightened her hand and gave a quick karate chop downwards. "Nur."

"Ahnonur?" Tuppence ventured with the glee of mock discovery. "Welcome Ahnonur!"

"Welcome, Ahnonur!" The class echoed.

What the hell was happening? *Am I being bullied by my teacher?* Nur sighed and shrugged. Tuppence *had* to know Nur's real name – she ran the school! At least, it was named after her! She must have gotten an attendance roster, right? So why was she trying to make Nur look like a fool? She was embarrassed by her name anyway. Why was this person making it worse?

Visions of The Crabshoe School For The Language

Of English as an oasis of pleasant conversation nestled into the screaming muteness of passive-aggressive family and incomprehensible strangers popped like methane bubbles in a tar pit. This place would be no different than the world outside. Perhaps slightly worse, because here she was being evaluated…by somebody who had something against her already? Or something like that? What had she done, that's all she wanted to know. And she *couldn't* know, until she learned.

Well, there was her incentive. Learn English, and she could figure out what Tuppence Crabshoe's problem was. As a bonus, she could perhaps ask her Uncle Dr. Bernard was *his* problem was too! Say, English was going to be very useful in working out why everybody here was always angry all the time!

Sure, she'd be Ahnonur. For now. But the day would come when she could set the record straight, in English. This she solemnly swore to herself.

Note to self: learn English swear words. If you're gonna do it, Nur reflected, do it right.

Class began.

CHAPTER 5

It was great that Nur had some internal impetus to master English, but she hardly needed one. She had more than her fair share of external ones.

Nur De Dernberg was born and raised on Seychelles, an island (well, 115 islands actually, but who's counting) nation floating in the Indian Ocean off the coast of Africa. Specifically, Nur lived on Mahé, the largest of the Seychellois islands, on which was situated the capital of Seychelles, Victoria. Nur didn't live in Victoria, but she often told people that she did, because nobody had ever heard of the town from which she hailed. This was a trick that worked perfectly well back home, but Nur would spend her year in America having mixed feelings about the fact that nobody here seemed to have ever heard about Seychelles at *all*.

Then again, she wasn't mingling with the sorts of people who would have, e.g. people who were on first-name terms with the proprietors of offshore tax havens. Seychelles did a mighty trade in tourism – specifically on Mahé, where tourism was the largest industry – and most of those tourists were sickeningly wealthy. Not so sickening that Nur wouldn't take their money when they palmed her an inordinately large sum for ferrying their bag up to their room, of course. Just sickening enough that she would grimace at their vainglory from the windowless break room.

The De Dernberg Towers were a luxury resort with history. One assumes, at least. The only piece of its history with which Nur was familiar was that in the fall of 2000, as the tech bubble was at its burstiest, the last member of the founding De Dernberg clan decided that tourism in this economy was a chump's game. So he cashed out and left the country to pursue a career in real estate. D'oh.

The Ramatoulaye family was all too happy to buy the De Dernbergs out; they had faith that tourism would recover before they knew it, and more to the point they didn't know what else they could do for a living. So they pinched pennies and tightened belts and took out loans and became the proud proprietors of the De Dernberg Towers.

…yes. The De Dernberg Towers is what the hotel was called, and the De Dernberg Towers it would remain, because after the dust had settled from the great penny/belt/loan maelstrom, the Ramatoulayes didn't have enough money to rebrand. It wasn't just about changing the signage, though they couldn't even afford to do that. The De Dernberg Towers were a know entity in certain circles (the sorts of circles who have animal mask orgies on a weeknight), and there'd need to be a concerted effort to inform said circles that the putative Ramatoulaye Heights was the same great product in a cool new package.

But alas, the coffers were empty. Meanwhile the De Dernberg Towers still trumpeted their status as "a family-run business since 1832" on every website, business card and little cardboard soapbar box. The Ramatoulayes didn't feel like having to explain to everyone who asked - and when your patrons were entitled, understated racists (the Ramatoulaye family certainly didn't *look* Teutonic) as theirs' were, people *would* ask – that management had changed hands but they just didn't have the money to update the signage and no you can't leverage that into a discount blah blah blah. Much cheaper and easier, then, to legally change their last name to "De Dernberg".

Nur was only three years old when this happened, and being told of the change was one of her first memories. Nur Ramatoulaye was a strange name, but it had a certain ring to that she'd always enjoyed. Nur De Dernberg was just plain dumb, and she knew it even then. She cried for what felt like weeks, and she likes to imagine that her sister, who would be born the following year, was given the stupid and pointless name of "Deirdre De Dernberg" simply so Nur wouldn't feel so alone.

Perplexingly, some of the extended Ramatoulaye clan began changing *their* last names. It certainly wasn't for euphonic reasons (exhibit A; Uncle Dr. Bernard De Dernberg). There was another reason for Nur to learn English: she wanted to ask her Uncle what in the blazes was going through his mind.

There had never been any discussion in the De Dernberg nee Ramatoulaye household about what Nur and Deirdre would be doing with their lives. They would be taking over the "family" business, and that was that. Nur was to be administrative, but obnoxiously, Deidre was given more or less free reign to choose her own destiny. She settled for wanting to be the head chef of the hotel. Best as Nur could determine, this decision was reached arbitrarily.

At any rate; the plan had always been for the sisters to visit their Uncle in America and learn English. The plan had not originally been "wait until 2016 to make the journey", but those coffers had been *really* empty.

Better late than never though; the time had finally arrived for Nur and Deirdre to come to America and learn the language common to a large majority of their patrons. They had a year in which to learn said language. Crabshoe's School wasn't exactly expensive, but it wasn't cheap, either. One year for two kids was all the De Dernbergs could afford. Woe to the child who failed to get a firm handle on English after one year.

So said the atmosphere in which the trip was discussed by her family. Nur had never been entirely clear on what sorts of woe would befall the prodigal daughter, but she had no interest in finding out. Grounding a young woman is easy enough, when she lives in a building with concierges and security cameras.

Three hundred and sixty-four days, Nur thought to herself as she tromped down the wooden staircase and out the front door of the school. The sun was just starting to dip behind the cityscape, and the breeze promised a pleasantly crisp evening. But Nur found little comfort in the urban idyll. *Three hundred and sixty-four days to master the language and preserve any semblance of a normal life at home...and all I've managed today is 'hello' and 'goodbye'.* At this rate, what could she reasonably expect to be saying this time next year? Maybe she would be able to chat about the weather with some greater specificity than hot/ light, cold/dark, but she had very little confidence that she would be able to field guest complaints regarding poorly folded bath towels, or whatever the heck those people found to grouse about.

She felt a bump behind her, and didn't need to turn to know it was Deirdre. With arms folded and brow sloped, the young De Dernberg was leaning into the "sulky teen" image so hard that she went straight through and out the other side, into the realm of "disgruntled mime".

Nur smiled, and that only made Deirdre sulkier.

"Goodbye, Nur."

She started and looked up the stairs to see Hyun-Woo traipsing down, trailing some of the other people he'd been smoking with yesterday.

Yuck. She'd forgotten he'd been smoking. Had he been smoking? Or had he just been hanging out with people who were? Not that it mattered, but she tried *very* hard to remember…

Nur started to wave, but stopped herself and instead opted for a casual nod. Why the latter should be preferable to the former, she couldn't say. "Goodbye, Hyun-Woo. Ah!" She held up a finger, then pointed it towards Deirdre. Made a walking gesture with her fingers. Shrugged. "Deirdre."

Hyun-Woo laughed and turned that radiant smile of his onto Deirdre. Nur wished he hadn't, because it was absolutely wasted on her. "Goodbye, Deirdre." Wasting his breath now, too.

Deirdre shrugged as though physically bucking off Hyun-Woo's pleasantries. She opened her mouth to say something, but no words came. Nur silently thanked whatever deities might be in the vicinity, and led her sister back to Uncle Dr. Bernard's house.

CHAPTER 6

Three hundred and fifty-six days.

Nearly a week and a half gone. Nur was experiencing the least appealing aspects of time's relativity: her days ground on and on and on, endless slogs of sullen wordlessness punctuated by spasms of vein-bulgingly taxing linguistic gymnastics. Were she a less empirically minded person, she might well believe that American days lasted closer to 30 hours.

And yet – time in macro was absolutely flying by. She started school eight days ago. Reveille, breakfast, class, home, sleep. Nur pushed for détente with her sister, hoping to entice her out on some fun excursions. There was stuff to do in Boston! They ought to be doing it! Classes only ran for about six hours on weekdays, and Beantown (a cutesy nickname she'd picked up from the Eastern European-looking woman in her class, a Croatian named Dunja) wasn't so large that a cross-city jaunt was infeasible in an evening. Plus, they'd had two days of weekend all to themselves. What had they done with it? Absolutely nothing.

They'd done nothing, and now they had *three hundred and fifty-six days* left. Nur looked at the clock.

12:03 AM, it displayed in merciless red LED.

Scratch that – three hundred and fifty-five days.

It was officially Friday. Their second one in America. Nur wanted to get Deirdre out and about, but she wasn't about to let that vain desire torpedo her free time. There would be an excursion this weekend, and that was all there was to it.

There was slightly more to it than that: Nur really didn't want to go alone. Call it fear or wisdom or something else, but the prospect of waddling off into a strange city in a strange country by herself sent a shiver jolting along her spine. "ILL-ADVISED", hummed the neon sign glowing behind her eyes. That about covered it. It wasn't necessarily a *terrible* idea, but it was ILL-ADVISED.

Deirdre had throttled back on her sulking. Well, the sulking had ebbed, anyway. Whether this was a conscious decision on her part, or merely the result of an inability to sustain such focused self-pity, Nur couldn't guess. Nor did she care to. Either way, Deirdre was now standing right next to Nur (seated, natch) on the T, as opposed to halfway down the car with her face smushed against the window.

"So," Nur ventured in her most affable tone, "I was thinking about maybe going out and doing something fun this weekend. What do you say?"

Deirdre didn't say anything, which Nur had expected. So she soldiered on: "There are all sorts of historical sights – this is a very important city in America's history – but I know you're not so interested in those. So maybe we could figure out something we'd both like to do? It's Friday night in America! There must be live music, or, I don't know, a wh-"

"Why do you want to hang out with me? So you can laugh about me behind my back again?"

The train screeched to a halt not due to some unforeseen obstruction on the tracks, but simply because the T screeched no matter what it was doing. Nur imagined the depot in which the (very stationary) trains were stored overnight was nonetheless a cavern of unholy iron caterwauling. The doors opened, some people got on, some got off, and the T screeched in to motion.

All this time, Nur was attempting to find a handhold in what Deirdre had just said. She hadn't, and so went plummeting from the Sisyphean summit of Conversation With Deirdre.

"What are you talking about?"

Deirdre leaned down to eye level with Nur, her bending back conveniently synchronized with a sharp bleat of the T taking a turn. "That Asian guy! When he came up and talked to you that day, you pointed at me and did some gesture and then you both laughed!"

"…" Good grief. Deirdre had been nursing that little nugget of nothing for over a week. Is *that* why she'd been so sullen this whole time? Nur considered responding with the bemused incredulity she was feeling, but had the presence of mind to catch a scoff in her throat.

Instead, she opted for the cooing, conciliatory approach. "Deirdre, we weren't laughing at you. We were laughing at a misunderstanding we'd had the day before. When you ran off…" Nur explained the whole situation, all the while watching Deirdre rebuilding her sulky bulwarks. *Why do I even bother.* It wasn't a question, just an observation. Still, she hued to the line of 'oh jeez what an unfortunate misunderstanding for which we are both equally culpable, I will apologize to you in the hopes that you will reciprocate (even though I don't feel I've done anything wrong)', hoping that her words might plant a seed of rapprochement (how curious, that Nur thought of her relationship with her sister primarily in terms of politics and warfare) that might grow under the warmth of her demeanor.

Nothing grows overnight, though. Nur would have to be patient. Which was obnoxious, because it was tonight with which she was primarily concerned. She wanted to go somewhere, but she didn't want to go alone. Who else could she ask?

"That Asian guy."

A different kind of shiver jolted along Nur's spine. This one lit up another neon sign in her mind, but this new one sure didn't say "ILL-ADVISED". What *did* it say? She couldn't be certain. It was written in a language she didn't understand yet. But it gave a lovely light.

After a week and a half, Nur could struggle through some very, very basic conversations in English, as long as the interlocutor didn't throw any curveballs. If she asked somebody how they were doing, and they said anything other than "I am doing well", then, well, she wouldn't be.

So trying to invite a boy out (not that she was *asking him out*, obviously, she was just *inviting him to join her* while she went somewhere that just coincidentally happened to be *out*, of course, naturally), a procedure that required great tact and forethought in her native language, was some ways beyond the pale. But the choices were either sit alone with Deirdre in the gloom of Uncle Dr. Bernard's house again (Aunt Amy was a welcome counterbalance, and would let slip some Creole from time to time. But the wry glares of disapproval Bernard threw her way ensured that those strategic slip-ups remained unidirectional), or potentially embarrass herself by asking this guy o…er, well, whatever.

Right! Whatever! It wasn't a big deal! They sat together in class, and often paired up for exercises. They were becoming friends, of course, and friends would go out with ea…friends would have fun togeth…friends would, um, pass time by simultaneously experiencing a given event in a sufficiently narrow geographical proximity as to permit it to be said that they were experiencing said event as a social bloc.

See? Not a big deal!

Tuppence Crabshoe, who despite Nur's hopes had *not* ceded control of the class to another teacher (why the owner of the school was refusing to delegate the beginner's class to somebody lower down the ladder, Nur couldn't imagine) and insisted on continuing to called her "Ahnonur", dismissed them and wished them a "GOOD WEEKEND." The words were written on the whiteboard in big block letters, which she underlined twice for emphasis.

Chairs scraped as students stood. It was imperative that Nur catch Hyun-Woo and ask him before he left the classroom – she wouldn't have the chance to ask him properly if Deirdre was lurking around, trailing grumbling thunderheads along with her.

Granted, there was no reason to remind herself of this imperative, because they were sitting right next to each other. Flagging Hyun-Woo down was a simple matter of looking at him and saying "Um." Still, this simple task seemed so unspeakably urgent that, when the time came, she looked at him (so far so good) and honked another word she'd picked up from fellow students: "HEY."

Hyun-Woo started slightly. "Yes?" he asked. Which, in as much as Nur was familiar with the word "Yes", didn't make very much sense to her. But it was already clear that Hyun-Woo was picking up English far more easily than anybody else in the class. Nur had heard that after one is fluent in multiple languages, acquiring new ones became a matter of less and less difficulty… which hardly seemed fair. Hyun-Woo already spoke a million languages – he didn't need one more! Why not let people like Nur have it? Why-

Education isn't zero-sum, you dummy. Now quit stalling and focus.

She cleared her throat. Oh, blast it all, she ought to have looked up some relevant words in the Creole-English dictionary!

But you didn't know you were going to ask him until you were already on the train.

Well then she should have the dictionary with her at all times, shouldn't she? And besides, she might not have *known* she was going to ask him until the T ride in. But that doesn't mean she hadn't been thinking about it, in the back of her mind…

Stop talking to yourself and talk to HIM!

Alright, alright! Jeez!

Hyun-Woo was staring at her with a look of focused concern. How long had she been staring at *him*? And how vacant must she have looked, as she bickered with her brain?

You are *your brain.*

Shut up.

"We go to…" where could they go? What places were there to go that she knew how to convey in English, wh-

"There are over 23 million things in there-"

"…the library?" Granted, not much of an adventure,

since it was all of a five-minute walk from the school. And, really, that was a thing she could probably have done herself. She didn't expect a library to be one of the dangerous corners of the city. She really should have worked out something better ahead of time, but now it was out.

Hyun-Woo smiled at her, a curtain of his thin black hair flopping rakishly across his forehead. What a smile! His upper teeth were perfect, straight and white. His lower teeth were just as white, but ever so slightly crooked, as though he'd leased his braces and hadn't been able to make the final payments. The dental idiosyncrasy was charming, and paired up with the cute little dimples set high up on his cheeks, th-

Friends friends just friends don't make it weird you don't even know this guy

He made an expansive gesture with his hands. "The Boston Public Library?"

"Yes," she nodded, using that word as an affirmative, the way she understood it to be used. "Tonight." She tapped her bare, watchless wrist. "Seven o'clock?"

Hyun-Woo nodded back. "Seven o'clock."

Nur nodded back to *his* nod. Or maybe she hadn't stopped nodding from before. Who could tell.

Tuppence Crabshoe, that's who. She'd been standing by the door, watching them like a sinister cross between Dr. Frankenstein and Geppetto. Nur gave her a "Not a big deal!" face and slipped out of the room.

Deirdre was waiting outside. Nur bounded down the stairs towards her, which enthusiasm caught her sister completely off guard.

"Come on!" Nur shouted over her shoulder as she practically skipped down the block. "Let's get you home!" There was just enough time for Nur to run home, drop off her sister, get changed and head back in to town. Deirdre had mocked her for packing the nice dress, but Nur was going to get the last laugh.

CHAPTER 7

He knows I wanted to meet at the library, *right? And not at the school?*

Does he know where *in the library I wanted to meet? Do I?*

Nur spent the train ride back into the city imagining all of the ways the meeting could go wrong. That's how it felt, anyway. So what a pleasant surprise it was to discover that she hadn't imagined literally *all* of the ways.

The Boston Public Library was closed, and had been since five o'clock.

Hadn't seen that one coming. Perhaps should have; alas, did not.

The universe was round, last Nur had heard, so she looked forward to the day when her hindsight reached back, wrapped its way around the fullness of eternity and returned to her from the other side. On that day, she might be able to boast of something approaching foresight. Thus, she looked forward to it. Or backward. Or something.

Until that day, she would be here, sitting in a lovely

white cocktail dress (upscale but casual, low-cut but tasteful) on the steps of the Boston Public Library's Dartmoth Street entrance, elbows on her knees, head in her hands. A group of rowdy boys passed by, and one shouted something in a tone that struck her as less than gentlemanly. She chose to believe it was "you are overdressed for the Library, which is closed, but your dress is still adorable and flattering". She was reasonably sure that wasn't what he'd actually said.

7:04. Maybe Hyun-Woo had gone to the school, or one of the other entrances. It was a *big* Library after all. And the *whole big thing* was closed.

Disaster.

"Nur!"

She was up on her feet like a shot, or two shots, thanks to the cracking of her knees. *I hope he didn't hear that,* she wished inexplicably. What would it matter if he *did*?

He came trotting up the steps, wearing exactly the same thing he'd been wearing to class. A nice off-white button up shirt, olive green pants. He'd been well dressed to begin with, but Nur still felt slightly foolish for having changed her clothes for a trip to the library.

"Hey!" he said as he made a show of looking at her dress, though he spun it out into "heeeeeeey!" Thankfully, there was nothing lecherous about his gaze. As most all women are, she was cognizant of how quickly the sun could set on even the most jovial of strolls. Of course not all men were of *that sort*, but there was often no way to know who was until the shadows had claimed their quarry.

She returned his smile, envying him, as she did all men, that he almost certainly had no such thoughts poisoning his pleasant evenings out. Once upon a time she would try to parse this feeling, to see if there was perhaps a hint of antipathy in it. She hadn't bothered with doing that in quite a while – she was well-accustomed to their obliviousness.

"Great!" he said, boldly offering her two thumbs up (for all he knew, she was from the sort of culture where a raised thumb meant 'I have lain with your most cherished female relation and found the experience unsatisfactory'). She gave a coy little curtsey, *like an idiot, what are you doing Nur,* and quickly recovered with another great popping of the knees. Perhaps she was being overly self-conscious, but very little was breaking her way this evening.

Nur pointed over her shoulder. "Library is closed." She knew enough, from her preliminary attempts at English study back in Seychelles and her nine days of intensive immersion, to know that "Library is closed" was syntactically graceless. But never mind that; she had a thought in her head which she conveyed in a language not her own, in a real-world context. This was a thrilling development.

So thrilling, in fact, that she nearly forgot that Library was closed.

"Aw," Hyun-Woo moped. But not for long – he took out his phone, punched a few buttons, and then gestured for Nur to follow him. Which she did, marveling that his phone apparently worked perfectly well without the ball and chain of free internet (*oof, what a child of my generation I am*). He led her back to Boylston, where they took a left and walked for several blocks. She was just starting to wonder where, precisely, they were going, when he gestured for them to cross the street. As they stepped out in the middle of the street, which was jay-walking, which was a crime, nine days in America and she was already committing crimes, which was insane because she was well aware of the state of American prisons…those thoughts vanished because as they stepped out, Hyun-Woo took her hand as though he'd been doing it every day for years.

That's when she knew the evening had changed. The original plan was to go on a little expedition with her sister, and here she was, *out* with a *guy*.

Correction: getting *drinks* with a *guy*.

He walked her right up to a bar, so packed that it spilled out onto the street, and made a 'how did I do?' face.

Nur almost gave him a thumbs up. But then she didn't, because Correction The Second: she was *not* getting *drinks* with a *guy*.

Because the drinking age in America was 21. Nur wasn't a big drinker, but she'd had a few in her time, and all of those had been legal. The drinking age in Seychelles was 18, and she had an entire year to grow accustomed to ordering adult beverages. She'd nearly forgotten that, for some reason, Americans drew the line at age 21, and it was a very bold red line.

Now goddamnit, *how to convey all of this to him*? She couldn't think of a quick way to do it without him thinking she was trying to shirk him. She *wanted* to get a drink with him, but she *couldn't*, legally.

She was taking too long to formulate a response: his puppy-dog face was starting to fall, less spaniel, more basset hound. Nur raised her hands in a placatory gesture (she sincerely hoped he wasn't from a culture in which this meant 'I have taken an informal poll of the individuals living in your vicinity and the consensus is that you emit an unspeakable odor, in case you haven't noticed all the wilted flowers and rotten fruit you leave in your wake')

"No! No, um…"

"Yes?"

Clearly Hyun-Woo had skipped ahead to the

lessons where 'yes' turns out to be an endlessly versatile word, because she didn't understand the way in which he kept deploying it.

"I am nineteen years old!" she shouted as one big word, as though blurting out an answer in a game of charades (which, in a way, she sort of was).

He gave another thumbs up. "I am twenty-two years old!"

Obviously, Hyun-Woo was intelligent. He knew a bunch of languages, and…well, that was the only thing Nur really knew about him, but idiots don't learn bunches of language! Still, though, she couldn't watch people struggling to scale a language barrier without thinking *they look like an idiot,* even as she herself was scrabbling for purchase on the damn thing.

It was a simple matter of him not knowing the drinking age in America. He was old enough, after all, so he probably read about it at some point and forgot. But Nur didn't know how to explain it to him.

This was perhaps the single most frustrating experience of Nur's entire life. That said a lot about the relative good fortune with which she'd navigated her nineteen years on Earth, as well as about how headache-inducingly awful this was.

I know what I want to say. It's sloshing around in my braincase. BUT I DON'T KNOW HOW TO GET IT OUT.

Hyun-Woo was looking confused. Nur managed to keep herself from slapping her forehead. Instead, she pointed to herself and decided to use the limited vocabulary she did have.

She pointed back down Boylston, the way the came. "Library is closed at five o'clock." She pointed to her wrist. "Eight o'clock." Shook her head from side to side. "Closed."

He nodded, looking at her like *she* was the idiot. They both thought the other looked like an idiot. This first date was going *very* well.

Oh shit is this a first date? Thoughts and events were all spiraling out in different directions, and at the center was Nur, looking like an idiot.

Too late to go back. The moment of truth: she pointed to the bar. *How do I say 'bar' in English?* Perhaps a plaintive look to Hyun-Woo would bring forth the proper word. After all, he'd known what to type into his phone…

Plaintive look didn't do it. So Nur scrunched her face up like The Thinker for the cheapseats and snapped her outstretched finger.

"Ah!" Hyun-Woo lit up. "That is a bar!"

"Yes!" Nur enthused. "The bar is closed at twenty-one years old." She pointed to herself. "I am nineteen years old." Pointed back to the bar and shook her head from side to side. "Closed."

"AAAH!" It was the Fourth of July on that smooth, dimply face. Comprehension burst and flickered, and then there were those little crinkly ones that were stupid but, in the context of the whole spectacle, were fine, she guessed. "YES!!"

"HA HA!!!" she exploded in kind. The press of an idea yearning but unable to be expressed had been relieved, leaving the expanse of an empty skull ready to be filled by new thoughts.

Nur turned them around, and they strolled back down Boylston. Around Copley Square, she grabbed his hand. They walked that way down to the Boston Common, not talking, not knowing how, simply enjoying the sounds of the cool, dusky city and the warmth of each other's company.

CHAPTER 8

What had happened there?

Nur had gone steady with guys, and Nur had hooked up with guys. She quickly learned that the latter was not for her, but hey, that's what experimentation is for. Finding what works and what doesn't. Point was, she was familiar with how both of those things felt.

Promenading down Boylston Street with her hand cupped in Hyun-Woo's hadn't felt like either.

The gesture was tender. *Intimate*, in such a way that dashing straight to holding hands was a multi-rung leap up her hierarchical ladder of intimacy. To her, kissing a fella was actually quite near the bottom. Making out was a bit of fun. Holding hands was *intimate*. The difference boiled down to physical versus emotional intimacy. The former was a respectable way for two consenting adults to pass the time, if they so chose. The latter was something more, more, so much more. It *meant* something. Physical intimacy could certainly mean something, but it didn't *have* to. Emotional intimacy necessarily implied a deeper connection. That was the way she saw it, at least.

The first time Hyun-Woo had held her hand, they were crossing the street. Perhaps that was why she let him, without giving it too much thought. It was a considerate, albeit anachronistically chivalrous, gesture.

But the *second* time, *she* had taken *his* hand. Still without giving it too much thought! It felt like the thing to do at the time. She had even interlocked her fingers between his, despite the fact that she had always found this approach made walking slightly more difficult (that always made her self-conscious, because it didn't make any sense and what, was she bad at holding hands or something?)

If Hyun-Woo had pushed her against a wall and started getting fresh, she'd probably have not only let him, but reciprocated with even greater enthusiasm. Finally scaling that idiocy-inducing language barrier had elated her, and the valence of said elation had an erotic element, no doubt about it. Who knew communication could be so sexy?

There was neither wallpushing nor freshgetting, though. Just handholding. Ding dong, emotional intimacy, straight away. She'd known him for a little over a week, and to think that was to make a mockery of knowledge as a philosophical concept. What did she actually know about him? Nothing. Literally nothing. He spoke a bunch of languages, seemed nice, and was handsome. She *guessed* he was from Korea, going by his name, but she didn't know for sure. So where was the attraction? She'd run grammar drills with him. There weren't exactly wedding bells pealing in the distance.

And yet, and yet, and yet she'd taken his hand and held the hell out of it. Their stroll was probably a solid thirty or forty minutes, and their grip remained unbroken that entire time.

Was it down to pheromones? He certainly smelled nice, and there was a radiant magnetism about him that she'd found lacking in the few casual relations she'd had in the past. It reminded her of her old boyfriend in a way that wasn't entirely unpleasant, and what a change of pace *that* was...

Over a half-hour of handholding with, for all intents and purposes, a stranger.

What had happened there?

What did it mean?

The T ride back to her Uncle's place wasn't nearly long enough to suss it out. So she utilized the time wondering if Hyun-Woo was running the same sort of play-by-play postgame breakdown.

She used the extra key her Uncle had given her and slipped in through the front door. Her Aunt Amy was nearly horizontal, watching TV and forcing a recliner to live up to its name and then some. She waved jovially. "Fun night out?" she inquired in her herky-jerky Creole. Nur loved her Aunt for not first casting furtive glances over her shoulder, checking for Uncle Dr. Bernard.

Sighing, she cast furtive glances over Aunt Amy's shoulders, checking for Uncle Bernard. She lacked her Aunt's courage in that regard; Uncle Dr. Bernard terrified her. "Yeah," she confirmed in her native tongue, "I met a friend from the school, and we just wandered around a bit." *Man oh man* those words had taste and texture. Chocolate and velvet, respectively. Not red velvet though. None of that bullshit.

Again, Nur loved her Aunt for not waggling her eyebrows saying 'oooooh a friend, really?' or any nonsense like that. Instead, Aunt Amy just nodded. "Are you looking for stuff to do? Stuff as in things. Activities. I'd be more than happy to offer some suggestions for both. All three, really. Stuff, things and activities."

"Thanks," Nur managed through a yawn, "I'd love some! I'd had a hard time coming up with things to do when I asked him…"

Whoops, she thought, but Aunt Amy didn't react in the slightest. *Why is it that the coolest relative I've got isn't actually related to me?* She didn't bothering wasting mental real estate with an obvious answer.

"I'll come up with a list and give it to you tomorrow. I might come up with the list tonight though. Still giving it to you tomorrow. Just one condition though, for the giving." Aunt Amy pulled the lever of her recliner, sliding back up to a regular seated position. It was as close as she'd ever get to sternness, Nur imagined.

"What's that?"

"You have to take your sister out. Sometimes. Not all the times, but some. With your friend, or just the two of you, you and your sister, either way. Just get her out."

Nur smiled archly. "She's annoying you too?"

Whoops again. A look of vague disappointment flickered on Aunt Amy's face, and it was all the more devastating for its formlessness. "No, I haven't seen enough of her to *be* annoyed. Or to be anything. In relation to her, I mean. She's always up in her room. Your room. Both of your rooms. Well, just the one room."

Aunt Amy rose from her seat, because, as Nur had discovered, sometimes movement helped Amy find order in the loose components of coherent thought that were always rattling around her brain. She walked up to Nur, reapproaching her thought from a different angle: "There's a chance you two might never come back to

America. We'd always love to have you, you being both you and your sister. We being us, being your Uncle and I. Your Uncle's asleep but he's still in the 'we' with me." She shook her head once. "But being candid, you and your sister might not ever come back. Deirdre's young, she is, and I think that's why she's so grouchy. But if she wastes her year in America brooding in her room, she's going to regret it for the rest of her life."

Valid points all, but Nur didn't want to be thinking about her sister right now. Her mind was still occupied by Hyun-Woo. Now they were sharing the same headspace, and Nur didn't see any good coming of the combination. "She's *so* tedious, though."

"Now you be candid: weren't you, at that age? Just a little? Tedious?"

Thinking back on it…several memories suggested themselves. And then several more. And more. Alright. Enough with the memories.

Nur nodded. "I suppose I was," she conceded dreamily, as though the time period under discussion was over half a century gone, as opposed to under half a decade. Deirdre *could* be alright, couldn't she? They'd had that moment on the plane, at least. Maybe there was a way to make more of those happen?

More to the point, though, she wanted Aunt Amy's ideas for things to do with Hyun-Woo. Going to a closed public library had worked out alright tonight, but Nur had her hopes on actually *doing something* next time.

She didn't notice that she was taking there being a 'next time' at all for granted. But of course she didn't notice it. That's what taking something for granted means.

"Okay," she allowed, "I'll try to get her out more. I can't make any promises, but I'll try my best."

"Thank you. I say that from myself, naturally, but also from Deirdre. One day she'll thank you too. Probably not for a long time. But eventually."

And, oddly enough, when Aunt Amy asserted this in her benignly confident way, Nur believed it.

CHAPTER 9

As August finally made good on the promise of September, so Deirdre emerged from her cocoon of huffy despondency and spread her gossamer, gossiper wings – a big, bold botherfly.

She'd found out about Hyun-Woo, and Nur had unintentionally blown the whistle on herself.

Not that there was anything on which to blow the whistle.

Sure, Nur had met him outside of class a few more times. These meetings mainly consisted of Hyun-Woo taking Nur somewhere she couldn't get in because of her age, like a boozy bowling alley or concert venue, and then the two of them strolling aimlessly through whatever neighborhood in which their would-be activity was taking place without them. These were pleasant evenings all, and Nur was indeed getting to see the city of Boston, just as she'd wanted. But those niggling concerns that maybe Hyun-Woo was, despite his brilliant multilingualism (and she still hadn't worked out just how many he knew), a bit of a bonehead. Like, after the second or third turn-away, a guy with a high-watt bulb in the attic would probably find a way to call ahead of time and ask if his nineteen year old...friend could get in, or look at their website maybe? Just in case he *were* a bit dim, Nur pressed the case to herself that there was something charming about that. Dimmer lights were always considered more romantic, weren't they?

Not great for reading, admittedly.

Only that metaphor devoured itself, because Hyun-Woo *was* reading. In English. Already! Running a few minutes late for the assigned meet-up time (and having been able, thanks to some helpful Starbucks Wi-Fi, to notify him through a text which read "five minute"), she rounded the corner to find him about half-way through an English language novel. It was a slim volume, and judging the book by its cover (she was still a ways away from tackling aphorisms) looked to be the straightforward sort about big men who used big guns and small words...but it was clearly in English. And he'd been here for a matter of weeks. Nur slipped back around the bend and simply watched him. He wasn't pretending to read the book. He was *reading* it, his eyes tracking along the page at a respectable clip. At one point he stopped, began mouthing a word, and pulled a much larger book out of his backpack and began flipping through. Nur couldn't make it out, and so decided to quit creeping. Upon approach, she recognized the book to be a translation dictionary. He had encountered a word he didn't know and was looking it up. *One word* he didn't know. More stunning was the realization that the dictionary was German-English. He hadn't even gotten a Korean-English one! Which, once again, was sort of dumb, but maybe also made him kind of brilliant? And whatever he was, he was intelligent enough to fold formal study habits into leisure reading.

And then he took her to a trendy little joint full of old board games, that, go figure, served alcohol. And for the fifth time, a big man who had big muscles and a small shirt asked for their ID's, and then frowned at them until they walked away.

A tough nut to crack, was her Hyun-Woo. Which only added a layer of fascination to her infatuation. *Not that he's* my *Hyun-Woo,* she was perhaps a bit too slow to clarify in her mind.

This was all fine and delightful until a Thursday in mid-September when Nur went to class to find Hyun-Woo's seat empty. Empty it remained for the entire day. After classes, waiting for her sister on the stoop of the school, Nur saw Hyun-Woo bouncing down the stairs. She waved to him. He waved back and made straight for her, arms extended like zombies used to do before they were cool. Before she knew quite what was happening, he enveloped her in a hug, which, stop the presses, was unprecedented. They'd never hugged before! Hyun-Woo had been bashful about physical contact; barring that first night out when he took her hand crossing the street, Nur had initiated all of their touching. He never recoiled from it, and he always seemed appreciative (nothing crude - squeezing her hand when she took his, or one time on the T leaning his head on hers, after she'd allowed her head to loll casually onto his shoulder). But he also seemed… cagey about it. Nur had absolutely no problem taking it slow – not that she even knew what the 'it' was. They lov- they *enjoyed* spending time together, but they still knew next to nothing about one another that couldn't be communicated via entry-level linguistics and bug-eyed semaphores. But the strangeness – could she go so far as to say *absurdity*? – of having sustained an emotional intimacy of the sort they'd been nurturing *without* more than a few glancing passes at the physical corollary finally came home to her with the hug.

Was Hyun-Woo ever going to make a goddamned move?

As they leaned back from the hug, Hyun-Woo kept his arms around her shoulders, and for a split second she thought he was going to kiss her. Which would have been a big-time bummer – Nur was not interested in exhibitionism, on either end of the exchange. Making out with somebody was great fun. *Watching* people make out was a hideous, squelching abomination that made Nur wonder if the human race should even exist anymore, if such a nauseating display of puckering and slurping was a part of its propagation.

For once, Nur thanked her lucky stars that he was such a chaste fella. He pulled all the way back, sliding his hands along her back and letting them lay on her shoulders. And then he said something, of which she understood very little.

"Tuppence mot govid me to the punnel acla."

He had a smile on his face, so it was maybe good news? Not quite knowing what was expected of her, she gave him what she hoped was a smile. If *his* face was anything to go on (and unfortunately it was everything she had to go on), what she actually gave him was something between *I hope this looks like a smile* and a death rictus.

She accepted that he was probably working hard to suss out whether or not she was actually a moron, as she had been for him.

"Understand?" He asked, opening his mouth to keep speaking. Nur knew he was going to repeat himself a bit louder and a bit slower, and was disappointed that she had no handkerchiefs or stray socks to stuff into his face before he had the chance.

"Tuppence mot govid me to the punnel acla," he repeated at the same speed and volume as the first time. The smile he got now was more genuine, though evinced no more comprehension.

Deirdre, who had at some point sidled up to Nur, stared at her fingernails with studied indifference (*ugh, she must have picked that gesture up from movies or something*) as she *aaal aaal aaal*ed a hunk of pink, sweet-smelling gum. "He said Tuppence moved him up to one of the more advanced classes," she translated with all due drollery and lip-smacking.

"WHAT?!" Both Deirdre and Hyun-Woo started at this reaction, and she couldn't blame them, but nor could she have helped it. She got to see Hyun-Woo every day at class, and about twice a week outside of it. Take away the class, they'd hardly have any time together!

"Also," Nur continued, which told Deirdre she was once again about to see where one of her sister's thoughts ended without ever getting to learn where it began, "how did you understand that?"

Deirdre relaxed. That *ex nihilo* "also" was easy enough to deal with. "Funny you should ask, I've been attending the Crabshoe School For Th-"

"Right, so have I, so why are ynnnnnnnn," she stopped herself too late. Her mouth got too big for its britches and thought it could bypass her brain, the result being her admitting inferiority to her sister. *You've done it again, Mouth.*

Stunningly, Deirdre *didn't* use the opportunity to gloat. Very matter-of-factly, she shrugged and reminded her sister, "I'm younger, I guess. It's easier for people to learn languages when they're young."

That seemed an insufficient answer, given how little time had passed, but Nur could hardly pay it any attention when there were so many precedents being set. First Hyun-Woo's hug, now Deirdre being not only reasonable but *thoughtful*?! Was there a gas leak in the Crabshoe School? What the hell was going on?

Knowing full well how dangerous this next move was, Nur made it anyway. "Do you think," she asked her sister in the least imploring way she could, "you could tell Hyun-Woo that..."

OBJECTION! cried the brain.

Overruled, returned the mouth, before shaping itself around more ill-advised words: "Could you tell Hyun-Woo that I'm just...I hope we can keep...why are you smiling like that?"

"Like what?"

Well, shit.

Of *course* Deirdre wasn't being nice. She was being *tactical*, to insinuate herself. She had probably suspected that there was something between her sister and that cute Korean fellow, and she knew that all she had to do was present herself as a plausible medium for turning "something" into a two-way bridge of communication.

Nur leapt at the bait headfirst. Rookie mistake! You'd think she'd never had a younger sister before.

The whole way home, Deirdre kept asking questions about Hyun-Woo in a mocking schoolyard croon. Ooooh, what's he *like*, what's his *sign*, is he a good *kisser*. It made her feel pathetic, because she realized she couldn't really *answer* any of these questions.

She felt a powerful attraction to this guy, and she couldn't answer a single one of her sister's stupid questions about him, questions that were intentionally superficial. If only Deirdre knew how much she were hurting her sister…well, she might stop, but then again, she might double down.

The final humiliation was that Nur still wanted to ask Deirdre to serve as interpreter for them. It was an objectively terrible idea…and yet it would make things so much *easier*. She would be able to *have a conversation with him*. If only Deirdre weren't so awful!

All the more reason to learn English quickly and efficiently.

Though that was neither easily said nor done.

CHAPTER 10

Feeling something that resembled – but was not – a pang of regret at her lackadaisical approach to getting Deirdre out of the house, as she had promised Aunt Amy she would, Nur spent more or less the entire weekend with Hyun-Woo. On Saturday she awoke early, ate a breakfast at which a few terse words were exchanged (Nur did her best to speak to Uncle Bernard in English, an effort for which the marble would sometimes warp into a smile, though predictably the more conversationally competent Deirdre kept shtum), and then slipped out of the house and headed into the city.

By the time Nur emerged from the Hynes station, she had made up her mind. Precisely when on the journey the mind was made up, she couldn't say. Not that it mattered. What mattered was that Hyun-Woo was clearly not going to make the first move, which meant that responsibility fell to her. Which was fine by her; Seychelles had the smack of the matriarchy in ways even America didn't, but that was starting to tip in her favor here, wasn't it? Hadn't she read that somewhere? True or not, she'd be doing her part to lean into the incipient tip. And come hell or high water, she'd be doing it this weekend. If she *didn't*, it was all too easy to imagine the tenuous but vivacious bond they shared evaporating as Hyun-Woo began his first full week of the advanced classes. It was time to put up or shut up, and Nur had had more than her fill of shutting up lately, thank you very much.

The difficulty was not in the will, then, but the way. Being as averse to public displays of affection as she was, Nur needed a nice, quiet place to be alone with Hyun-Woo. So where to find one? She didn't rule out Uncle Bernard's house, because she never even considered it. Aunt Amy seemed like the type to be cool with it, but even if she'd lived there alone, Nur felt her tummy go runny at the prospect of rumors floating across the Atlantic, around the Cape of Good Hope, and into the homey halls of the De Dernberg Towers, be it ever so Hopeless.

The senior De Dernbergs had never *explicitly* told Nur that she was to marry a Seychellois man...but it was clear enough. They expected her to take up the reins of the business. That meant they expected her to *stay in Seychelles*. Unless her man were willing to relocate for her, parental approval would not be forthcoming. Which shouldn't have mattered, except it did. Because even once Nur stopped being a direct dependent of her parents, she would forever be one indirectly, for as long as she worked at the Towers. She could always quit, of course. It'd just be a matter of finding new employment. And new housing. All without references, she'd imagine.

So Uncle Bernard's was out in the same way that the front lawn of the White House was out; it had never been in to begin with.

What about Hyun-Woo's place? She didn't actually know where he lived, or with whom he was staying. Plus, well… how quickly the sun could set on even the most jovial of strolls, remember? He seemed like a consummate gentleman and all-around great guy… but there was always that off chance that he *wasn't*. And she would prefer not to tell anybody where she was going, or with whom. So even if he *did* invite her back to *Chez*…whatever Hyun-Woo's last name was (*I've gotta have a straight-up informational session with this guy, as soon as I can get the vocabulary down…*), she'd have to decline. And that would probably be seen as a great discouragement, a mixing of the messages. All the more reason to make the move sooner rather than later.

So when? Where? How?

On the bright side, at least 'what' and 'why' were easy.

They walked over to the Prudential Center and went up the eponymous tower. The views were staggering, though like the skyline of the city itself, didn't seem like they *ought* to have been impressive as they were. It had something to do with being fifty-two stories above a city that seemed mostly content with four or five. The skywalk ran the full perimeter of the Pru, and the morning had the crisp clarity unique to mornings after a rain long in the offing. They could see for miles, perhaps dozens, perhaps a hundred or a thousand. It hardly seemed to matter; there was so much to see from up here, there wasn't a chance of taking it all in. Many of the trees still held their leaves, leaves which in turn held the hues of the Promethean sunrise that had only just yielded to the more traditional blues of the afternoon, and so Boston resembled nothing so much as a handful of mighty rocks standing their ground against an endless floe of molten lava. In a matter of weeks the fire would cool and calcify, but the city would remain. And in case there was any doubt, behind them was a mini-museum full of pictures and trinkets, of which they understood the general import if not the finer details, like 'what the hell is this supposed to be'.

So much for history: the present rolled out in all directions. *There* was the John Hancock building, to which Deirdre had taken a shine upon discovering that it used to shed fatal panes of glass. Up *that way* was where Uncle Bernard lived, a fact that Nur was proud of being able to convey. She did have to say "my house is there", which was 100% inaccurate because it wasn't her house and, now that she was looking at it, Uncle Bernard's was actually probably more *that-a-way*.

Hyun-Woo ran a finger across the skyline, following it around to just about the other side of the Skywalk. Eventually, it settled on a particularly flushed patch of the city. "My house is *there*," he stated with a confidence that implied a more respectable percentage of accuracy. He was clearly using words he knew Nur would understand (which was considerate but, if she was being honest, also kind of obnoxious and patronizing), but something about the declarative tone made Nur think that perhaps Hyun-Woo *did* have his own place here. Or *there*, as the case may have been.

They could go there to be alone…eventually. Once she could turn *Hyun-Woo is probably not a sex murderer* into *Hyun-Woo is ~~probably~~ not a sex murderer*. Or, at the very least, *Hyun-Woo is <u>probably</u> not a sex murderer*, which she happened to believe was the best you could do until you'd been going steady with somebody for, oh, a few years or so.

A hundred-mile view of a crisp morning…this

would be a *great* spot for a first kiss, wouldn't it?

As if in response, a portly tourist shouldered up to the window next to them. Too many people. There were too many people. Nur spotted a few in loving embraces, even a few locking lips, and bully for them. She was hardly a prude herself, but still, something about public affection rubbed her the wrong way, when she would have much preferred it not be rubbing her *any* way, at least until they were in a space of relative privacy.

Split the difference, then. Absolute privacy would be exceedingly hard to come by. But *relative* privacy must be doable, right? Somewhere they could get away from the sweaty press of humanity that seemed to fill every inch of public space in an American city, somewhere they could perhaps feel a different sort of sweaty press of humanity that might, if not fill every inch of public space, then scratch the itch around a pubic space.

Depending on which way the wind was blowing, Nur could be a buttoned-up prude or a button-popping lecher. It was good to have range, she reflected as they resumed their meandering lap around the Skywalk.

So where c-

She looked down and saw it. A public space that wouldn't be overly crowded, and as a bonus, had a cute bookend-y quality to it, ha, ha, but also let's hope there was a great deal of *book* and a noted paucity of *end* to it.

Nur pointed down to the Boston Public Library. "Open, maybe?"

"Let's find out," Hyun-Woo replied with a smile, and Nur was pleased to discover that she had understood that.

CHAPTER 11

Nur was nervous. That was the sort of phrase she might come to appreciate for its loose, homonymic playfulness once she got a stronger handle on the English language, but for now would go zipping past her.

For her – Nur - nerves were *de rigeur*. The making of romantic moves always proceeded along well-worn ruts. The journey began smoothly, with bold bluster. *I'm just gonna lean in and kiss this clown right on the mouth.* In her mind's eye, the situation played and replayed itself, with infinite variations of the central theme: Nur as unshakeable, unflappable, effortlessly self-possessed and to hell with everyone else. Nur as she wished to be seen, in short.

The next leg of the journey was always a jittering, restless one, which is why she avoided sitting down next to the object of her affections as much as possible. She got fidgety, her stomach tightened, and she wanted little more than to curl into a ball and roll into the nearest storm drain. Her limbs seemed to go cold, and the closer she came to the prospect of a kiss, the more she would shiver. It was either embarrassing, or in those cases when she managed to keep it under control, it was merely a mortifying tic that threatened to *become* embarrassing. Which may well have been worse, really.

The most frustrating part about this whole rigmarole was that kissing was still not that big of a deal to Nur. But that was an intellectual position, and she had never been able to actually act in a way that reflected how she felt.

Stop being nervous, she ordered herself, achieving the same results she'd have gotten issuing that command to her sister (though without reply by way of a desperate, barrel-scraping swipe at wit or sarcasm).

The third and final stage of the journey, well…she hadn't gotten there yet.

For now, she and Hyun-Woo were wandering the reading room of the Boston Public Library (BPL, as the local toughs presumably called it). It was tall and silent, but not an abandoned silence. It was a crowded silence, heavy with concentration. Every clearing of the throat, each turning of the page, sent a shock wave of sound rippling up to the vaulted ceiling, where it colonized, birthed echoes, and let gravity bring them back down. There was a direct correlation between the amount of noise someone made and the depth of the focus with which they were drilling in to their book. You could tell from looking at them that the quietest people weren't actually reading – they were trying very hard to not make noise, and a book happened to be open in front of them.

Their footfalls rolled through the hardwood hall like approaching thunder, as they strolled between long polished desks at which green reading lamps outnumbered readers by a solid 4:1 margin.

"Literate" is how Nur would describe herself. Not a frequent reader by any means, and certainly not a speedy one. She enjoyed a good book here and there, but mostly there: reading was rarely a diversion for the home. She found it more useful as a way to pass the time in waiting rooms or on public transit. Nor was Nur religious in the least. Her parents were Roman Catholic, which all but guaranteed that Nur wouldn't be. Almost all of her friends had Roman Catholic parents, and almost none of those friends shared the faith of their elders. It was a wonder the religion survived.

Despite being neither religiously nor literarily inclined, the only thought Nur could sustain about this place was that it was like a cathedral. Not necessarily from an architectural standpoint (though it was big and had open spaces, which sounded like a cathedral to her; incidentally, she wasn't architecturally inclined either), but in the sense of being a larger symbol for an abstract concept that gave people succor. Now that e-readers were a thing, books, much like gods, were everywhere. You didn't *have* to go to the library, any more than you *had* to go to church (well, that didn't apply to Catholics, actually). But you could, and she could understand why people did, if that was their thing. The advantage of a library, of course, is that membership is free, and there's more than just the one book.

Her fingertips were cold. Was her jaw chattering? *STOP BEING NERVOUS.*

Hyun-Woo started to lead her past a much smaller room off of the nearest hall. Quietly, she fell back a step and slipped behind him through the door into that room. That way, he would come to her, and she would be waiting for him.

Was it weird to be self-consciously constructing a romantic moment? Isn't that what romance was all about? It was certainly capable of arising spontaneously, but there was often an element of calculation in it. Couples don't just *happen* to wind up atop hills at sunset, or on a gondola beneath the stars. One or both of them decide "this would be a lovely, romantic experience", and then do it. That was normal. Right?

stopbeingnervous

Planning only gets one so far, though, and apparently planning had gotten Nur into a small room full of technical manuals for large machinery. Not as romantic as a room full of, like, ancient maps of a flat world, or erotic woodcuts from the twelfth century. But, silver lining, also a room less likely to be visited by unwanted interlopers.

Or Hyun-Woo, apparently. She had positioned her back to the door, hoping he might come up behind her, gently lay a finger to her shoulder, and with just the slightest pressure and a hint of his nail, trace a line along her arm as he wrapped his own arms around her. For a minute or two, nothing of that sort happened. And then; nothing continued to happen. So she let slip the façade just enough to shoot a glance (sultry as she could make it) over her shoulder.

The room was empty, save her. Where the hell *was* he?

She turned and poked her head out of the room, looking left and right down the hall. No sign of him anywhere.

The best-laid plans go to waste, but this wasn't a very well-laid plan. Though it was a plan to get well-laid, eventually. There was another English turn of phrase Nur wouldn't be able to appreciate for quite a little while.

Back in the reading room, Nur scanned the downcast heads for one with that familiar slick of jet-black hair. No Hyun-Woo. She doubled back to that room of technical manuals and continued to the hall on the other side. Not there, either.

Where the hell was he?

As she was walking back to the reading room for a second survey, she found him. In the technical manual room. He didn't appear to be searching for her, unless he expected to find her in a thick leather-bound volume with what appeared to be a monster truck engine on the cover.

He looked up and smiled that smile of his. She stomped up to him, clapped the book shut, and put it back on the shelf. The face he made was so innocently clueless, Nur nearly laughed right at it. Instead wrapped her arms around his neck and made the last leg of the journey to Smoochville: say fuck it and *go for it*.

That's how it always was. She thought about it thought about it thought about it until her head was positively ringing with neurotic self-doubt, right up until the moment when she said fuck it and *went for it*.

Because once that happened, she'd be able to think straight, and remember that kissing isn't such a big deal after all.

Nur reeled herself in at headbutting speed, but slowed her approach once the critical distance had been closed. His lips were soft, but pulled taut. She wasn't the only one who'd been nervous, but now she was the only one who seemed to have calmed down.

Hyun-Woo's hands hovered over her shoulders, as middle-school boys will do when they get their pictures taken with *girls*. As a bit of encouragement, Nur gave his lower lip another peck, this time opening her mouth juuuuuuuust the slightest bit. He got the message, and his hands stopped hovering. They were still clamped tightly to her upper arms, the way American movie stars did in the 40's, but hey, progress was progress.

They kept it at that speed for a while, and eventually Hyun-Woo relaxed and ran a hand up to her cheek (taking a roundabout route that let him glance her left breast with the edge of his hand – she could only grin at the collision between his natural reticence and baser instincts), while the other hand slipped down to the small of her back and pulled her in close. Turned out Hyun-Woo hadn't relaxed *too* much.

Patience, Nur counseled the both of them mentally. Physical intimacy of this sort wasn't a big deal to her, but assuming the horizontal was, right up there with handholding.

He didn't press his suit though, and so it remained a romantic moment, if not one achieved in precisely the way she'd intended. Nobody came into the room, and they weren't certain how long they were in there. But they remained there until they had sated themselves on each other, and that took long enough for them to have gotten a running start at learning the basics of fuel injection, were they interested in the books above them as anything more than a surface to lean on. If nothing else, Nur could have learned a thing or two about double entendres.

There was a direct correlation between the amount of noise someone made and the depth of their focus. Nur and Hyun-Woo had been *very* focused, and remained largely unaware of just how much sound carried in the halls of the BPL.

Suffice it to say that many readers that day came to appreciate Nur's position that making out was great fun, but *hearing* other people make out was a hideous, squelching abomination.

When the slurping horrors finally reemerged into the shining afternoon sun, Nur considered herself educated. The education pertained, specifically, to how essential it was that she learn more about Hyun-Woo. This guy was something special; now it was all down to working out how and why. Nur knew her English wasn't up to snuff – but the good news was that this didn't have to be an obstacle anymore.

The bad news was that the solution was to run head first at a different obstacle, this one having sharp edges and an attitude problem.

CHAPTER 12

She just stared at Nur for several silent seconds, her face less a comprehensible expression and more a protean potentiality that contained a multitude of expressions.

"I'm *serious*," Nur reiterated, in case that hadn't come across. "This is important to me, and I am asking you to be mature and sisterly about this. And if you don't think you can do that, I'm asking you to be a decent human being and tell me so."

Precisely *how* to ask Deirdre for her help had been a vexing conundrum, one over which Nur had fretted away several weeks. In the meantime, she and Hyun-Woo had continued to see each other most evenings after class, stealing moments of intimacy whenever they could. The speed with which Hyun-Woo was picking English up was nothing short of remarkable. He was conversing freely and easily with Americans, apparently telling them *jokes* – which meant he was starting to pick up not just language but *culture*. Humor varied wildly amongst peoples, and Nur had always considered 'making an American laugh' the threshold for fluency. Clearly that *wasn't* the case – she could still see Hyun-Woo grasping for words in ways even the slower native speakers didn't – but it was still a testament to an inborn talent. She couldn't be sure how long he'd been here, but he had been in the beginner class when she showed up about two months ago, so it was...

Two months gone.

Which left just a little over *three hundred days to master the language, or face the consequences at home.*

She was getting better, for certain. Her verbal communication was much stronger than her written, and that was alright. But it still wasn't great. Case in point; Hyun-Woo was a regular chatterbox now, happily talking up a storm to her. And perhaps it would have been better if he had just made loud *whoooosh* noises like a storm; it would have made exactly the same amount of sense to Nur, with the bonus of not making her feel like a complete idiot.

The problem was daily transmogrifying, from 'they couldn't communicate with one another' into 'Nur couldn't understand what Hyun-Woo was communicating'. And the worst part of this was that Nur's feelings towards Hyun-Woo were shifting just as inexorably. At first it frustrated her that he would blather on at her in a language that *surely* he knew she couldn't understand, save every fifth or sixth word, but the frustration was diffuse, at the situation more than anything.

One day in early October, though, she realized that frustration had whittled down to a point, with a very specific direction. She was coming to resent Hyun-Woo, ever so slightly, because he was no longer just as culpable in their failure to communicate as she was.

The onus was now entirely on her, the laggard. Did he actually feel this way? Impossible to say for sure, and Nur was inclined to say no. But she couldn't help but project it on to him, because that's how *she* felt, and she knew it was unreasonable for herself to think, so perhaps somebody else could think this unreasonable thought instead.

It was ludicrous, a ludicrous idea if ever she'd heard one. She was essentially mad at him for ceasing to be confused in the same way that she still was. Selfish, anti-intellectual pettiness! But she couldn't *stop* feeling that way, and she grew increasingly frustrated that she couldn't.

So why not just stop seeing him? she asked herself after one especially disheartening dinner. Two months in and they still hadn't done anything much more adventurous than send their hands out on reconnaissance missions to lower climes. It was, in the argot of this land, 'casual'. If he was starting to be a greater source of anxiety than positivity in her life, why not simply divest herself of him as anything more than a friend?

This was a good point – but not one that she needed to face just yet. Hyun-Woo was, completely unintentionally, making her emotional life slightly more arduous of late. But, on the whole, his presence was still overwhelmingly positive in that indefinable way it had always been. He could sometimes be a bit stingy with eye contact, but when he gave it to you, and when his lips spread into that great big grin…the rest of it melted, right along with her.

But how long would this last? The fact remained that she needed to be able to talk to him. Even if she didn't grow overly annoyed by his superhuman acquisition of English (which, boy, it sounded even *more* ludicrous when phrased so plainly), she could quite easily imagine him growing bored with her, spluttering and struggling her way through asking the waiter if they could split the check (*that* had been embarrassing, particularly as her effort climaxed with Hyun-Woo paying the whole damn thing).

Desperation did what Aunt Amy couldn't; compelled Nur to invite Deirdre out of the house with her.

And here she was, in their shared bedroom (Uncle Bernard was home, so having a Creole conversation downstairs was out of the question), standing in front of Deirdre, her arms folded defensively, as though expecting the inevitably sarcastic retort to come with a physical assault tacked on.

That quivering, unreadable face of Deirdre's finally started to coalesce into…nothing. A flat, affectless mask of apathy.

"On one condition," Deirdre replied.

Not apathy – calculation. Her sister was bargaining.

Nur had to bite the inside of her cheek to keep from bursting in to song. 'On one condition' was highly unexpected, on account of it being the most promising reaction she could have imagined. Had Deirdre simply *agreed* to act as translator between Nur and Hyun-Woo, all the polyester in the world couldn't have spun a red flag big enough. But Deirdre wanted something in return, which gave Nur some leverage, and could potentially act as a guarantee against her two greatest fears: deliberate mistranslation in the moment, and indiscretion after the fact.

Hoping she was matching her sister's straight-mouthed anti-expression, Nur inquired as to what the one condition was.

Deirdre jerked her head towards the door. "They

won't let me out alone. You can come and go as you please, but no, little Deirdre's gotta be locked up for her own safety."

"What? Since when? I had no idea!" Which was true, but how could she have even entertained the alternative? Deirdre was fifteen. No way would Uncle Bernard let her go out alone – and even if *he* had been comfortable with it, their parents certainly wouldn't be, so the injunction would have remained.

Try this one on for size: she *hadn't* entertained the alternative. She had just *literally never thought about Deirdre's experience.*

"You think I wanted to be sitting up here by myself every night?"

"Yes, I did!" This had flown off the rails in record time. Nur raised her hands, showing Deirdre her palms. "Wait, wait. I'm sorry, okay? Really. Sorry. You were getting on my nerves and so I walked away from you, and I shouldn't have done that."

Deirdre sat on her bed, mouth open and finger raised. She'd been poised and ready to strike, only to see her prey vanish into thin air with little more than a *ping* to mark its passage. She slowly curled her finger back into the rest of her loosening fist and lowered her hand. "Yeah, well…that's right. You shouldn't have."

Typically, Nur would have needled her sister more about her role in what had happened, but that had less to do with actually expecting her sister to acknowledge how awful she could be, and more to do with letting her know that she hadn't won ('Won what?' ask only-children everywhere). But right now, conflict resolution was the name of the game. One didn't rescue hostages by running down the hostage taker's rap sheet and asking them to just *admit* that they're not very nice.

"Can we put that to one side for right now and try

to move forward? Please?" she added for good measure.

Deirdre made a show of thinking about this for a second, but she wasn't a great actress. Her mind had already been made up. Whatever she wanted from Nur trumped her sense of being slighted. And as that perceived slight was a two-month affair, and certainly remained untempered by any acknowledgment of her having perhaps brought it upon herself just a bit…well, there was more than enough polyster for *this* red flag.

"Alright," Deirdre imbued with considerable portentousness.

"So what's your condition?"

Again, her sister jerked her head towards the door. "They won't let me out alone…but they really want me to go out with you."

"Uh-huh."

"But I really want to go out alone."

"You want me to talk to them for you?"

"No, and you couldn't even if I wanted you to."

Nur shrugged defensively. "They'd listen to me."

"Not in Creole, they wouldn't."

"S-" And then Nur figured out what Deirdre was gearing up to ask. Her response was self-evident. "No."

"Why not?"

"Because what if something happened to you?"

"You could just say that I ran away from you, you wouldn't get in tr-"

"*I'm* not worried about getting in trouble, stupid! I'm worried about *you* getting into trouble. *Real* trouble."

"You're not that much older than I am, and you don't speak English as well as I do, yet you get to go wherever you want all on your own. It's not fair!"

"No, you're right. It's not. So what?"

Deirdre shook her head. "Well, that's my condition.

You want me to play interpreter, I'll do it. But you have to give me a night out to myself. And that's final."

Though she professed nothing but fear for her sister's safety (fear that was genuine and deeply felt), Nur was painfully aware of the peril she herself would be in, should she tell her Aunt and Uncle she were taking Deirdre out for the night, only to let her run off and do her own thing. Even if the night went absolutely beautifully, and her sister returned safe and sound… well, Deirdre wasn't a picture of discretion. She could let word slip, or perhaps grease the floor a bit to *make* word slip. Because while Deirdre would certainly get in trouble, Nur would be *punished*. Fantasies of a totalitarian curtail on her social life should she fail to learn the English language in a year were a dawdle compared to the perpetual Hell into which she would be thrust, should her parents discover what she'd allowed Deirdre to do.

And on top of that – assume everything *did* go perfectly well, Deirdre comes home with a spring in her step and a smile on her face, etc. What are the chances she would be satisfied with that single night out? A precedent would have been set. She would fully expect to have more nights to herself, and since she rolled double sixes the first time, she'd fully expect each night to go just as well as the first. A second roll of the die, and then a third, and a forth…how many could she manage before one night comes up snake eyes? And if Nur tried to draw the line at the first night, and were happy to have just the one translation session with Hyun-Woo (and what were the chances of *that*, talking of likelihoods), Deirdre still had the lever with which to move the world. She could tell about the first night, and no doubt she'd have had the presence of mind to get some proof, demonstrating Nur's absence. A little slice of trouble for her, the rest of the dire pie for Nur.

Perhaps Deirdre was aware of how fiendishly brilliant this seemingly simple request was, of how it would completely shift the power dynamic of their relationship for the foreseeable future. Or perhaps she wasn't. She wasn't a great actress, after all, and for once her face seemed to have all the edges filed off.

No, perhaps she wasn't aware *yet*, but that softness was fleeting. Deirdre was sharp, through and through, and she'd work all of that out in time. Consenting to her request would be one of the worst decisions Nur made in her entire life.

On the other hand, she would *finally* get to know Hyun-Woo a bit better.

Nur tapped her foot on the *blah* tan carpet, scarcely aware of the muted *ff-ff-ff-ff* with which this was filling the silence, like a fluffy helicopter struggling to get airborne.

She curled her nose and bobbed her head from side to side, making a great show about thinking about this for a second. But she wasn't a great actress. Her mind had already been made up.

Deirdre's smile curled up into points.

CHAPTER 13

It was going to be awkward no matter what; the challenge was in finding the least awkward way for it to go down.

Nur was quite certain she never found it.

They met at a charming little coffee spot on Newbury. Upon arrival the only available seats were along the elevated bench just in front of the window, which wouldn't do at all. It was unsatisfactory from a spatial standpoint, but the view wasn't adding much either; it was deep into October by this point, and the city palled in resignation to the ferocious winter coming its way.

So Nur had them wait until one of the smaller, circular tables that had caught her eye during last week's prodigious joint-casing session opened up.

They all three sat down, and Nur was pleased to see Deirdre adhered to the predetermined choreography. Without the slightest hint of embarrassment, Nur had literally drawn her sister a picture of what she wanted her to do. This was *important*, damn it!

It was important to Nur that she and Hyun-Woo be sitting next to one another. *But* Deirdre had to be between them; otherwise it would feel like she was just one or the other's interpreter, and as Nur was certainly not going to allow her sister to have the seat of honor next to Hyun-Woo, having her sister sat next to her would send the subconscious message that Nur needed the translator, as opposed to them *both* needing someone to translate between them.

She remained very sensitive about the disparities between their English.

But, Nur didn't want Deirdre to be physically between them. *But* nor did she want her sister plopped on the opposite side of a square table, as it would make her feel removed from the conversation, and as she was the necessary conduit through which the conversation was to be conducted, that would serve to put a sense of distance between them, when she was after the exact opposite effect.

Circular was perfect, though. Nur and Hyun-Woo sat close together on one "side" of it (call it 2 and 4 on a clock face), with Deirdre canted off to the opposite side, tending towards Nur (say, 9 or 10).

For obvious reasons she wasn't about to bring Hyun-Woo in on this extensive pre-production process for Sitting Down At A Table, so the De Dernberg sisters' placements would have to be relative to him.

It went off without a hitch, which was down to luck because when the time to sit came Nur just sat, without the least reference to clock faces. She was too busy thinking about the first thing she wanted to say.

Rather tediously, she had forced Deirdre to review the general shape of her acquired English – things she did and didn't know how to say, concepts she could and couldn't articulate, the limits of her vocabulary, the extent of her conjugation. This latter section was the most fraught; Nur was advised to steer clear of any temporally-fluid tense, your *was going to do*s and your *will have been doing*s.

So Nur had a rough idea of what she *could* say, and still expect a certain degree of fidelity in the translation. But she'd not given a great deal of thought, prior to this moment, to what she actually *would* say.

'So where are you from?' Nah, too obvious, answer and question alike.

'What do you do for a living?' Nope, she didn't think she could manage pretending to be interested via translator.

'When are we going to...' no no no, she'd given Deirdre more than enough ammunition by her very presence.

So what?

As if by magic, a question suggested itself. It was 'how long have I been sitting here furrowing my brow in thoughtful silence?' She was loathe to hear the answer, and so decided to open her mouth and be surprised by whatever came tumbling out.

That whatever was "What is the most American thing you've done since you've gotten here?"

She and Hyun-Woo both looked expectantly to Deirdre, who was surveying the ceiling through wink-squinted eyes. Nur nearly snapped at her – *pay attention!* – before realizing that what she was seeing *was* attention. Deirdre was puzzling over the translation as though it were a calculus problem she was trying to solve upside-down.

Finally, she turned to Hyun-Woo, and said what sounded like it was probably a faithful translation. Nur heard and understood familiar words, like "what" and "you" and "American", and a heretofore unacknowledged knot of tension made itself conspicuous by its unraveling. She'd been anticipating her sister to mistranslate, even with the promised solo night out as collateral. But those fears appeared unfounded, and what a relief that was.

Hyun-Woo laughed quietly, but that laughter slipped effortlessly into a look of good-natured concentration. It was a silly question, but he was taking it seriously. And, much to Nur's surprise, she couldn't wait to hear his answer. Hopefully it would lead to an amusing anecdote (*poor Deirdre*, she thought without sarcasm, recalling her sister's look of pinchfaced cogitation), but if nothing else it would give her an idea of what he thought of as quintessentially "American".

Cynicism, she realized, would annoy her. She was quite taken by the melting pot, even if there did seem to be the odd rotten apple or overripe squash floating around.

She'd find out soon enough, anyway. He said something to Deirdre, something with multiple, distinctly-voiced characters and hand gestures, and as that something got longer and longer, so too did Deirdre's face. Hyun-Woo chuckled out the last few words, and Deirdre laughed. A whipcrack of petty jealousy shook Nur – Hyun-Woo had told a joke meant for *her*, and *Deirdre* had gotten to enjoy it first! – but as always, rationality quickly reasserted its control, much as a pilot will always clutch tightly to the controls as the plane flies into the side of a mountain. Bummer that Deirdre got to hear it first, but if not for her then Nur would *never* get to hear the joke.

Still, rationality could only do so much. "What did he say?" she snapped at her sister.

Deirdre scratched her chin. "Um, well he said 'I think the most Ameri-'"

"At the end! When you laughed! What did he say?"

"-can…wah? Oh, um, he just said he could tell by

my face that maybe he better stop talking and let me translate." She punctuated this sentence with a pointed look.

Nur raised her hands and shrugged.

"Anyway, he said, basically, I think I have this right, he basically said 'I think the most American thing I did since I got here was I was at a red light one car back from the intersection…'"

So he has a car, Nur noted.

"'…and I saw a woman on a bicycle crossing the street when the red hand light said she should not be crossing the street, but she did and then the old man in the car directly in front of me pressed the gas and moved forward a little bit and tapped her, and she fell off of her bike and screamed like a whistle.' I – and this is me, Deirdre – I think that might be a colloquialism I'm just not understanding or mistranslating, anyway…"

"You're doing great," Nur whispered in genuine awe.

"Thanks, full disclosure, there was some stuff I didn't understand so I filled in the blanks as best I could from context. I don't think I'm too far off the mark with any of them. ANYWAY, all the cars stop and this…I guess he used a word that'd translate as *greasy*, this greasy guy leaps out of his car and points at the lady on the bike who fell, and starts screaming 'Hey lady, you ran the light!', and she didn't seem to mind except to give him a rude gesture, so he turned to the people around him, which included Hyun-Woo, and started telling all of *them* that the lady ran the light.

"And then this bald guy comes out of nowhere, and gets right in the greasy guy's face, and starts shouting about how never mind the bike lady, because 'I saw you go barreling through that last light back there!', that was the bald guy saying to the greasy guy, who replied by saying 'no you didn't', which was nice of him because it just disputed that the bald guy *saw* it, not that the event actually took place.

"Now this pushy lady, probably about 50 or so, gets out of *her* car and just starts saying 'Sir, sir, she did not run the light, I will give you my name and information', and she wasn't really saying this *to* anybody, she was just sort of saying it for the benefit of anybody who could hear her. And all the while she's saying this, the bald guy pulls out his camera and points it at the greasy guy, and shouts 'I'm gonna take your picture!', and so the greasy guy asks "Oh yeah?" and then tells him to go right ahead, except you can tell he didn't mean it because he also called him a word that's like 'anus', only worse, or maybe better depending on what you're after. He rescinds the offer to go right ahead when he sees the bike lady, who's still just lying on the ground in front of the old guy's car, turn the phone she had been using to take pictures of said old guy's car towards *him*, being the greasy guy, to start taking his picture.

"And he goes 'You're gonna take my picture? Well I'm going to take *your* picture!' and then he proved it by pulling out his phone and taking everybody's picture. All this while that pushy lady is saying 'sir, sir' and offering her name and information to whoever wants it, and he – Hyun-Woo – said there was a solid fifteen seconds of just two lanes of traffic frozen at this intersection while they all took pictures of each other, and then he realized that the 'sir' the pushy lady has been talking to is the old guy in the car that hit the bike lady, and the old guy hadn't said a single thing in this whole time. He'd just been sitting there, dead quiet, staring at the lady lying on the ground in front of his car, taking pictures of two guys who had nothing to do with anything, other than being behind the old guy when he hit the lady who was crossing when the red hand light said she shouldn't have."

Deirdre took a deep breath and nodded, looking utterly pleased with herself. And Nur couldn't blame her for feeling that way. She also couldn't help but wonder if leaving Deridre home alone with Aunt Amy all this time had led the latter's…linguistic imprecisions to rub off on the former.

"Wow…wow, um, thanks for translating all of that."

"Yeah, sure."

"Um…can you ask him what happened after that?"

She did. He responded.

"He says nothing. He managed to squeeze by them by driving a bit through the parking lane and then he just went on his way. He heard sirens approaching as he was leaving, so police and an ambulance probably showed up. But that's the entirety of his story. He says it's the most American thing that he saw."

Perhaps that wasn't *quite* what Nur had asked him, and perhaps it wasn't *quite* the answer she'd been expecting (she didn't wholly understanding what he was even getting at with that answer)…but she loved him all the more for it.

IT!

She loved *it* all the more for it.

It being the *answer* he gave. The first it, anyway. The second it was how unexpected and unique the answer was.

She loved *the answer*.

Well, word that's like 'feces', only worse, or in this case better, given what she was after.

CHAPTER 14

Nur was a romantic who had never been in love. She read books and listened to songs and watched movies by people who, she could only imagine, *had* been in love, all with an eye towards fabricating the feeling in herself. Naturally, there was no way to check her results against the real thing, having never felt the real thing before. Which led to another dilemma: how would she know when she *was* feeling the real thing, if all she had to compare it to was the lumbering quilt-monster she'd stitched together from the shreds of devoured pop culture?

An even more troubling thought had given her some sleepless nights – what if she already *had* been in love, and the real thing was so underwhelming as to pass by unnoticed? She'd certainly been infatuated before, and lust was well…well trod ground, let's say. But nothing had come close to the full-body furnace feeling she'd been led to expect from love. What if the rarified pronouncements of song and literature were the adult equivalent of Santa Claus, a lie for the uninformed perpetuated by the disillusioned, in a pointless attempt to inject some magic into reality?

Troubling questions all, but not nearly as troubling as the answer which was now suggesting itself.

This can't be love, she assured herself, *because that would be stupid if it were.*

Stupid because she didn't know him that well. Or at *all*, really. Were she called upon to count the ways she loved him, she would make it to "number one", which would be "one time you saw a lady on a bike get hit by a car or whatever". Yes, please, marry me.

Were she to count the ways love towards this man in this moment would be stupid, however, she'd graduate from fingers and toes before she'd gotten her shoes off. Point one was already covered; how about that they lived on different sides of the Equator? How about that her prospective career tied her to that location for the foreseeable future? How about that they couldn't speak to each other without Deirdre as intermediate?

Once again, all together: How about *they didn't know each other at all*?

Sure, the workings of the mind had little sway over matters of the heart, she knew that perfectly well. She'd only heard it a billion times. What the poets of yore had failed to mention was that the heart needed more than the gentle course-corrections of the higher faculties; the heart was a first-class twit who needed a shaking of the shoulders and slapping of the face, or ventricles or whatever.

And yet…and yet she felt *something* for Hyun-Woo that was unlike anything she had ever experienced. It was both ecstatic and matter-of-fact, a glorious affirmation of something she could easily take for granted. Nothing about it made a single lick of sense, which was more annoying than anything else. And yet it didn't bother her, because hey, what's one more counter-intuitive sensation among friends?

Hey.

Or *more* than friends.

HEY.

Wait a second-

"*HEY*," Deirdre repeated once again. "Are you trying to relive that story in real time? Say something!"

Christ, they were both still sitting there. So was she. Nur had just vanished into the depths of her own navel while Deirdre and Hyun-Woo were just sitting there, staring at her.

Mortified, Nur inhaled deeply, as one does upon waking from a surreptitious classroom nap. She recommended the facilitated conversation, which took a very long time and is hardly with recounting in full. The highlights are as follows:

They found out where they were each from. Nur knew exactly where South Korea was, and much to her surprise, Hyun-Woo knew all about Seychelles, which on the sliding scale of foreigners' understanding of African geography meant that he recognized Seychelles as a place that existed somewhere on the planet. While Nur had lived her entire life in her native land, Hyun-Woo had spent precious little time in his.

They found out what they each did. Nur was a student and worked in her family's hotel after school. Hyun-Woo had tutors but no consistent formal education, as he was constantly traveling the globe with his parents. It didn't feel right to think of this as "not doing *anything*", but from an occupational standpoint, that's what it sounded like to Nur.

They found out what their parents did. Nur's were in the hospitality racket. Hyun-Woo's were both diplomats (Nur almost asked what their domestic disputes were like, but decided not to hinge a risky zinger on Deirdre's translated delivery). This explained all of the traveling Hyun-Woo did, as well as his outrageous fluency in so many languages – he had spent his formative years bopping across the globe, soaking up customs and tongues. Nur envied him his fortunate birth, and quickly stamped out the embers of resentment smoldering within the envy. Hyun-Woo was a child of *privilege*. Hardly an endearing quality, though he couldn't well help it, and he at least seemed aware of the unearned nature of his happy station.

They found out what they each *wanted* to do. Nur wanted to follow her parents into the hotelier business. Which wasn't *entirely* true – she wanted to make her family proud, and it just so happened the best way to accomplish that was donning a stupid vest and bidding tourists welcome to the De Dernberg Towers. Were she to write her own ticket, it would likely be one-way out of Seychelles, to forge her own path. But the thought of letting her parents down overwhelmed her self-interest, and so hotelling it was.

Hyun-Woo, meanwhile, wanted to do… something? As far as Nur could gather from Deirdre's translations, the man wasn't a particularly political animal. Trying to reverse engineer his tone from the timing of the translation, he seemed to view diplomacy the way most people looked at vacuum cleaners – necessary for keeping things clean, but never as clean as they promised on the box, and they made a god-awful racket I'd rather not have to hear, thank you very much.

So what did her maybe-love want to do with his life? What was his ambition? Nur hadn't the slightest clue, which put her in good company, because apparently neither did he.

Well, it must be love, she realized, because lack of ambition was a terrifically unattractive quality to her, and yet here she was, continuing to be attracted to him.

Perhaps 'lack of ambition' wasn't fair. Lack of realistic expectations? Hyun-Woo knew he wanted a job that would allow him to keep travelling, and he knew he wanted a job that would pay well, and he knew he wanted a job that would be enjoyable, and he knew he wanted a job that would be fulfilling, and he knew he wanted a job that would be exciting, and he knew he wanted a job that would leave him with a lot of leisure time.

What he didn't seem to know was that *everybody* wants these things, but nobody gets them all because that job doesn't exist.

His naiveté was charming, she supposed. That was probably why she was still attracted to him.

Or because it's love.

Alright. Or that.

The chatted for a bit longer, moseying right up to the four hour mark of their marathon conversation. "Chat" was the right word for it, because their discussion mainly covered the topics of "this" and "that". Nothing profound, nothing deep. They both wanted to – at least, Nur wanted to, and she got (or projected) the impression that Hyun-Woo did too. But it was tough to muster the requisite enthusiasm when those needling questions and revealing answers would be running the gauntlet of Nur's younger sister. Admirable though her translation job had been so far, Nur wasn't about to give Deirdre any more dirt than she already had.

And so, through some unspoken agreement (and how painful it was to know that they'd have to return to the arena of the unspoken once again), Nur and

Hyun-Woo both embodied the essence of 'wow would you look at the time', said their prolonged, three-person goodbyes, and went on their ways, feeling as though they had crested a low hill of interpersonal understanding, only to be afforded a sweeping vista of All The Things I Don't Know About You.

On the T ride home, Nur put her arm around her sister. She'd be hard pressed to say whom this surprised more; it certainly hadn't been planned, and she could feel Deirdre recoiling from her embrace. Once Nur recovered from her own shock, she gave her little sister an affectionate squeeze.

"Thank you," she managed, with a sharp formality that disappointed her. "Really."

"Yeah, yeah," Deirdre replied dismissively. But her shoulders slackened under Nur's arm, and she didn't try to buck said arm off for the entire ride back to Uncle Bernard's. Nur was so touched by this gesture that she, for the duration of the journey, forgot all about the debt she now owed to her sister.

She would have been even more touched to know that Deirdre did as well. But then the journey ended.

CHAPTER 15

Deirdre's big night out came three sunsets later, when Deirdre said "tonight's the night" and Nur bit her tongue before it could form the word "no". A promise was a promise, a deal was a deal.

A promise and a deal were also both opportunities to exploit loopholes opened by imprecise phrasing.

To wit: it was, at no point, stated that Nur couldn't follow Deirdre on her night out, from a distance. Sure, they did say it would be solo, and she'd be going out alone, but that was still true! She would get to wander the city of Boston all on *her* lonesome, and Nur would be wandering the city of Boston all on her lonesome. It would just be coincidence that their paths would be one and the same, just as it would be nothing but personal eccentricity that would see Nur ducking behind parked cars and hiding in bushes, if it came to that.

And really, come on: Deirdre had to know Nur would be following her. She was a smart girl, and she knew her big sister well enough. So by failing to add the stipulation *and by the way you aren't allowed to follow me*, wasn't Deirdre tacitly *inviting* Nur along as a shadow?

Hardly worth answering, that.

More worth answering was the question Nur asked her sister after they had laid on the 'well we're heading out see you later' song and dance for their Aunt and Uncle.

"So what are you doing with your night out?" she asked with enough innocent curiosity to put several cats to death.

Deirdre shrugged and replied "oh, you know," which, like, come on.

"Actually I don't."

"Well," was the beginning and end of Deirdre's riposte.

After a lapse into silence, Deirdre returned fire: "What are *you* doing with my night out?"

Nur's shrug was but an echo of her sister's practiced gesture. "I'll be wandering around, I guess." Which was true enough.

"Mhm."

Thus ended their second song and dance of the evening. About ten minutes after that, Deirdre lost her tail.

"Well," the young De Dernberg reprised as she turned to the doors, "this is where I leave you." She weaved between the closing doors of the T, leaping out of the train at the Hynes stop.

Nur leapt up from her seat. Curses! She had thought nothing of it when Deirdre remained standing, because that was the posture they'd always taken. *How did I not see this coming?* she wondered as the Hynes stop, and a waving Deirdre, made a speedy exit stage left.

Shit shit shit shit shit, she added as the T sped through the grim, dim tunnels of Boston. *Shit.*

Of *course* Deirdre had anticipated that Nur would be following her. So she had planned on losing her. Why hadn't Nur anticipated *that*? She had been blinded by a temporary feeling of sisterhood, that's why. The translation thing had gone so well! Was a good faith performance too much to ask from her sister? Nevermind the fact that Nur herself had been planning to act in ways that fell short of 'good faith'; she was the big sister! She was supposed to look out for her little sister! Ends justifying means, and what not!

She alighted at Copley, nearly shouldering the accordion doors off their runners in her haste. Taking the steps two at a time, she emerged into a dusky, cold evening, the Old Church now fully visible between the palsied, cracked fingers of the denuded trees. The sight that had so impressed her that first day failed to register in the slightest, except as one of many material obstructions that could well be concealing Deirdre, directly or indirectly.

Scratch that – unlikely. She looked to her left, down Boylston, in the direction of the Hynes Convention Center. Two paths suggested themselves: sprint down the street, head on a swivel, hoping to catch a glimpse of her sister…or cross the street, catch the first outbound T and get out at Hynes. For all she knew, the timing could well work out to be approximately the same. The only advantage to the former plan was that, if Deirdre had come wandering this way, Nur might spot her…but in all probability, Deirdre would have anticipated *this* as well, and so taken her one-woman uh-oh roadshow in the exact opposite direction.

"How did I not see this coming?" Nur reiterated for the benefit of everyone in earshot who understood

Seychellois Creole, which is to say nobody. She added, "aaaaaaaah…"

Every moment of indecision was a moment in which the distance between Deirdre and herself grew. That was not a helpful thought to think, but it was the thought she thought.

"Aaaaaaah….ha!" There was triumph in that *ha*, because coming to a decision was a small victory and she'd take what she could get.

Swinging her upper body like a runningback, she teetered to the left until the teeter turned into a sprint.

The deciding vote had been cast by that unhelpful thought. The idea of sitting around and *waiting for a train* in a moment like this would have been more than she could bear. Even if it took her slightly longer, running along Boylston would give her the illusion of being actively *on top of* the situation, rather than being passively ferried along by the wretched public transit system that caused this whole mess in the first place. Damn the MBTA, that's what Nur had to say about this!

Or would do, once she got her breath back. Wheezing her way along semi-crowded sidewalks, she wasn't looking to say much of anything just then, except maybe *how did I not see this coming*, because she couldn't imagine it being possible to say that too many times.

Deirdre looked the wrong way when crossing the street and was hit by a truck.

Deirdre slipped on a banana peel and fell into an open manhole.

Deirdre took a pamphlet and joined a cult and spent fifteen years worshipping a stinky man in a bathrobe and then committed suicide.

Deirdre fell through a portal to an alternate

dimens-

This line of thinking was not productive, but Nur couldn't much help it. These and other mortifying images of mortal peril came to her unbidden, and hung along a burning thread of rage like sheets so soiled they needed to be dried before they could be washed.

Deirdre could be anywhere was also not the start of a productive run at deducing her whereabouts, so with her overtaxed heart thudding in her throat, Nur decided to narrow things down as best she could.

Where would Deirdre definitely not go?

Uncle Bernard's, duh.

The School…almost definitely not. But that would be closed anyway.

The Library, which would also be closed.

The café they'd done their translation stuff…

Deirdre would probably not go to any of the places they had already been before. So, yeah. Was that helpful? Did that narrow things down?

Not really.

Deirdre could be almost *anywhere*, Nur concluded, which was progress of a kind.

She rounded the corner and skidded to a halt at the gaping maw of the Hynes stop, currently disgorging a mess of harsh yellow light and soft white people. Gasping for air in short, snatching gulps, she slapped her hands on her knees and leaned until her upper body was nearly parallel with the splotchy concrete beneath her, because that felt like the thing to do.

Take a breather, look at the problem from a different angle, OH NO.

Here was a different angle: Deirdre would eventually have to go home. Her sister was a rascal, but she wasn't an idiot. She wouldn't try her luck at shacking up with some stranger, and besides, Nur was relatively certain her sister was a virgin, and still retained enough of a romantic streak to keep that record intact until she met 'the right guy'. So Deirdre would go home.

She would go home alone.

She would go home and Uncle Bernard would ask, 'where is Nur?' And Deirdre would respond, 'I don't know.'

And then they would both be in a world of trouble. Deirdre's would just be a small, small world; the Wide, Wide, World of Pain would be reserved for Nur.

The worst part about this was that Nur felt certain Deirdre hadn't planned this particular hitch in the plan. It was just that they had clearly expended so much mental energy on trying to outmaneuver each other, they'd forgotten about the final, essential step of needing to, uh, inmaneuver back together at the end of the night.

And then, the ultimate cackling horror of the situation revealed itself to Nur, backlit by giddy shafts of lightning. If one of the De Dernbergs has returned home alone, both would get in trouble. That was for certain. But whoever returned first could also control the narrative, and minimize damage for themselves. Deirdre could sing of Nur's negligence, but Nur could just as easily spin the yarn of Deirdre's deception. Perhaps the latter case would have been the more disastrous, as it implied willful chicanery.

A classic Prisoner's Dilemma, then. Each sister could secure herself a measure of immunity from familial wrath by compromising the other. Not knowing what the other was going to do, it was in both of their best interest to go home immediately, before the other had the chance to get in first.

Nur froze and pondered this for five eternal

seconds…and without quite knowing how, she arrived at her decision, without realizing the degree to which it would set the tone for their relationship into the foreseeable future.

She smote her thighs and took off running around the station, back the way she came on Newbury Street. "How did I not see this coming?!" she shouted out loud once again.

"See what coming?" asked somebody at a bus stop.

"It's a long story!" Nur replied.

Halfway to the café at which Deirdre had been so helpful just three days ago, Nur realized that by some stroke of impossible luck, that man back at the bus stop could understand and speak Seychellois Creole. She came as near to screeching as a halting human can, made a violent about-face and ran back to Hynes.

The guy was gone, presumably on a bus to wherever Deirdre and Amelia Earhart and the crew of the *Mary Celeste* had gone as well. This was the old De Dernberg luck! Nur said a rude word before it was back to wheezing.

CHAPTER 16

Luck once again broke Nur's way: the café where she had heard about the most American thing Hyun-Woo had ever seen was open, and getting onto their Wi-Fi was relatively quick work. She didn't know the word for "password", but knew the words "this" and "please", so it was a simple matter of pulling up the password entrance page on her phone and pointing.

She got on and sent Deirdre a message: "I'm at that café from a few days ago, *please meet me back here ASAP.*" The italics were implied, of course, but Nur liked to think that the ones and zeroes that comprised her message could retain the urgency of their inception as they zipped across the city to wherever the hell Deirdre had gone.

Then came the hardest part: she had to wait.

While she waited, she ruminated.

It was slightly disheartening that she should have not the foggiest idea of where Deirdre would go, wasn't it? She thought she knew her sister relatively well, and would have said so to anyone who asked (though what an odd question that would be). But being forced to prioritize Deirdre's interests, in the hopes of distilling them into places she might go as a result of those interests, made Nur realize that her conception of her sister was at least half a decade out of date. The dolls and baubles with which Deirdre was once so enamored had long since taken up a dusty residency in the closet, obviously, of course, and the adolescent fascinations had gone the same way. So why, as Nur struggled mightily to come up with the things Deirdre *did* like, *now*, in the *present*, couldn't she put her finger on anything other than Pokémon and sharks (Deirdre used to know everything about sharks, for some reason) and Lisa Frank?

What the hell did Deirdre enjoy nowadays? Scratch "slightly disheartening" – this was shattering. Having the sibling close at hand meant she could always just hold something in front of Deirdre's face and watch how it shone or contorted. *Knowing* what Deirdre liked had never mattered before, because finding out was so simple. *What do you think of this? Nur would ask.* Deirdre's face would attain the Platonic ideal of Frown. *Alright, not a fan then.* It was as though she had treated her sister as an outsourced memory bank. There was no point in *both* of them remembering Deirdre's likes and dislikes, after all!

Idiot. Nur nursed the wounds of the self-flagellation still in progress, staring out the window at the shafts of tree-sliced streetlight raking across Newbury like searchbeams. Masochism wasn't usually her style, but she needed to be doing *something* proactive.

The café closed an hour and change later, at 10:00PM. Nur could at least understand that the helpful woman behind the counter was apologetic about the eviction, though that fundamental decency ended up being more frustrating than anything. *If only I could explain the situation, this helpful woman would probably, well, be more helpful.* Simple words trapped in her skull, yet again. Instead, Nur stalled long enough to compose a second message to Deirdre: "I'm getting kicked out of the café, so if you get this *meet me...*" where?

Where the hell could she have gone!? She won't be able to get into half the stuff to do in this town, being a minor. And most businesses are closing, or already closed. So where?!

"...so if you get this *meet me at the café anyway.* I'll be sitting out front like a chump." Angels from the Cloud whisked the message off into the night, and Nur followed it with a final nod to the helpful (and real) woman from the café. Tugging the lapels of her coat, she hugged it closer to her body and hunkered down on the café's frigid stoop. Unsurprisingly, the café's Wi-Fi didn't extend this far, so she was once again incommunicado.

A few days later, she would reflect with rueful mirth upon how wholly Millenial she was in that moment. Sitting on a stoop, waiting for something to happen, wracked with an existential sense of disconnection because she didn't have any Wi-Fi service. Also wearing a terrifically fashionable coat she bought for a scandalously low sum, almost certainly the product of offshore labor conducted in deplorable conditions.

But this was a sneering grin for another time. In the moment, Nur could only bemoan how little she actually knew about her *sister*, her own sister, and how pathetic it was that her primary concern was not actually for said sister, but for *herself*, and what parental hell would rain down upon her if word of this wretched evening made its way across the globe, as it most certainly would if Deirdre went tottering home alone.

What an unspeakably short-sighted decision, to agree to this! And why? So she could have a mindless, nattering small-talk marathon with a crush?

(not just a crush)

Shivering on the top step of a commercial brownstone, the night was cold but her self-loathing was on *fire*, for all the good that did her, and the street was quiet and the passersby were lonely and the cars were fuel-inefficient and everything was garbage. Was English really *that* important? She was going to be working and living in Seychelles for goodness' sake! Give it a few years and she'd be running the De Dernberg Towers – she could *hire* people to speak English *for* her! Or the guests could damn well take a stab at Seychellois Creole, how about that? Damn to them! They could and should be damned!

Deirdre sat down on the stoop next to Nur.

"…" said Nur.

"I got your message," Deirdre replied.

Nur considered this carefully, and then said "…"

She wanted to be angry, but that would be stupid, because technically what had happened was precisely what she'd agreed to. Deirdre had simply bucked her attempt to get cute with the terms of the agreement.

Frustration seemed fair enough, just on the basic principle of 'it's frustrating to be deceived'.

But then there was relief. Mostly relief. Relief that Deirdre was safe, obviously, but also relief that *she* would be alright, and she wouldn't catch hell from her family and be grounded until the sun exploded.

So there was also disappointment, that she could be so selfish.

Mostly the relief, though.

Nur leaned her head on Deirdre's shoulder, and Deirdre leaned back. They sat that way for a long time, even though the night was cold.

On the T ride back, Deirdre told Nur about her big night out. It mainly consisted of riding high on the novelty of solitude for about fifteen minutes, and then a slow descent into the ennui of the same. Having a night out alone was fun in theory, but she had nothing to do. And sometimes those can be the best nights, as long as you've got someone fun with whom to do nothing. Instead, she just wandered around Back Bay for a while, until she realized precisely what Nur had about the catastrophe that would be Deirdre returning home alone. So she ended up spending most of her night out looking for a place with free Wi-Fi, to send Nur a message, in the desperate hope that her big sister would have the same thought and do likewise. Happily, she discovered that Nur had beaten her to the punch.

Now having something to do ("find my way back to that café"), Deirdre took a leisurely but purposeful stroll through a hushed late-autumn weeknight in Boston, all on her lonesome. It was revivifying in its simplicity: alone time, *real* alone time, for the first time in months. Humans are sociable creatures, and despite her trendy, pouty poses, Deirdre was no exception. But she also came by her desire for privacy honestly, and found the odd night alone to be essential for her mental health.

So she sat on the stoop next to Nur feeling completely refreshed, and that feeling carried her all the way back to Uncle Bernard's. The two sisters spoke easily and amicably, whispering and giggling in the silence more commonly filled by the thunderous cracks and snaps of thin ice and eggshells.

Nur was genuinely glad to hear that Deirdre had a good night, and let her know. Privately, she could only be disappointed to know that morning would almost certainly burn the goodwill off like the mists over a dead bog. But until then, she could admire the way the will-o-the-wisps looked through the happy haze.

And then she felt like the biggest asshole on the planet, because the next morning Deirdre was still in a highly agreeable mood, and Nur had just a few hours ago compared her to a dead bog.

CHAPTER 17

There's a scene that pops up in most modern crime fiction, where character A needs to earn the trust of character B. Both characters are hardened criminals (naturally), tough customers who shave with dull razors (invariably male, are the characters in these sorts of scenes) and take their coffee black. Character B says something to the effect of 'give me one reason why I should trust you', to which Character A pulls out their gun, turns it around, and hands it to Character B grip-first. 'Because I could have just shot you in the dingus there, yet now I am giving you the opportunity to shoot *me* in the dingus', comes the unstated reply. The moment when each could have killed the other passes, ferrying the miasmic paranoia off with it.

Chest-pounding machismo of this sort always rang hollow to Nur – as if eliminating the most dramatic forms of betrayal left no room for the less grisly offenses – and yet, something of this sort had passed between Deirdre and her…and taken a large portion of their reciprocal suspicions with it.

The logic of the Prisoner's Dilemma dictated that each of them ought to have rushed home before the other had the opportunity to. Instead, they exchanged messages, met up, and went home together, thus obviating any trouble for either of them.

There passed a moment when they could have shot each other in the metaphorical dingii, but didn't...and gosh and darnit if this didn't instill a certain degree of good faith in one another.

A trial period of sustained circumspection might well be what was called for then, but Nur was growing impatient. Deirdre had already amply demonstrated that she was capable of facilitating progress in Nur's romantic liaison, and there was so much progress yet to be made. Nur considered the issue and decided that, despite its intimately personal nature, Deirdre could help, and she ought to strike while the links of the sororal irons were hot.

Alright, no sense dressing it up: Nur wanted Deirdre to help her get laid.

"You *what*?"

"Please don't make me ask again."

Deirdre rose her palms to her temples and very pointedly failed to conceal a smile. "I've...I...I'm-"

"This isn't about you!"

The smile widened. "No, I know, of course not." Deirdre lowered her hands to her lap. "I, er, *it's* just surprising, is all."

Nur couldn't quite bring herself to look at her sister's beaming mug, so she let her gaze settle on Deirdre's right ear. "If I could handle it myself, I would."

"That big, huh?"

"What?"

Deirdre's grin split open, revealing her brace-straightened teeth.

Nur would have done a spit-take, if only she'd been drinking something. "No! The *it* is the, the circumstances, not-"

"I know, I know. I'm messing with you."

"Well, don't!"

Mercifully, Deirdre picked up on this and adopted a dignified pose more becoming of the situation's sensitivity. "Right. Sorry. What do you expect me to be able to do though? I can't imagine having your little sister play pimp is going to get him in the mood."

"You wouldn't be 'playing pimp'. You'd be…" she tried to lock down a phrasing of Deirdre's putative role that didn't sound like a florid euphemism for pimp. She failed. "Well, anyway, I just need you to help with the translation for a bit, then peel off. We'll arrange a meet-up ahead of time, and-"

"Where am I going to sleep though?" The concern was genuine.

Nur scratched her chin. "Huh?"

"I can't come back here, so where am I go-"

"Oh. *Oh.* I wasn't planning on spending the night with him."

"…then what are we talking about?"

Nur walked over to her bed and sat down across from her sister. "No, I mean, I'm planning on 'spending the night with him' in the colloquial sense. But I wasn't going to literally stay the whole night. That'd never fly with Uncle Bernard."

A wretched little smirk alighted on the corners of Deirdre's mouth.

Nur sighed. "What?"

"Nothing."

"That's something. What."

"Just that I'm *definitely* playing pimp here."

Despite her frustration with Deirdre's lack of gravity, Nur gave a dramatic "ah!" gasping noise, like an old dowager fixing to faint. "Why, just because I'm not staying the night?"

"You're gonna do the deed and then scram, right?"

"Well he's not paying me!"

"Of course not. But is he paying *me*?"

"Ah!" Nur grabbed a pillow and hurled it at Deirdre's head. It was a good-natured hurl. "You little shit!" That was a good-natured 'you little shit'.

The levee broke and Deirdre's laughter came roaring forth. It was catching, and Nur was receptive.

CHAPTER 18

They had something approximating a plan, and Nur didn't feel great about that. A scheme to get into a guy's pants…that was a simplistic formulation of things, but it wasn't *inaccurate*. She did love him. Probably. Most likely. And he was very timid, clearly not apt to make many first moves beyond hand-holding. Fold these in with the extenuating circumstances of their limited conversational opportunities, and a little pinch of calculation wasn't so unreasonable after all. Was it? Of course it wasn't.

Probably. Most likely.

And anyway, it's not as though it was some masterpiece of Machiavellian manipulation. "Get Hyun-Woo to invite us back to his place". That was it, in totality. From there, they had a little rigmarole put together, by which Deirdre would excuse herself and leave the lovebirds to their tender ministrations. If, on the walk up, the area looked like a halfway decent one, Deirdre would get the night to herself once again, wandering and exploring to her heart's content, as long as her heart could find contentment by 11:30PM. The T closed relatively early, after all. This time limit also presupposed Nur could find contentment of a more glandular sort before the train carriage turned back into a pumpkin, but she'd never been the 'go all night' type anyway. Get in, get the job done, get out. Anything more was just loitering.

The pumpkin was before the horse here, though. They had to get invited to Hyun-Woo's, and as he hadn't extended the invitation on his own, the issue would need to be forc...facilitated. That was where Deirdre came in. Deirdre and the calendar, which turned out to be a capable co-conspirator.

Halloween wasn't unknown in Seychelles and South Korea, but it was more acknowledged than celebrated. Nur speculated that she had an uncommon familiarity with the holiday, simply because it was observed by so many of the tourists who spend the ass end of October vacationing at the De Dernberg Towers.

October 31st fell on a Monday this year, which meant much of the mischief went down on the 28th and 29th, so working stiffs could drink themselves silly without condemning themselves to jockeying a desk with ringing ears and splitting head. This unspoken preemption of the Big Night caught Nur unawares, but also served as a helpful reminder that she needed a costume. She herself had never dressed up for Halloween, or as the case seemed to be, dressed down for it.

Some people dressed as characters from pop culture; some dressed as real people, historical and contemporary; some went as inanimate objects; some went as animals. The common thread running between all of these seemed to be a paucity of threads. America was still recovering from a recession, she knew this, but how striking it was to see that *nobody* seemed to have enough fabric to complete their costumes!

Nur would never self-describe as a prude, but fits of sarcasm like that made her wonder if that was just because she lacked the self-awareness to do so. If people wanted to dress up as sexy versions of, say, a child murderer (Darth Vader) or a corporate CEO (Harold Westmore), that was their prerogative. And more power to them for doing so in such a frigid clime. Would that Nur could feel so committed to anything, as these people did their igloo eroticism.

This naturally opened an avenue of seduction; parade in front of Hyun-Woo in something revealing. What that something was remained undetermined, as she'd had very few costume ideas, and even fewer that she hadn't seen in the days leading up to Halloween executed far more, how to phrase this, *successfully* than she'd be able to. Nur had nothing to be ashamed about with her body, and nor was she (usually, anyway). But it also wasn't the sort of body that got along with skin-tight leotards and crop tops. Seductive in the confines of a bedroom, sure, she could manage that. But stood next to some of the stunners Nur saw clomping around Copley in six-inch heels, she wouldn't have been able to entirely blame Hyun-Woo for a wandering eye. She had self-awareness enough for *that*, at least.

The costume was the hard part. The rest was fairly straightforward.

Inviting oneself to someone else's house was a no-no, Nur knew. And even if it were more acceptable, she still wouldn't do it; there were few things she hated more than people inviting themselves along with her. On anything. It baffled her why anybody would ever just *assume* their presence was wanted, despite not having been requested.

How to get around this? Well, on one of their semi-regular threesome dates on the Friday before Halloween, Nur and Hyun-Woo and Deirdre as translator, Nur got up to go to the bathroom. As she passed her sister, she gave her a little tap on the shoulder. This served no purpose other than to say *look at us, with the surreptitious gestures, except don't actually look.*

Running out the clock on the porcelain throne, Nur tried to ensure Deirdre would have enough time by running a projection of how she imagined the conversation would go. She knew Deirdre's opening salvo well enough; they'd rehearsed and refined it over a period of days.

Deirdre: *Hey, while Nur's in the bathroom; we're gonna be trick-or-treating on Halloween, and I thought it'd be a fun surprise if one of the doors we knocked on happened to be yours. Where do you live? I'll sort of nudge her your way, and we can pretend it's just a crazy coincidence.*

Inviting him into her confidence, making him feel as though he's inviting them when he's really not.

And he really *isn't*. They're sort of inviting themselves, putting Hyun-Woo in that awkward position of either feeling obligated to accommodate or having to uncomfortably rescind an invitation he'd never extended.

So, yeah, they were inviting themselves over to his house. But desperate times, and so on.

At this point, the conversation would naturally go wildly off road. Nur and Deirdre had rehearsed that opening line, and settled on a variety of follow-ups based on the numerous possible responses they could imagine Hyun-Woo giving, but of course they couldn't imagine *all* of the possible responses. He could well surprise them both by saying something utterly out of the blue, in which case Deirdre was on her own. Nur had to trust her sister's extempore talents, and she was pleased to find that she did. She really did.

Hyun-Woo: *Yes,* she imagined him saying, *this is a wonderful idea, perhaps the most wonderful idea I have ever had the pleasure of hearing. Why not skip the pleasantries of trick or treat, and have Nur ascend to my penthouse where we will dine on the finest seafood fresh from the harbor, and smush our genitals together.*

(Nur expected that saucy talk would get jumbled and unsexified in the act of translation)

Deirdre: *I expect Nur will be exceedingly pleased to hear this.*

Hyun-Woo: *I, in turn, am exceedingly pleased to hear that.*

Deirdre: *This has been a conversation conducive to exceeding pleasure.*

Hyun-Woo: *What an exceedingly pleasurable turn of events.*

Deirdre: *I concur.*

Hyun-Woo: *Terrific.*

Jealousy shot through Nur for a split second; the moments of exceeding pleasure should pass only between Hyun-Woo and herself! And then she remembered that that conversation hadn't actually happened, or at least, hadn't actually happened *like that.* That was all imagined.

She got up to find out how the conversation actually did happen.

She sat back down, wiped, and then got up to find out how the conversation actually did happen.

Not right away. She had to sit through the rest of the date – not that the rest of the date wasn't enjoyable.

They chatted through Deirdre about ways in which they would not want to die, and the ways in which they would kill themselves, if they were so inclined. A morbid conversation to be sure, but oddly unifying. They had moved beyond the small-talk phase, and Nur was unutterably pleased with this development. Small talk was boring. Strange conversations about whether you would rather jump out of a plane with a faulty parachute, to watch the Earth go from a far-off hypothetical to a terminally tangible fact, or go scuba diving with a faulty tank, struggling to shake off the dead weight and kick up to the shimmering surface, as the dancing sunlight slowly collapsed into an endless tunnel…this was an Interesting Conversation, of the sort one doesn't have with just anybody. And Hyun-Woo was having it with her, freely and easily. She wasn't just anybody to him.

On the walk back home (they'd had this get-together in a cute little faux-French eatery near Uncle Bernard's place), Nur did something she hadn't done in years: she put Deirdre in a headlock and gave her a noogie.

"Gah, stop it!" Deirdre sputtered.

Nur released her sister and laughed. "You're amazing, Deirdre. It was like I was talking directly to him. I forgot you were even there."

"Gee, thanks."

"I mean that as a compliment! You're a natural interpreter!"

"Oh, of course," Deirdre replied with an ostentatious, hand-spinning bow. "I knew that."

"So what did he say?"

Deirdre regained the vertical with a fiendish glimmer in her eye. "About what?"

"You know what!"

"He liked the idea."

Did he find it exceedingly pleasurable? Deirdre having information that she didn't was maddening. "And he gave you his address?"

"Mhm. He did."

"What is it?"

The fiendish glimmer bloomed into a spotlight. "It's meant to be a surprise."

"…"

"Don't you want to be surprised?"

"No!"

"If I tell you where he lives, and which house, then you're going to have to pretend extra-hard to be surprised when he opens the door. But if I *don't* tell you, you'll only have to work half as hard."

Deirdre had a point. If Deirdre wasn't a great actress, she came by it honestly. Nur was no better. Retaining an element of the unexpected would keep her from having to feign shock, which would likely take the form of screwing her palms into her eyes and shouting "WWWHHHAAAA?!"

But still…this meant Deirdre had information that Nur didn't. Which was *maddening*.

Also…

"Also, if you're gonna keep it a secret, now we have to actually go trick-or-treating!"

Deirdre feigned shock, only just falling short of how Nur fancied she would have done it. "But that was always the plan, wasn't it?"

"No! We would have gone straight to his place!"

"With empty bags?"

"Empty bags of what?"

"…empty?"

"What *would* have been in them?"

"Candy!"

Nur lifted a finger, ready to make a great point, before realizing that Deirdre had beaten her to it. The illusion would be incomplete if they showed up to Hyun-Woo's without candy. So now they had to actually go trick-or-treating.

"...good point. But I'm too old to trick-or-treat," Nur opined as she slowly lowered her finger.

"*I'm* not. And neither are you." As Nur's finger fell, so too did her shoulders. Deirdre shook her head. "It's free candy!"

It was in moments like these when Nur remembered just how young her sister was.

"Alright," she allowed, hiking her shoulders back up to their normal position, "but promise me you won't hold Hyun-Woo's place out until the end of the night."

"I would have thought the night was over when we got to Hyun-Woo's, no?"

"...good point."

CHAPTER 19

The two criteria by which Nur assessed potential Halloween costumes were sensuality and insulation. It was a notably cold October in Boston, getting down to the 30s, and there was no sense revealing skin if it would be mottled with goosebumps. Particularly with her having been born and raised in a tropical environment, Nur had little truck with the cold.

Were a film to be made of her life, this would be the point at which a jaunty pop song would come tinkling in, obliterating the diegetic sound and signaling a montage during which all manner of garments and household accessories were repurposed into a series of increasingly preposterous costumes which escalate, in comedic fashion, to the point at which the final costume is discovered.

But were a film to be made of Nur's life, it would have subtitles, and Deirdre would probably be more reliably amusing than she actually was, and both herself and Hyun-Woo would have abs (as would Deirdre, as would Uncle Bernard and Aunt Amy, as would

Tuppence Crabshoe – everybody would have abs), and they (Nur and Hyun-Woo, *not* any of the other people just mentioned parenthetically) would have had sex within the first thirty minutes of their meeting, thus rendering this whole Halloween misadventure moot.

Without the magic of montage, finding a suitable Halloween costume was more dirge than lark. Deirdre had asked around and discovered that the secret was to come up with a thing that you wanted to be, then just put the word "Sexy" in front of it, and yank away the fabric around the legs.

Uncle Bernard took a hard pass on any fabric being yanked or torn, so Nur was left to cobble something together from the materials she found around the house, as they were.

Lucky for her, her Aunt and Uncle had acquired the tackiest trappings of their respective cultures. Which is how, at the end of what would have been a rather prolonged and humorless montage set to something like The Rite of Spring, Nur wound up dressing as Sexy Bear from The Revenant (being "From The Revenant" was Deirdre's suggestion, as she insisted that just plain 'sexy bear' meant something specific in America).

The "costume" was really just a single item, a thick pelt that belonged to some poor bear or wolf or whatever, but now found new life as a throw blanket meant to represent the fur traders that dominated some distant portion of Aunt Amy's family tree. The dimensions were modest enough to drape over Nur's shoulders like a cape without dragging any surplus pelt behind her. Plus, it was warm! Granted, it would take some explaining for which Nur was hardly prepared, but there weren't many alternatives.

Deirdre, happy to have a costume that took some explaining, fashioned a little hat for herself out of tin foil and went as An American Conspiracy Theorist. Her costume would prove significantly more popular throughout the evening, leading Nur to wonder if America wasn't more heavily populated with the tin foil hat types than she'd realized. Perhaps they had some kind of cabal or society at which they met under cover of night.

Thusly attired, the two sisters bid their Aunt and Uncle a good night and stepped outside. Deirdre assumed the lead, and Nur followed, legs shaking less from the cold and more from nerves.

Tonight was the night.

They meandered around the neighborhood for a while, collecting candy in the canvas Trader Joe's bags they cadged from the cupboard, nodding and smiling to the other trick-or-treaters who hadn't gotten the holiday out of their system over the weekend. Most of the Monday night crowd appeared to have significant crossover with the juicebox crowd, Nur was slightly embarrassed to note. But she and Deirdre perhaps represented the median age, if only one took into account the parents and chaperones trailing the giggling throngs of prepubescents.

On second thought, that made her feel *worse*.

Once they'd taken on enough candy to start engaging the forearm muscles in more direct ways, Deirdre ushered Nur onto the inbound green line. This they rode in silence, sat between Sexy Yellow Nattering Tic Tac Monster From That One Children's Movie and what Nur first took to be Sexy Indira Gandhi, India's First And Only Female Prime Minister, but upon further inspection was probably meant to be Sexy Bride Of Frankenstein (vertical hair and a little white streak, anybody could have made that mistake).

So baffling were the costumes, Nur completely

failed to notice that Deirdre had sat down next to her, for the first time in the nearly three months they had been here.

A quarter of a year, one fourth of our time here gone, Nur realized with a concussive jolt. Already nervy at the prospective turn she meant the evening to take, this realization hit her especially hard.

Fortunately, the T pulled in to Park Street, and Deirdre shot up with a smile. "We change here!" she called over her shoulder as she leapt down the two steps to the platform.

Nur buried the temporal anxiety and followed her sister. After alighting, she paused. "Wait…we're changing?" She couldn't imagine why she would give up this costume, so perfectly balanced between sensuality and insulation.

"To the red line!" Deirdre once again called over her shoulder, weaving through the colorful crowd of Sexy Sitcom Characters and Sexy Patio Furniture. Nur processed this for a moment, before remembering that the T had its own array of colors; she had merely been limiting herself to the green one.

For the first time, she was going to get on a different line. Wherever Hyun-Woo lived, it was off the red one. And didn't the red one lead to Cambridge? And wasn't Cambridge where the brainiacs and rich kids lived? Hadn't she heard that somewhere?

Her anxiety redoubled. Perhaps her fantasy hadn't been far off the mark – perhaps Hyun-Woo *did* live in a penthouse. Not that it would matter if he didn't, but, well, she wouldn't turn her nose up at him if he did. She'd certainly never been in one, other than the one atop the De Dernberg Towers. But she only went in there to clean it after some rich asshole had wrecked it. Would she finally get to participate in the wrecking?

Oh, to see how the other half lived…

Nur pursued her sister around the stairs to the street, and down a stairwell that led to the deep, rushing warmth of the red line platform. Her costume was doing her all sorts of favors aboveground, but down here, with a volcanic breeze unique to subway tunnels tossling the fur of the long-dead coyote or marmot or whatever she had draped over her shoulders, she was starting to sweat. And her candy was starting to melt.

"Say," she said, "why did we spend so long around Uncle Bernard's place, if Hyun-Woo lives off the red line?"

Deirdre smiled and answered by way of shaking her bag of free treats gone runny in the heat, which caught the perpetual sigh of the tunnels and made an unpleasant, whooshing squooshing noise like somebody with a cold trying to breath through their mouth while eating macaroni and cheese.

Nur frowned, and Deirdre couldn't blame her, because that was a sound so far from appetizing it made a mockery of the petty deception that netted such an unhappy chocolate slop. "Free candy," Deirdre reiterated without conviction.

"Uh huh," Nur granted as the baseline sigh became a thunderous yawn, portending an incoming choo-choo. "Well let's maybe minimize the amount of time we waste getting more free candy, please? I think we have enough."

Deirdre grinned. "Biological clock is ticking, eh?"

"I think you know perfectly well that's not how I'd phrase it."

"I do."

The train came, they got on, and off they went.

Much to Nur's chagrin, they did waste about a

half hour wandering around Cambridge, which was charming in theory but frustrating in practice. It was indeed where the rich folks lived, and the rich folks always bought the big-ass Hershey bars. As Deirdre was running the show, Nur had to endure the onslaught of sugar. It was such a mindless exercise that she actually *had* forgotten why they came out in the first place. So when they knocked on a door and Hyun-Woo opened it, she didn't have to feign surprise in the least.

CHAPTER 20

"Oh!" Nur shouted. She managed to stop short of "WWWHHHAAAA?!", but only just.

Instead, she looked up at Hyun-Woo on the porch, dressed as…himself…and asked "why are you here?" in English, because it was all she could think to say without recourse to translation (thank heavens they had that class on dealing with doorstep missionaries).

It was, in hindsight, a dumb question. It was a mark in favor of Hyun-Woo's natural tact that he answered it as though it weren't.

"This is where I live," he returned gently. Nur was struggling enough to understand the English, so the fact that she understood *that* led her to believe that Hyun-Woo was managing to speak with a normal American accent. Whatever that meant.

There he stood, clutching a plastic jack-o-lantern full of sweeties, in a solid blue T shirt and plaid, unbuttoned overshirt, over deep blue jeans…and there *she* stood, Sexy Bear from The Revenant. He had stayed in to hand out candy to children. And she knocked on his door.

From go, this scenario had been erotically charged for her. So it wasn't until now that she realized precisely how unsexy the entire situation was. Ascension to the penthouse was far from a foregone conclusion, to say nothing of a collision of naughty bits.

As sneakily as possible, Nur tried to strike a sexier pose. Nur wasn't well accustomed to being sneaky or sexy, so the pose she struck was instead both uncomfortable and unattractive.

Hyun-Woo hardly noticed, though. He just kept staring her straight in the eye. That was gratifying. Maybe salvaging this moment wouldn't be so difficult after all…

He nodded to her bag. "Lots of candy?"

Was that innuendo? Seemed like it might have been, but Hyun-Woo had never struck her as the overly flirtatious type. Or maybe he *was*, and flirting was wildly different in Korea than it was in Seychelles than it was in America. *Screw it, tonight is about making the first move.*

"Not enough," she replied with a saucy roll of the right eyebrow. She was so immensely proud of that, she could hardly be bothered to worry about it being too much.

Or, go figure, not enough; Hyun-Woo just nodded, pulled a handful of candy from his plastic basket and deposited it into her bag. "How's that?" he inquired with a lack of irony that was equal parts charming and, in the current situation, frustrating.

From Nur's right, an evil witch cackled and tin foil crackled. She turned and showed Deirdre her eyebrows, nary an echo of the saucy roll on them. Her sister got the message and sat on the cackle. Nothing to be done about the tin foil, however.

Deirdre then loosed a stream of babble in which Nur could find little to nothing comprehensible. She aimed the spray directly at Hyun-Woo, and his face betraying understanding on his part.

Nur clutched her sister's arm as sneakily (but not sexily) as she could. "What are you saying to him?"

The younger De Dernberg shook Nur off and kept rattling on. A smile dawned on Hyun-Woo's face, and that's when Nur started to get *really* worried. Did Deirdre still fancy herself a little pimp? This was not working out at *all*.

Finally, Deirdre stopped, and now it was Hyun-Woo's turn to talk. He said some stuff, then Deirdre said some more stuff, then Hyun-Woo said some more stuff.

"What are you guys saying?" was all Nur contributed.

After a few back-and-forths, Deirdre turned to her sister. "I told him we've been out for hours and you're exhausted and have a blister on your foot."

"That's all you told him, is it? Took you that long?"

"Well, I may have said some other stuff. But the upshot is he wants to invite you in."

She nodded to Hyun-Woo, who nodded to Nur.

Mixed feelings, instantly. She was going in, private time with Hyun-Woo. At long last! That was the one hand. On the other hand, she was going in on the pretense of having an imaginary blister what needed treating. So the invite wasn't so much sexy as it was humanitarian. Not to mention, she didn't actually *have* a blister. So unless she could slap on a bandage large enough to convincingly cover a blister, she'd have to see to her purpose this evening with her socks on.

Far from ideal, but it'd do in a pinch.

And a pinch would certainly do, she mulled

privately, as she wasn't about to embarrass herself with more public attempts at innuendo this evening.

Hyun-Woo turned and opened the varnished wood door wider. And he gave her one of those smiles, with a little something extra. He knew what was up, surely. Right?

Nur patted Deirdre on the back and leaned in for a whisper. "Harvard T station at 11:30, right?"

"Yeah. Go get…get that…fuck his…go have sex."

"…"

"…"

"I appreciate your help on all of this but I'm really not comfortable with you talking t-"

"I'm not either. I just wanted to see where the boundary on our relationship was."

"You found it."

"I know that now."

"…"

"…"

"See you later."

"Yep."

Nur went upstairs with Hyun-Woo, and Deirdre went back to explore Cambridge, and they never spoke about that, or like that, to each other ever again. Their relationship was so much the better for it.

Hyun-Woo's apartment building was three stories tall, with an exterior of brick and moss that almost demanded all tenants have two sets of hand towels, because one set is antique and *for display only* so please use the cheaper ones that also look like antiques but are not.

His apartment was up a curved marble staircase on the second floor, behind a big black door that could well have been painted yesterday, and almost certainly looked that way every day. As Hyun-Woo opened it, it creaked precisely as much as one would want it too; it wasn't an ear-splitting whine, but nor was it a tedious silence. It was a door with character, and Nur felt reasonably confident that the hinges had been seen to and were maintained by specialists in the field of aperture acoustics.

Before even stepping inside, in other words, Nur was assaulted by such a display of wealth as to be ever so slightly repulsed. She'd always imagined it would be fun, falling into the stiffening lap of luxury, but in practice it was making her feel slightly…icky. It might well have helped if Hyun-Woo had shouted "ta-da!" every few seconds; at least that way she would have known that *he* felt like it was all a bit much as well. But he kept his head down as he held the doors for her and led her into his not-so-humble abode, like this was all the most ordinary and unremarkable thing in the world.

Which meant to him, it probably was.

She wondered, not so idly, just whose apartment this was. His parents were both diplomats, so was this an apartment allotted for foreigners on political business? One might expect it to be in, say, Washington D.C. then, right? Or were they renting it for the duration of Hyun-Woo's study at the Crabshoe School For The Language Of English? Or did they *own* it? How wealthy were they, exactly? Did they make all of their money on diplomatic business, or did they have thumbs in other pies?

The question of love came circling back. If Hyun-Woo were just a hook-up to her, she wouldn't give two hoots about the answers to those questions. She'd done the 'no strings' thing before, and while it wasn't her favorite, she'd done a good job at snipping those strings.

For a little while, she saw a guy who giggled every time he reached climax. And a proper *giggle* it was, *tee-hee-hee* like he was being tickled. It was harmless but unnerving, especially when Nur flipped the causal chain and wondered if maybe he could only reach climax by giggling himself up to it. Still, the guy was great, and often brought her to a similar conclusion (though she never marked the occasion with a giggle, you can be sure about that), so she bundled that unfortunate characteristic up with all the others (for reasons all his own he insisted on calling her "Bee-Baw"; he had a grandmother's grasp on texting etiquette; his hair always felt sort of greasy) and partitioned them. They had both agreed it was a purely physical relationship up front, and so the rest didn't matter.

Now here was Nur, forming questions about 'the rest' as pertained to Hyun-Woo, and finding that she cared deeply about the answers. How disappointing it would be, to find out that he was not only unambitious (oh, she'd managed to make herself forget that assessment of him, but now it came roaring back) but entitled as well. He seemed so kind and well-adjusted… and if he weren't, well, it wouldn't matter if this were purely physical. But it did matter.

So was this love? She had no way of knowing. Maybe. It hardly seemed worth wondering, at this stage.

But it was most definitely *something*.

Hyun-Woo swung open the door to his/his parent's/the US government's/somebody's apartment. Where Nur expected buttoned leather and odorous mahogany, she saw modernity. Sharp angles and glass tabletops and space-age curvy chairs and minimalism minimalism minimalism, so much minimalism it bore repeating even if that did sort of defeat the purpose.

The place was so sleek and shiny, it seemed an almost perverse refutation of the building's exterior.

Not that any of this implied a lesser degree of wealth or privilege than antique stained oak armoires and cuckoo clocks with golden pendulums would have, of course. This whole classed up Sharper Image look may well have cost *more*, when all the electronic doodads and gewgaws were factored in. It was just, to Nur's slightly biased mind, a less ostentatious form of wealth. It was *progressive* wealth, wealth aimed toward the future, as opposed to wealth turned toward the past.

This was a largely arbitrary position to hold, she knew perfectly well. But that did little to minimize the intensity with which she felt it.

Or perhaps it was just a convenient stance to take, given her ulterior motives.

Recalling the motives, she dropped her bag of candy, hoping to get Hyun-Woo's attention. The bag went *thwack*, and Hyun-Woo turned, and then they stood silently for a moment as the contents of the bag went *krskrkskrskrskr* for what felt like a billion years, until they finally settled.

Hyun-Woo favored her with his resplendent grin. "Do you-"

Krskrskrskr said a rogue bar of chocolate.

"...do you need to dress your _____?"

Ah, right. She had nearly forgotten that she was flying solo here. What was the last word he had just said? He was talking about 'dressing', which was certainly on topic, though she was more concerned with undressing at this point. What would she have to dress? *Does he think I'm cold because of this costume? He maybe thinks I need to dress in more clothes?*

"No," she gambled, "I am, maybe, *too* warm." She shrugged the animal skin blanket off onto the floor. It fell with a refreshingly soft and brief *wshhhh*. Underneath, she was wearing a dark tank top. All the 'flesh colored' garments she could find were apparently for wan cave monsters with the complexion of a snake's egg, so she'd had to bust out her tie-dying skills and tint a top to match her own skin tone. Judging by Hyun-Woo's face, the illusion of nudity was effectively attained, at least for a moment.

"Haaah," Hyun-Woo exhaled. He nodded for a moment, then pointed to her ankles. He started to repeat himself, but he didn't need to.

Damnit.

Do you need to see to your wound. Dress meant applying a bandage in that context.

Nur cocked her jaw to the side, and reset it with a little *pop*. "Oh, yeah." She picked up the fur coat and tossed it on the nearby Christ-like sectional, which instead of sins had taken on all of the fluffiness and cushionitude of the rest of the apartment. *That'd be a prime spot to start,* she noted as Hyun-Woo showed her to the bathroom, which was surely the opposite end of that spectrum. She thanked him, closed the door, and pondered her next move as she wasted a perfectly good bandage on a decidedly healthy portion of her left heel.

She was exceedingly surprised to find that she wished she could have talked to Deirdre just then.

CHAPTER 21

Seychelles was hardly a matriarchy, but it did skew that way. So Nur was well-accustomed to being the carnal Prime Mover Unmoved, and it had never felt unusual to her. The fact that Hyun-Woo was retaining such passivity led her to speculate that South Korea may have had a similar social-sexual setup.

Then again, some people were just timid. This she reminded herself as she lay flat-out on one arm of the fluffy, puffy sectional. It was only by the tremulous energy of her goal for the evening that she avoided falling asleep instantly. This was one comfy-ass couch.

She got comfortable (how could she not), resting one ankle atop the other (remembering in the knick of time to inhale sharply as she brushed the bandage across the top of her right foot), and gazed up at Hyun-Woo with what she hoped were eyes in which a fella could get lost. Or at least diverted enough to make him swallow his pride and ask for directions.

After that, she was really counting on him to react. She had no problem leading, but even the world's most magnetic leader couldn't shift a, hm…

There was no way to finish that analogy without insulting Hyun-Woo, especially if she'd gone with her first thought, which was "a bucket of dirt".

She needed him to follow her lead, that was the point. And far from following, *very* far, was Hyun-Woo, all but hugging the wall opposite the sectional.

And thus, they reached a stalemate. Nur had made a big show of flopping onto the comfy-ass couch, so she couldn't well get right back up without looking like a fool. But the couch was a passive place to be. He was up and on his feet, but more interested in squat-scratching his back like a gorilla on a thick frame, which displayed a large white matte, which displayed a small grayscale picture of a dock at sunset or some shit.

She had no words. How frustrating, then, that she should have so many things to say. Words locked in the skull, yet again.

It's alright, she strained to convince herself, *just break the ideas down to their component parts. Figure out what you* can *say.*

…

What can I say?

…

How long have we been staring at each other?

…

This is getting weird.

…

Somebody should say something.

…

You're somebody.

…

SAY SOMETHING!

"Bbbbhhhhlllll!" Nur cried, because she had so many things she wanted to say all at once.

The worst part about the eternity that followed was that Hyun-Woo didn't react. If he had recoiled or grimaced or attacked, Nur would at least be able to understand why. He had invited her into his home, and she had started gibbering. There probably wasn't a particular protocol observed by the higher classes in moments like these, unless the uppity books on etiquette were far more comprehensive than Nur had ever imagined, but surely human nature would dictate *some* sort of response in such a situation.

But Hyun-Woo just stood there, staring at her with exactly the same look of skeptical perplexity as he'd been rocking for, oh, who knows how long. Time flies when you're trying to cultivate your romantic prospects and accidentally end up drowning them in molasses.

And then she remembered that she was wearing an eroticized version of a very bad bear from a very bad movie, and she wished she had died in her mother's womb.

He broke the silence that had descended after *she* had broken the silence, and his silence-breaker was hardly more substantial. Though, to be fair, that was mostly on Nur, because at least he said words.

Three of those words she knew and understood. The fourth she didn't, which was a bummer because that seemed like the really important one. It was the word that the other three words were about.

"I've never had" were the first three. What had he never had? What's never-having-been-had-ness would be germane to this agonizingly protracted moment?

Did bbbbhhhhlllll sound like something else in English that he'd never had?

Had he peeked in her bag and recognized a type of candy he'd never had?

Was he oh wait no hang on a second right oh okay

well *that* explained a lot.

In all of her excitement, her scheming and dreaming, Nur had never bothered to look up the English word for what she was after. She couldn't be *certain* that the English word of which she was ignorant was that fourth word Hyun-Woo had said. And she wasn't entirely sure how best to seek clarification on the topic.

It would certainly frame his hot-and-cold approach to intimacy in a more comprehensible light, and maybe a big white matte to draw the eye.

Well, she could think of one method of clarification.

She felt a smile creeping across her face, and watched Hyun-Woo's drop in perfect counterpoint. It was a grin directed at her two methods of detection, though for all poor Hyun-Woo knew she was smirking at his never having had the fourth word.

"No, no," she corrected. "Um...I didn't understand. You've never had..." And then she went with her second method, which was to touch the thumb and forefinger of her left hand, and poke her right index finger through the resultant hole.

Hyun-Woo's face was a patchwork of emotions that had been run through the wash a few too many times. "Right," he replied in a completely unreadable voice. "I've never had sex."

"Sex," she repeated diligently. And then Nur De Dernberg, hopeless romantic, self-appointed bulwark against the hordes of cynicism that would seek to divest Love of its nobility, poor study of the English language, said "you wanna have it?"

And Hyun-Woo said "sure".

And then they had it.

And it was just alright.

The hardest part (wakka wakka) was after, when Nur had to get up, collect her costume and leave, without knowing how to mumble "whoops, can't stay, gotta run, gotta meet my sister, so sorry". She *did* want to stay, and she got the distinct impression that Hyun-Woo wanted her to stay as well. The wordless post-coital extraction (well, technically the *second* wordless post-coital extraction of the evening, heyo) made her feel cheap, even if she knew there was a perfectly good reason for it.

Well, maybe that was the second worst part. The worst part was, in the beginning, when Hyun-Woo was, erm, still asleep at the switch, and Nur spent a hot second terrified he'd be the sort of guy who couldn't perform unless he was being strangled or cut. However he wanted his first time to go, Nur was less than thrilled at the prospect of *their* first time being conducted under the aegis of a safeword like "race car" or "recycling bin" – of the words they both understood, not too many were especially sexy. Unless their safe word had been "sex", which Nur had just learned, though for some reason she'd much rather have had Hyun-Woo start shouting LAUNDROMAT LAUNDROMAT than SEX SEX SEX. Fortunately it was just good old-fashioned performance anxiety, and Hyun-Woo was quick to regain his confidence without being put in a half nelson.

So, in hindsight, having to once again become Sexy Bear from The Revenant and tromp off into the cutting chill of October (though with a toasty afterglow to dull the needling breeze)…*that* was the hardest part. Because she wanted to stay. Not even to do it again… not that she'd say no if he'd wanted to…but just to be with Hyun-Woo. For it being his first time, he had been gentle and attentive. And while she certainly hoped she'd have the chance to teach him the occasional virtues of vehemence, the obvious effort he'd put in to baseline adequacy was endlessly endearing, in such a way that made her want to bury her face in the crook of his neck and fall asleep. Then again, she was a cuddler, so she may very well have wound up feeling that way no matter how it turned out.

Even still – it was 11:13, and she had to be going. There were mumbled farewells, hers far more generic than she imagined his were, a prolonged hug, and a few chaste kisses, followed by a prolonged not-so-chaste kiss and another hug.

By the time she left his apartment it was 11:29, because that not-so-chaste kiss was *very* prolonged. As was Hyun-Woo, Nur couldn't help but notice. On second thought, a second time would have been just fine by her. But it was 11:30. Time to go.

After one more kiss.

CHAPTER 22

It was a good job they'd set up those sisterly boundaries earlier in the evening. They'd keep the ride home relatively painless. Nur was happy to provide the headlines, but the gory details would remain classified.

She didn't get back to the T station until a little after 11:40, and she'd been hustling to make that. As she arrived tardy, sweaty (maybe this costume was a bit *too* warm) and panting, there was some good-natured ribbing from Deirdre, variations on the theme of "that good, was it?" Nur weathered these gracefully as they descended the stairs and awaited the train.

And then, a shaft of regret pierced her bosom, because she realized she'd left her bag of candy at Hyun-Woo's. Not that that mattered, because free candy was for children like Deirdre. But still. It was free candy, and she wasn't a *sociopath*, which is what you'd have to be to lose a bag of free candy and not feel *something*.

He'd probably bring it into school tomorrow. Cold comfort, given how hard she would murder something with chocolate and peanut butter right now.

"Enough about the candy," Deirdre snapped, which was when Nur realized she'd been having those thoughts out loud. "Tell me about the *sweets*."

"..."

"I thought that was tactful."

"On the cusp." Nur jumped as the train took a corner and made a loud farting noise.

"Is that a type of foreplay?"

Despite a valiant effort to retain a mask of frustration, Nur smirked. "It happened, and it was nice, and that's all I'll say about it."

Deirdre opened her mouth to pose a follow-up, but slowly closed it, respecting the line Nur had drawn. The older sister was proud of the younger, and even though that didn't happen often, it always felt just right when it did.

On the few times that did happen, it never lasted long. Case in point: before they'd even made it back to Park Street to switch back to the Green Line, Deirdre clapped her hands together and informed Nur that "now, we switch."

"I remember. At Park Street."

"No, I mean you and I switch."

"..."

"I wingmanned for y-"

"No."

"-ou, now you have t-"

"No way."

"-o wingman for me."

"Absolutely not."

"Why not?"

The train pulled in to Park Street. They debarked, ascended the stairs, awaited an outbound C train, boarded it, sat down (well, Nur sat; Deirdre stood) and waited for the train to start moving.

"Because," Nur resumed as though there hadn't

been seven minutes of electrical silence just then, "you're fifteen years old."

"So?"

"Age of consent in this country is eighteen."

"And?"

"It'd be illegal!"

"Not if I do it with somebody else under eighteen!"

"I'm not going to help two children have sex with each other!" Nur shouted into car full costumed people too old to be in costumes, suddenly quite glad that her English wasn't good enough to support this conversation.

"Nobody's asking you to help us have sex, j-"

"Just get to a point where you can *have* sex, yes, I get it, I see where you're going with that. I'm not joking."

Deirdre stomped her foot, which rustled her bag of candy. She'd seldom looked younger to Nur that she did now. "I helped you! I did almost all the work on setting that up!" She pointed indiscriminately to her left, which Nur was fairly certain was completely the wrong direction if she meant to be pointing towards Hyun-Woo's place in Cambridge, but all the same she knew perfectly well where the trembling digit was directed.

"And I've told you, multiple times, how much I appreciate that." The dusty snapping sound creeping into Nur's voice was her patience fraying to the breaking point. She'd shot for a reasoned tone of diplomacy, but her frustration betrayed her. Deirdre's face was busy betraying *her*, and what was burning in her belly was a bit more than frustration. So Nur broke the glass in case of emergencies and yanked out the ire extinguisher. "Look, I'm sorry," she cooed, not quite know what she was sorry for just yet. "I'm sorry that, ah, well, I know how much you helped me out here. But this was a specific…thing, with a specific guy. I really like him. Are there any boys you've met who you really like?"

This was a four-alarm blaze of fury on Deirdre's face. Where had this come from? They had been getting along so well! Just *minutes* ago, they had been getting along! Good-natured ribbing! Where did that go? Why was this happening?

How can I make it stop *happening?*

"That's not the point," Deirdre mumbled. She knew she was in the wrong, and Nur was glad to see her sister wasn't facing this realization with the belligerence of her youth. "I just…it's what's fair! I helped you, you should help me. It's…I want it to happen."

A question occurred to Nur, largely because it was a topic near the front of her mind. Even as the words had clumped together in her brain and gone sliding down the mouth-spout, she knew that saying them would be a terrible, horrible, catastrophic thing to do, and she wished with all of her might that she wouldn't say them. But inertia's a hell of a thing.

"Have you ever even *had* sex?" she inquired as gently as one can with that question.

Deirdre blinked hard enough to crack walnuts between her lids. Nur was almost positive she could hear wet little *bink bink bink* noises over the rumbling and grumbling of the train.

There was hardly any point running damage control; the rickety edifice of sisterly affection they'd been laboriously constructing over the past few weeks had just collapsed in on itself, and sieving through the ruins for encouraging crossbeams wasn't going to bring it back.

But still, Nur tried, because she didn't quite understand why this had happened. Couldn't quite believe it *had* happened. Hadn't she just thought to herself that the ride would be relatively painless? "Deirdre, if this was something you wanted we should have discussed it. It's not as though I agreed to help you, and now I'm refusing."

Deirdre said nothing.

"I'm really sorry I said that. I didn't say it to be mean, I'm just thinking, you should try to have your first time be special, you know? Not with some stranger in America."

Deirdre said nothing.

"I'm just trying to look out for you. I'm really, really sorry I said that. I'm an idiot."

Nothing, said Deirdre.

"I don't understand what just happened! We were getting along!"

Nothing is what Deirdre continued to say.

"I can't thank you enough for helping me with Hyun-Woo, but you can't honestly have expected me to help you lose your virginity to a stranger, could you?"

Guess what Deirdre said to that.

"What did you expect I would say to that?"

Deirdre scoffed. "I expected you to be my friend."

"That's exactly what I'm doing!" And then they both said enough nothing to fill a three-week philosopher's symposium.

Someday, Nur assured herself, *Deirdre will look back on this moment and know I was right. Even if she doesn't thank me for it, she'll know I had her best interests in mind.* That was a nice thought, but the thing about 'someday' is it's a day that never really comes. Not really.

CHAPTER 23

Nur had a lot of time to think, because she had a lot of time and thinking was all she could do.

Hyun-Woo returned her bag of candy the next day, with a great big smile on his face. After some labored English and a three-minute panto, he managed to ask where Deirdre had gotten to, and Nur had managed to respond that her younger sister wouldn't be along to translate anytime soon. There were a few more frustrated stabs at conversation, but after becoming accustomed to the friendly intercessions of the junior De Dernberg, it was difficult to maintain any great enthusiasm for the sort of halting, gesture-heavy exchange to which they one again found themselves limited. And that was alright, because it was time to go to class. Hyun-Woo to his advanced session, Nur to the one just barely above the beginner level.

She hardly paid Tuppence Crabshoe any attention. Had she thought about it, she might have made more of an effort, as the words and concepts the venerable namesake of the school was writing on the board and tapping with a stick were just the sorts of things that would help Nur communicate with Hyun-Woo. But she was too busy thinking about other things. Thinking about how much she wanted to say to Hyun-Woo, about last night, about tomorrow night, and about today, and about the two of them. Thinking about all of the things she wanted to say but didn't know how, not in the melodramatic sense but in the more prosaic, enragingly literal sense. Thinking, because that was all she could do.

Somehow, Nur had gotten it into her head that relations with Deirdre would thaw under the first sunrise of November. This was quite emphatically not the case. Deirdre simply reverted to her old self…well, her old *old* self. Her old *old* self was bubbly and fun and pleasant to be around. It was her old *new* self, the dour, gloomy teen, that Nur had desperately hoped she'd seen the back of for good. Alas, not so much. Deirdre had stepped up her cold shoulder game from mute glaring to mute eye-contact-avoidance. The amount of effort and attention she was putting in to ignoring Nur was surely unprecedented in all of teendom. And, though Nur would never in a million years admit it…Deirdre was getting to her. Distracting herself on the endless T rides to and from the school by making the acquaintance of every bleat and screech and moan and groan the train made as they complained their way around Beantown proved fruitless; the only reprieve she could find from her sister's deafening silences was in the classroom, where her ears rang with the conversations she wasn't having, and was unable to have, with Hyun-Woo.

The only constant left in her day-to-day existence now was a closed-circle parade of thoughts, with leering, over-inflated floats tethered together by used dental floss and prayers to the gods of forgotten civilizations.

Why had Deirdre turned so suddenly against her? What was her sister's problem? And *why wouldn't she translate anymore*? Hyun-Woo was growing more distant, Nur could feel it. They still hung out after class, they still explored the city, and every once in a while Nur would head back to Hyun-Woo's inexplicably trendy pad and see to the solemn rite of buggery that kept a single man a "bachelor", as opposed to "lonely".

But whatever they were up to, it only occasionally involved speaking to one another. Not for lack of trying, at least not at first. But then, yes, slightly for lack of trying. Slamming their heads against the brick wall of incomprehension was exhausting, and Nur could hardly begrudge Hyun-Woo for making friends with some of the people from his advanced classes, and preferring to hang out with them after class.

Actually, it was more accurate to say that she knew she *shouldn't* begrudge him that. But she did. It made her slightly jealous. Yeah…slightly. To begin with, he would invite her along with them, and would make a real effort to include her in their conversations. But the conversations were so far beyond her that, even as Hyun-Woo's accommodating new friends joined in the 'let's all throttle back our vocabulary so Nur can join in' routine, Nur could understand them to a certain extent, but remained incapable of formulating responses. She couldn't help but resent the ostentatious patience with which the friend group regarded her, and she couldn't blame them if they felt a similar exasperation with her. So she stopped coming to these soirees, so Hyun-Woo stopped inviting her. Which was on her. And she knew that.

But still. Jealousy crept in and made a bed, and she was nothing if not a gracious host.

This to the one side. On the other, Deirdre was

making friends just as effortlessly. They were all learning to speak English with startling rapidity; how useful was the youthful soup of their swimmy, ill-formed grey matter! In theory, Deirdre couldn't go out without Nur present as chaperone. In practice, she would sprint out the door as soon as classes were over, cackling down the street in a phalanx of quite literally fast friends, and then send Nur a message to the effect of "I'll be at X place at X time." And Nur would have no choice but to futz around alone (save those rare afternoons when Hyun-Woo wasn't otherwise engaged with his new buddies) until X time, at which point she would go to X place. What choice did she have? She couldn't well go complaining to her Aunt and Uncle. As she'd already established, Deirdre would get in big trouble, but Nur would still get in little trouble. And in the De Dernberg family, a little went a long way.

She spent these comfortless afternoons thinking thinking thinking, naturally. To begin with, she thought about Hyun-Woo and Deirdre. As November withered and snow began to fall, the thoughts turned to generalities. Big Question type stuff, about communication and relationships and love, always love, what did love feel like and what did it mean and was this love or was that love (but never *what is love*, because even at her most introspective Nur was sensitive to the threshold of pure pretention) and how could you love someone who didn't even seem to make time for you anymore and right along with love she thought about time which was slipping through her fingers, every passing day brought her back to Seychelles just a little bit more, brought her back with what seemed to be a stagnant store of English that was bound to disappoint her parents, and infuriate them as well because what had they spent all that money but to have their daughter learn English, and of course they would point to Deirdre and ask why she couldn't have buckled down and studied hard like her younger sister clearly had, and was any of this love or was it business, this was a *family* business after all, and did that leave any room to view one's children as anything other than an investment, and would they care if she told them she thought she had fallen in love, and that she'd really *tried* to learn the language but she just hadn't been able to, the language being *English*, in case they needed clarification…

November slipped on the ice and cracked its head open, and December came dribbling out. Nur's thoughts took a similar tumble, from rarified generalities into abstract self-absorption. Thoughts about thoughts. Thoughts for their own sake. Productivity hit a nadir, at least as far as her relationships were concerned. She'd stopped trying to sort them out. Had this thing with Hyun-Woo become purely physical? It was starting to seem that way. They rarely spent time together that didn't culminate in them mussing up Hyun-Woo's always immaculately made bed (a bed he always remade as soon as they got out of it – had he always done that, or was that a recently acquired affectation? Nur couldn't be sure). Wasn't that what people did when they were in love? Consummate their emotions in a more tangible way? She certainly still felt *something* for him, and the something was still quite intense. But it was tinged with bitterness, because now his new friends weren't so new anymore, and she felt blocked out. Some of his once-new friends were girls. Nur couldn't help but wonder… and she hated herself for doing so.

In spite of her perpetual distraction, English began to sink in. Tuppence Crabshoe first stopped called Nur 'Ahnonur', and then graduated her from the rookie classes near the middle of December (it was only then that Nur realized why the head of the school taught the beginner courses – to personally monitor the progress of the neophytes from 'go'), which gave her an ephemeral but nonetheless uplifting rush of slow-burning adrenaline. The low-intermediate course thrust her in to no less motley an assortment of classmates, mostly middle-aged folks who looked like they had a number of interesting stories they could tell you and a few *very* interesting stories they never would. It seemed the young, attractive people were all in the advanced courses.

Nur learned, neither quickly nor heroically, but she learned. Comprehension remained far easier than conversation. She went and saw a movie one afternoon when Deirdre was off doing whatever it was she did when she went off (Nur hardly cared anymore, though she did feel periodic *ping*s of worry like enemy submarines caught out under the sweeping green arm of radar), and understood most of it. Granted, most of it involved the world blowing up, but sometimes a character would shout "look out" or "no" or "here's what's going to happen", and she understood most of that stuff.

The city drowsed under a heavy white blanket that fell as crisply as Hyun-Woo's duvet, after he'd tugged and slapped and yanked out the wrinkles they'd so lately pushed into it. And then, about five minutes later, the snow would be pockmarked with bootprints and plowed into grey mounds along the slushy streets, conspiring with the ice to annihilate the human race, one clumsy, puffy-coated grocery-carrying man at a time. There was one day towards the end of the year when clouds tall with incontinence dropped their business in undeniable quantities, and Boston cried out, in one voice, "fair enough". Public transit shut down, businesses and schools closed, and the city grew warmer than Nur had ever seen it. Coolidge Corner, a quaint little intersection near her Uncle Bernard's, was full of people, families and lovers freely wandering the intersection ordinarily so heavily congested with cars and trucks and trains, laughing and catching falling flakes on their tongue, packing those few flakes that escaped their gustatory defenses into balls and hurling them at their friends (for some reason, it was not just acceptable but encouraged to pack snow into tight, icy projectiles and whip them at the faces you love most, which made Nur wonder if love was all it was cracked up to be anyway).

Surrounded by friends, families and loved ones taking the air, Nur wandered alone. Deirdre had refused to go out with her, and Hyun-Woo was who knew where. Actually, she suspected she did; he was probably up in Cambridge. With the T out of commission, connecting today would be nearly impossible…but it still hurt her a bit that he didn't shoot her a text, to say hey, look how beautiful the snow is today. She could read most texts now. He knew that.

Look how beautiful the snow is today, she'd written in a text just before heading outside. An hour after that, she leaned against the glass façade of a coffee shop whose Wi-Fi she'd used quite a lot. It was closed, but fortunately they hadn't bothered shutting their router off. Not that it mattered; Hyun-Woo hadn't responded to her.

This was the first time Nur had seen *snow*. She didn't count the earlier flurries, because, well, she hadn't wanted to. It was more romantic to say that *the first time I saw snow, it was from the center of a hushed town square, under the Tudor-style clocktower with the brown witch's hat for a roof, the hands of the clock frozen in this magical moment, and there I stood, swaddled in wool and down, toasty despite the windless chill, watching through the curtain of thick, falling flakes as friends and families and loved ones took in the day, lit by somnolent sunlight made otherworldly by the diffusion of the clouds,* and so on and so forth, tapping this vein of uncharacteristic poetry all to avoid the unhappy fact that she stood in the center of the hushed town square all alone.

Hours later, after she'd taken a few laps and done some more thinking about nothing in particular, she returned to Uncle Bernard's, her extremities numb despite the wool and down. Hyun-Woo still hadn't responded to her text, and Deirdre was asleep with her head stuffed under the pillow. So Nur drew herself a warm bath and sat in it until her fingers pruned, at which point she continued to stew in it until the sun went down and she deemed it privately acceptable to go to sleep.

CHAPTER 24

Hyun-Woo invited Nur to his New Year's Eve party, and she accepted. She couldn't quite escape the feeling that the both of them were making decisions based on good form rather than genuine enthusiasm. What was she actually contributing to Hyun-Woo's life? Certainly not sparkling conversation, of the sort he got from his advanced classmates. Sex? Well, yeah, but it wasn't *just* that. They weren't bootycalling one another (that was one of the words she'd picked up in the intermediate level – once one surpassed the basics, one's classmates had just as much to teach as the teacher, if not more); they still went on 'dates', though Hyun-Woo did seem slightly bummed at the restrictions placed on where they could go. All of his advanced buddies could get into bars and clubs, after all. Nur had plenty of fun pregaming (Ibid.) at his place and having a dizzy eighteen at mini-golf, and she thought he did too. But she couldn't be certain, and that that doubt had claws.

So it was decided: what Nur brought to Hyun-Woo's life was something between linguistic connection and sex.

For some reason, standing on his stoop on that final, freezing evening of the old year, eagerly anticipating the moment when he would swing open the door, that they might commence the boozy baptism of the new...not the forthcoming moment of admittance but *this* one, the one in which she shifted her weight from foot to foot in a vain effort to keep warm, the one in which she soaked up the gratified silence of a spent year counting down to quitting time, the one in which her only company was the tinkling of silver chimes tickled by the breeze and the distant, premature pops of firecrackers so recently in the hands of overeager drunkards and children, both factions knowing perfectly well they'd be sound asleep before the real fireworks went off...it was *this* moment that Nur would always come back to. Why *this* moment should be the one upon which she pinned her plaintive retrospection, she never quite worked out. Oh, she had some ideas, mostly to do with how the new year began, though they didn't explain the clarity and purpose with which this moment would become *the* moment in her mind, arguably the moment upon which her entire American experience pivoted. And perhaps that was an apt analogy, because the pivot point is always passive and static, just as this moment was. It was the stuff furthest from the pivoting point that did all the moving.

However she thought of it, she always *did* think of it, coming back to it time and again to wonder why she never bothered to invert the question: what was Hyun-Woo actually contributing to *her* life?

It's not that the answer was negative, not at all. It's just that, had she ever bothered to stop and ask herself this simple question, things might have turned out very differently.

The curtain was thick and blue, but it wasn't flush against the wall, so the sunlight rushed the sides, spilled in through the gaps like a Jackson Pollock painting that had exactly the wrong idea about what frames were for, and punched Nur in the eyeballs.

"Mmmrrrp," she rumbled. Somebody inside her head was trying to play "Ave Maria" with depth charges, and the sunlight brought with it an accompaniment like moist chimp fingers tracing the rims of wine glasses filled with vinegar and DDT-rich surface runoff.

"Don't mix your liquors," that had a lovely ring to it in English. One of Hyun-Woo's classmates kept saying that to her, but neglected to underline the ecstatic truth beneath the snappy rhyme. Though to be fair, she probably thought she was underlining it by repeating it over and over. Unfortunately Nur missed the emphasis, and had arrived at a rather dramatic punctuation point.

Why did I drink so much? she might have wondered if she had been capable of coherent thought just then. Instead she wondered *hhhhnnnnnngggg*. But she knew what she meant.

She turned to Hyun-Woo's friend, the one who had warned her about not mixing her liquors. What was her name? Something pretty plain. Sally, or Debby, or something like that. Sallydebby was from…Russia? Or Brazil? She was from somewhere, anyway, and they had had a lovely conversation. In English! Nur had conducted herself relatively well – to her surprise, alcohol had loosened her up, and peeled away the gauzy self-consciousness that smothered her usual attempts to speak English fluidly. Or maybe the fluid she'd consumed just let her *think* she was doing better than she actually was. Which

OH.

OH GOD.

OH FUCK (thanks, intermediate classmates!).

OH FUCKGOD (profanity had a learning curve like anything else, natch).

Nur had stayed awake until the big ball in New York dropped, at which point she followed suit.

At Hyun-Woo's house.

Overnight.

She pulled out her phone and utilized Hyun-Woo's wireless internet to check her messages, of which she had approximately one million.

The depth charge hymnal had, it turned out, not been in her head. It was in her phone, vibrating endlessly all through the night. As it was right now. One million and one messages.

She punched in her password and made a quick survey, reconstructing the evening.

Deirdre had sent the earliest messages; a warning, that Uncle Bernard and Aunt Amy were starting to make agitated noises. It was touching, in a way, that deep in whatever pique Deirdre had been lounging the last few weeks, she was still looking out for her big sister. The tone of the messages was slightly glib, "you better hurry back or you're gonna be in deeeeeeeep trouble," that sort of thing, but the fact that she had about an hour lead on any of the other messages was heartening.

Deirdre sent her first message just after midnight, after Nur had already collapsed into her booze cocoon. Aunt Amy's first message and come just before 1:00AM. It was softly concerned, with a stern permissiveness just beneath the surface. "Send us a message to let us know you're alright. The T is closed by now, so let us know where you are and we can come get you."

Then, at 1:30 *on the dot*, Uncle Bernard started sending messages. Well, he started by sending *message*, one massive disquisition on the nature of outrage and disrespect, and how he and Nur embodied each respectively. "Invited you into our home, this is how you repay us," that sort of thing. Nur suspected that he'd punched this out in a blind rage, and stayed his finger from the 'send' button only by Aunt Amy's request. "Wait until 1:30", she must have said, and Nur could just imagine Uncle Bernard boggling at the clock, sweat trickling down his brow as he tried to steam the minutes off in the furnace of his righteous fury.

But then, Deirdre was still sending messages all this time, giving Nur a fly-on-the-wall perspective of what was happening. Aunt Amy was trying to defend Nur to her Uncle, or rather from her Uncle's punitive instincts, Deirdre assured her, but in point of fact *Amy* was the angrier of the two. It was an anger borne of disappointment, which was more agonizing than any punishments Uncle Bernard could hand down from high horse. "I always thought Nur was a sensible girl" was one phrase Deirdre reported via text, and that was one phrase that would haunt Nur for years to come.

Amy wasn't even mad that Nur had stayed out all night, Deirdre cabled. She was mad that Nur had stayed out all night and *hadn't let them know*, because it left them no choice but to assume something bad had happened to her.

Which, by about 2:30AM, they did.

They discussed calling the police, Nur read, and at that point her phone split into two and went all runny, at least until she dabbed at her eyes with clumsy, slightly chafed palms (and what was *that* about?). They had discussed calling the police but knew they couldn't, because they watched cop shows or something. Deirdre was iffy on that part. They also talked about calling her parents, which split the phone into about sixteen and necessitated more than a few dabs.

But they didn't. Deirdre was very clear about that. They didn't.

But that didn't mean they *wouldn't*.

Nur shot off a text without quite knowing what she had written, something about sorry and didn't mean to and nothing wrong and shouldn't have and sorry once again, grabbed up her coat, her purse and somebody else's scarf (raw deal, because the one she came with had been way better) and rushed out the door without saying goodbye, or indeed without thinking that she ought to.

She would have been gratified to know that Hyun-Woo awoke four hours later, and his first thought was "where did Nur go?" But she never found out, because as was always the case, Hyun-Woo's natural introversion meant he tended to keep thoughts, even those that would make other people happy, to himself.

He would probably have been less gratified to know that, as Nur sprinted back to the T and fretted her way back down the red line, onto the green line and out past Coolidge Corner, where she'd had that magical, lonely moment in the snow, she was thinking of a hundred and one things, and none of them were him.

She wouldn't realize that herself until quite some time later.

CHAPTER 25

Uncle Bernard and Aunt Amy responded to Nur's accidental overnight in the second worst way imaginable. The worst way, of course, would have been finking her out to her parents. The consequences of that would have followed her for *years*. But with that apocalyptic option safely put to bed, there still remained a myriad of ways her extended family could make the next seven-and-some months of her time in America (nearly halfway gone – *that* was a startling thought, though one that found little purchase amongst all the others she was having lately) superlatively unpleasant.

The way they chose to respond was the only one she hadn't forseen. Which, she supposed, actually meant it wasn't the "second worst way imaginable". It was the "first worst way unimaginable", which sounded pretty dumb in both of the languages she knew, and more than likely in all the ones she didn't as well.

What they did was this:

...

...

…

Nothing.

They didn't say anything to her about it, they didn't make a show of *not* saying anything to her, they didn't even have the decency to give her nasty looks as she came slinking back into the house feeling as though she were glazed in shame…they just gave her exactly the same sort of greeting she always got when she came home. "Hi Nur."

HI NUR?! After what she'd done? That's all? She winced her way up the stairs, knowing perfectly well that they were waiting for her to clean herself up. Then, she would come back down, and the hammer would fall. They'd really let her have it this time. Yes indeed.

She took a shower, changed, and descended the stairs in extreme slow motion. Each footfall was registered by a wince, as though she expected the steps to be sown with broken glass.

Finally; the bottom step. She swung out into the living room, about-faced towards the kitchen, and saw her Uncle Bernard slurping up soup and periodically swiping at the iPad propped up before him. He looked up at her, smiled…smiled, he *smiled*, he SMILED, that same smile he used to give her on other afternoons, without a hint of venom or irony or condescension, just that wretched *smile*, when he should have been FURIOUS with her…

Sometimes, in cartoons, a coyote lays some dynamite for a roadrunner, tiptoes behind a rock, depresses the plunger, plugs its ears, and then…

…

…

…

Nothing happens, at which point the viewer knows the coyote is really in for it. The question is *how*. Will the plunger itself explode? Will the coyote peer around the rock, only to have the rock explode? Will the coyote be run over by a freight train because the explosion knocked it off its tracks? Will a space shuttle fall from the sky and flatten the coyote because the dynamite didn't blow up and for fuckgod's sake this means *the coyote must be made to suffer*?!

Nur imagined the coyote depressing the plunger, nothing happening, and then nothing *continuing* to happen. The coyote would roam the desert, expecting to find itself on the receiving end of some outrageous act of violence without a moment's notice…and nothing would happen. It might think itself in the clear, but in the back of its mind, every action it took would be fraught with the weight of the depressed plunger that yielded no kaboom. Looking both ways when crossing the street wouldn't protect it against an underground explosion. Walking outside would always leave it open to meteorite strikes. Staying inside would always leave it susceptible to gas leaks. And the coyote would live out the rest of its agonizingly long life in a state of perpetual expectation, expectation of a gruesome promise upon which the laws of Whimsical Animation never made good…

That's how she felt.

She asked Deirdre why they hadn't said or done anything, and her sister could only shrug. "I guess they said everything they had to say in the texts," she hypothesized.

Which should have made Nur feel better, because that was plausible, but it didn't. Uncle Bernard had a temper on him. Surely he wouldn't miss a golden opportunity to let it rip. Would he? Of course not! Almost certainly not.

SO WHEN?! For a week and a half, this drove her

halfway to genuine, gibbering madness. Why weren't they saying anything? She had worried them sick, stayed out all night, and they *surely* must have smelled the alcohol on her, an *underaged* girl, who by the way they must have known was staying with a *male*, and good heavens maybe they could smell the sex on her too (nevermind that she hadn't had any that night), and yet they wouldn't say a single thing out of the ordinary to her.

Her social life fell apart. She stopped wanting to go out with people, fearful that allowing an unspoken curfew to lapse would send her Aunt and Uncle into their well-deserved rage. Because that must be what they were waiting for, right? Another slip-up. All it would take was one more night out, and she would feel the heel of their boot.

So she stayed at home every night, smothered and gasping in the viscous atmosphere of Everything Being Perfectly Normal. And *that* certainly didn't help things.

After a week and a half of feeling like a sweaty sponge being wrung out over a bucket, soaked in her own excretions and wrung out again and again and again, she bounded down the stairs, rushed up to her Uncle Bernard, and blubbered apologies for a solid two minutes straight.

For the first minute, Bernard kept his eyes fixed tightly on the television, which was playing a show about dancing chef decorators looking for love or something. Eventually, he hit the pause button (Nur would later wonder if he had simply shelled out for that feature or if Bernard had DVR'd that show, which would have been a fascinating insight into the Real Uncle Dr. Bernard De Dernberg) and turned to look at her.

When she finished, he nodded appreciatively, embodying an avuncular warmth of which she would never have suspected him capable.

"It's alright," he cooed in Seychellois Creole, breaking his own nearly half-a-year old rule. "Everybody makes mistakes. Your Aunt Amy and I certainly had our fair share of wild nights. Sometimes we still do," he added with a wink, and Nur couldn't decide whether to explode with laughter or sick, but she knew she most certainly wanted to explode. "But you scared the hell out of us."

And just for a moment, there was the anger Nur had expected to see. Bernard's face *flexed*, there was no other way to put it. It hardened and bulged, then relaxed once again. "We know you're better than that."

(I always thought Nur was a sensible girl)

Uncle Bernard waved a permissive hand. "So next time – not that I'm hoping there *is* a next time, it's only that I know you're young and away from home and I'm not an idiot – keep us in the loop. Please. Alright? Otherwise I'm going to have to tell your parents what you've been up to."

Had they been speaking English, Nur likely would have missed the nuance in her Uncle's tone just there. But they weren't, and so she understood in perfectly well. She mumbled a few more apologies, ran back upstairs, smushed her face into a pillow and decided that laughter was the explosion she was after. She laughed until she cried, she laughed so hard she started to curl into a ball, she laughed so hard her abs were sore for the next two days.

She laughed because "Otherwise I'm going to have to tell your parents what you've been up to" wasn't a threat. It was a *plea*.

Uncle Bernard was just as frightened of Nur's parents as she was. That's why they were all being so eminently reasonable. Nur was her Aunt and Uncle's responsibility, as far as her parents were concerned, and while they could certainly get her in trouble by reporting her indiscretions, *they* would get in trouble as well.

So what kind of trouble could he get into? Well, Nur was still never quite clear on why Uncle Bernard changed his surname to De Dernberg when her parents did, as he had no affiliation with the hotel. Unless he *did* have some connection of which she was unaware, in which case...

I have some leverage, she allowed herself to think in some far corner of her mind. Not leverage to do anything crazy. She hadn't been so anxious because she worried about punishment for her new year's debacle (well, not solely); she genuinely felt bad. And she wasn't about to double down on that.

But she did have some leverage to stop having to treat Hyun-Woo as a secret. If she was going out with a boy, and it was all above board, well, that was alright, wasn't it? If they didn't like it, she would insist, they could phone up her parents and see what *they* thought about their little girl getting bonked all across America.

And maybe not having to sneak would change things between Hyun-Woo and me. Only it wasn't until that point that she'd admitted the 'things between them' needed changing.

CHAPTER 26

How about this, then: Nur hadn't even considered that Uncle Bernard might be afraid of her parents, because she hadn't considered her Uncle at all. She'd been through this before with Deirdre, hadn't she? Yes, of course she had. But had she learned her lesson? No, apparently not. She had still been thinking like a teenager, *me, me, me,* with nary a thought spared for anyone else. Only that wasn't quite true. She did think about other people, and what they might be feeling. She *had* learned that lesson with Deirdre before. Only it was a limited lesson, or else she had been so immature as to draw limited conclusions from it, because she had only started thinking about what other people might be feeling *as pertained to her.*

What could Deirdre be feeling that would make her act this way towards me? *What might be driving Uncle Bernard to behave as he has* towards me? It was an ostensibly thoughtful position to take, as long as one was willing to shut the inquiry down before it reached the end of the sentence. She had continued to, without the slightest hint of intentionality, place herself at the center of the social orrery. That complete lack of deliberate selfishness made it worse, really. That meant the selfishness was so deeply ingrained as to be second nature.

Nur had never thought of herself as a selfish person, for whatever *that* was worth.

If only it could be as easy as having her younger, immature self booted from the pilot's seat in favor of the older, more mature Nur. There was no clean divide between two selves that way; she was a unified whole, existing on a spectrum of immaturity, and any daydreams to the contrary were simply proving what they set out to contradict.

So she had recognized it. It was time to stop thinking about people's rich, complex personal lives as tools to explain how they were acting towards her. Instead, she needed to accept that how people acted towards her were byproducts of their rich, complex personal lives that ticked away with, in all probability, little to no consideration of Nur when she wasn't directly in front of them.

Which was, if she was being honest with herself (and why not be, this late in the game), sort of frustrating. But it was only fair; how often did she think about Uncle Bernard in the day, *really*? Not too much, in any sense other than a logistical obstacle.

But it was also, in a way, incredibly freeing. No, her every move was *not* being scrutinized and judged by everyone around her. No, every embarrassing thing she had ever done was *not* inscribed in the stone tablets of the witnesses' long-term memories. No, she was *not* foremost on everyone's mind when they made decisions that would affect her.

Youth had seen her dancing under the spotlight,

crying for everyone to look at her and pay attention, then crying because the harsh single-point, single-mindedness of the light was so unflattering. Why did it take so long to realize that not only was this *not* the case, but that she didn't *want* it to be?

What a profitable round with the thinking cap she'd had that day. She had discovered something about herself, and felt prepared to take a massive leap into the greater maturity of adulthood.

Naturally, she went on to behave exactly as she had before this long dusky late-afternoon of the soul, because personal epiphanies are great but old habits die hard. She did, however, feel little pangs of conscience when she had a selfish thought or did a selfish thing. And that's how progress always starts; not with dreams, not with daydreams, not with bathtub epiphanies or scales falling from eyes, but with the conscious mind thwacking the unconscious one on the snout with a newspaper until a new routine became old hat.

After a week or so of said schnoz-bopping, Nur was pleased to see the first budding chutes of personal progress.

CHAPTER 27

Nur could have apologized to her sister again, or sat her down for a lengthy heart to heart about the life lessons she had learned by finding out what Uncle Bernard was scared of and then having some dreams or something, but instead she went up to Deirdre and suggested they get a big-ass breakfast and then go sledding. Except first they'd have to get a sled. They went, they had a good time, though for a hot second Deirdre almost lost her big-ass breakfast, at which point she too learned a life lesson that had to do with scarfing down a full-and-a-half stack of chocolate chip pancakes with thick home-made whipped cream and maple syrup, and then trying to do anything other than hibernate for the rest of the winter.

Still, it was fun. And the following Monday, Nur ducked out of her own class early to peek into Deirdre's. *The old Nur just stood outside the school, expecting Deirdre to come to her,* thought the new, proactive Nur, whose proactivity saw her creeping through the halls and peering at children through the tall rectangular windows set into the doors.

She saw what, in some oblique way, she had expected to see. Deirdre talking to friends, one of whom was a handsome young man taking every opportunity to touch her. Strictly PG, nothing untoward. Practiced casual is how Nur would have described his moves. A hand hovering in for a gentle landing on her shoulder, or a playful tap with the back of the hand when he's suddenly got something witty to say, or the floating knee that just happens to brush against hers when he leans in to listen to what she has to say.

Well, no shit. While Nur had been obsessing over her life, and her relationship with Hyun-Woo, she had been blithely blind to the story in which her sister was the lead. Deirdre and her boy had, arguably, an even *more* star-crossed romance, because Nur had only to contend with her Aunt and Uncle, really. And those days were at an end. Deirdre had hidden this from *all* of them.

Which was sad to think about. Even in their good stretch there, Deirdre hadn't dropped even the slightest hint that she had a brown-haired beau. Or maybe she *had*, and Nur had simply been too self-absorbed to notice them. That was even sadder: that Deirdre hadn't been concealing it from Nur, but Nur still never noticed…

…so if Deirdre hadn't been hiding it, and assumed Nur therefore knew about this guy, and then asked Nur to return the favor of acting as wingman, a request which Nur refused…

…on the grounds that she didn't want Deirdre losing her virginity to a stranger…

…which, in hindsight, was really none of her fucking business, was it? Even if the guy *were* a stranger, which she supposed he wasn't, if she wouldn't consider

Hyun-Woo stranger, wasn't that Deirdre's decision? Nur should have asked if the situation was safe, and then butted the hell out.

Well maybe that was going too far. She had *some* sisterly responsibilities. But the point was, the guy wasn't a stranger to Deirdre. Just to Nur.

And, well, she still didn't feel *super* excited about helping her sister lose her virginity. It was one of those gut-level intuitive judgments that most people are fortunate enough to have. The Venn diagram between Thoughts About Family and Thoughts About Sex should be two unbroken, non-overlapping circles on opposite sides of a football stadium (one time she had been masturbating, and just at the moment of climax, received a text message from her sister. It was a solid three weeks before Nur felt the slightest hint of loin-stirring again).

But somehow, Deirdre had held her nose and dragged those two circles atop one another, so it was only reasonable that Nur return the favor. More than an apology, more than a long-winded explanation for the dreams and reasonings that led to this reversal, simply helping Deirdre out would be the way to mend this particular fence, between Thoughts About Family and Thoughts About Sex. And if, in the mending process, she reinforced it with steel and concrete, so much the better.

Nur wandered back outside to wait for her sister, as per usual. But as per unusual, she waited on the stoop of the school, just outside the front door. As the students trickled and then rushed out, she shot out an arm and snatched Deirdre by the elbow.

"Relax!" Deirdre cried – in English, Nur couldn't help but notice. That was slightly frustrating. Half a year in America, and Deirdre was already managing to make her sudden outbursts in English. "What's your problem?" That in Seychellois Creole – so *that* was alright.

Nur patiently surveyed the docent runnel until she spied her quarry. She elbowed Deirdre softly and gestured toward the brown-haired beau with her head. "That's him?"

Deirdre followed her sister's gaze and marked the terminal point with an explosive procession of emotions. The one she landed on was optimistic confusion with a soupçon of anger. "What do you mean, 'him'?"

With dread inexorability, the TAF and TAS circles threatened eclipse. So Nur replied to her sister with a suggestive, eyebrow smile, and rolled the dice: "The one you told me about?"

The lurid liberality of that expression got through to Deirdre, alright. The creases in her brow smoothed themselves out. "Yeah," she finally admitted.

Not so deep down, they both knew Nur was bluffing. She hadn't heard a word Deirdre had said about this guy. But going by the look on her younger sister's face, Nur had an impression so strong as to be something close to certainty that, by the very act of bluffing, she had conveyed the amount of thought she'd put in to Deirdre's situation, without explicitly saying as much. Because why bother pretending to have heard something she hadn't, unless she had become cognizant of said something's importance to the person who said it?

Maybe that was projection, or pure fancy. Either way, it didn't much matter to Nur. Because Deirdre seemed gratified by the exchange, and the two sisters once again found common cause in trying to get one of them laid.

It was a point of no small frustration that the circles TAF and TAS seemed so drawn to one another, but perhaps a little bit of overlap would help stabilize them both. Just a little bit. Not too much. Nur just hoped that one day, she would learn to live with that little bit of overlap without wanting to sick up her lungs.

CHAPTER 28

The kid's name (and he *was* a kid, Nur acknowledged only in passing, as she zipped that thought straight into the mental garbage can) was Kamal, and that was really all Nur needed to know about him. She couldn't keep calling him 'the guy' or 'the boy', certainly not 'the kid'. But hot on the heels of "his name is Kamal" came a biography of such exhaustive triviality, Nur began to once again despair of whatever connection she felt she had with Hyun-Woo. At bottom, they really didn't know anything about each other. Not if the things Deirdre and Kamal knew about each other was the benchmark, at least. Granted, the youngins had more of the common language down, but Nur had never let a well-reasoned point stand in the way of self-doubt.

Kamal was Pakistani, and Deirdre seethed with genuine outrage as she recounted the flaming hoops through which he was forced to jump upon immigration. Kamal was in Boston on a $20,000 scholarship to Boston University, where he took night classes towards a degree in archaeology, and Deirdre swelled with proxy pride as she expounded upon the ancient Soanian leftovers near Islamabad, which was to be Kamal's specialty. Kamal always seemed to smell great, even on days when he claimed he hadn't showered, and Deirdre flushed with timid recollection of the furtive whiffs she'd stolen.

Had Nur been asked early last August to describe what love *looked* like, from a purely behavioral standpoint, she would have outlined the Deirdre before her accurately enough to help a police sketch artist capture her visage and bring her to justice. Did it cheapen the things she felt – or *thought* she felt – for Hyun-Woo? She was ashamed to admit that she thought it might. Looking at him had filled – and still did fill – her heart with a bewildering stew of emotions. She looked at him and wondered what he had been doing one year ago today, when the two of them hadn't the slightest inkling that the other existed. She looked at him and wondered if he felt the same way as she did when he looked back. She looked at him and wondered where they would be one year from now, if they would continue along the paths they had set out for themselves, or if they might prove so drawn to one another that their paths converged and took an entirely unexpected but breathtakingly picturesque detour...

She looked at him and thought all of these things, but it was a purely internal combustion. Unless there were some fugue states for which she couldn't account, and about which nobody had told her, Nur had never jabbered and babbled about Hyun-Woo the way Deirdre was doing now for Kamal. What did that mean?

Deirdre was younger, of course. Was it just youthful enthusiasm? Maybe...but she seemed so *sure* of her feelings for Kamal. Nur was constantly waffling, scrutinizing her motives and second-guessing her emotions. Was Deirdre doing the same thing, and simply finding more reliable conclusions than Nur was? Or had she neglected to engage in the same critical examinations?

And who, in that case, had the right approach to being in love? Were either of them *actually* in love? Was there anything to gain from asking these sorts of questions?

Was Deirdre still talking?

"...time out of Pakistan, which made me think, like, we've got so..."

Yes, she was.

One thing was for certain, at least: Nur understood why Deirdre had gotten so angry at the flat dismissal of her carnal ambitions. Her baby sister was all grown up, and she was, as the Americans say, *thirsty*.

Nur let Deirdre run out the charge of giddy affection, not knowing that this would take several days. When that reservoir finally ran dry, they began to talk logistics, which once again seemed like a dirty word where love was concerned, but some things just couldn't be avoided.

To wit: unlike Hyun-Woo, Kamal was not possessed of mysterious riches. The only reason he could come to America was because of the scholarship, and the only reason he could stay in America was because his mother lived here now. His parents were divorced, that was another thing Nur found out from Deirdre, and Pakistan wasn't exactly the best place for a divorced woman with a child to be setting up shop. So she moved to America, remarried, and was finally enjoying the company of her son for the first time since her expatriation. They lived in a small, one-bedroom apartment, just a ten-minute walk or so from the language school.

A small, one-bedroom apartment. Kamal slept on the fold-out couch in the living room.

So Kamal's place was out.

Despite the gentle leverage Nur now held against her Uncle Bernard, him being equally afeared of her parents and all, she wasn't about to try to turn his house into a fuckpad. They were his guests, and even if she could somehow convince him to keep mum about the whole thing, and not tell *her* mum (which she doubted very much), she wasn't about to lean on him for something like this. He would be helping his niece, a legal minor, get her cherry popped under his roof. Bernard seemed like the kind of guy who wanted not a football stadium between his TAF and TAS circles, but a continent, or perhaps a solar system.

So Uncle Bernard's was out. What did that leave? Get a hotel? And how would they explain that charge to their parents? They certainly didn't have the money to cover it in cash, and besides, if the hotels in America were anything like theirs in Seychelles, it was nearly impossible to get a room without a card now. They could try to call it a night of research, which in a sense it would have been. But again, Nur felt slightly gross about making her family even unwitting accomplices to this. She felt more than slightly gross about her own involvement, but she loved her sister and that's what people who love each other do. They help each other have sex. But also there are a lot of different kinds of love, Nur added for her own mental well-being.

So what did that leave?

Nur could only think of one possibility, and it was arguably the grossest one.

CHAPTER 29

Hyun-Woo didn't say anything for several seconds, and that was to be expected. Nur had been silently hoping that he would have as much trouble with the age for sex as he had with the age for drinking, but his ruminative stillness dispelled that hope. Two minors having sex was all well and good, but what did the law have to say about helping said minors have said sex? Was that what he was wondering? Or was it just the strangeness of having to provide a pad for your lover's younger sister to do the deed with a boy he'd never met? Or was it the added absurdity of having the person translating the plea be the interested party herself?

Deirdre had equipped her sister with a few English prompts, hoping she wouldn't have to be present for the pitch. It'd save everybody a lot of discomfort, they agreed. But ultimately, even if Nur was reasonably confident she would have been able to understand Hyun-Woo's responses (he was getting pretty good at anticipating Nur's problem areas and avoiding them, which made it a pleasant surprise when the areas stopped being problems), she couldn't remember the entire spiel Deirdre prepared, and the prospect of starting the hard sell and not being able to finish it was mortifying to both of them. So Deirdre went along, and allowed Nur to make the pitch in Seychellois Creole, translating for them for the first time in weeks. It was awkward not only for the subject matter, but for the fact that Nur and Hyun-Woo had grown accustomed to communicating without a middlewoman. Reintroducing her was a bit like slapping training wheels on a motocross bike. Even if the driver still had a tendency to fall down a lot, two little extra baby wheels aren't gonna help on a hairpin turn.

He looked from Nur to Deirdre, back to Nur, held her gaze for a little while, darted his eyes to Deirdre and then straight back to Nur, then at his feet. He made an extended study of his shoes.

Just as she was losing heart, Hyun-Woo lifted his head as though he'd found the lost heart down on the floor and needed desperately to let her know. "It's important to you?" he asked Nur directly. The question came in English, but the language of its delivery didn't even register with her. Nor, really, did the content of the question. What she latched on to was the aching finality with which the question was asked; she knew in that instant that however she replied, Hyun-Woo would proceed accordingly.

All of the risks, all of the personal reservations, all of the variables of which she couldn't possibly be aware, were sublimated into a single question aimed not at Deirdre but at *Nur*. He cared what *she* thought, and her word would be law.

She still had a million questions, about what Hyun-Woo wanted and needed and expected and thought and felt…but that one extra question from him turned out to be a satisfactory answer to hers, at least for a few beautiful seconds there.

Nodding, she suddenly developed a great interest in her own shoes. "Yes," she replied in effortless English. "It is." Her eyes rose to meet his again, and there they remained, and there they would have continued to remain, and Deirdre not cut in.

"It's also important to *me*," she pointed out quite reasonably.

Hyun-Woo once again favored Nur with that unrivaled smile of his. "Well alright then."

"Ahem," said Deirdre, because for once she thought she could forward a strong moral argument that she should be the center of attention in this conversation. And eventually, she was. Eventually.

There was a perverse (in the sense of 'odd', as opposed to 'lecherous', though one could be forgiven for making that mistake) fascination to be found in watching Hyun-Woo orchestrate a sexual liaison. For one, he was trying to *orchestrate* it, as though there were dozens of moving parts that needed to be wrangled and synchronized. Quite the opposite: unlike Nur and Hyun-Woo, Deirdre and Kamal had had conversations about sex, and the gist of those conversations had always been theory with an eye towards practice. There were only two moving parts, and given the opportunity they would lock into complimentary, repetitive motion all by themselves.

For two, Hyun-Woo was still slightly reticent with regard to sex. Nur suspected this would be a lifelong affliction, not that there was anything wrong with it. Not having the vocabulary necessary for such a sensitive conversation, she wasn't entirely certain why Hyun-Woo had retained his virginity into his second decade of life. Choice, circumstance, or something else, all she could say for certain was that Hyun-Woo as he was now had some difficulty staring down sexuality. And yet here he was, taking something like charge of the situation. A sexual situation. The Hyun-Woo of last August would never have gotten involved in such a predicament, Nur was certain, and merely implying the sorts of particulars now being bandied about freely would have caused him to blush until his face burst into flames.

Then again, the Nur of this January-almost-February (Christ, where was the time going?) felt nearly face-flushed into the danger zone as they discussed all the surfaces in the apartment upon which Nur and Hyun-Woo had come to know one another biblically. Deirdre didn't want sloppy locational seconds, but was quickly discovering that this left her the choice to making her own scriptural introductions inside the fridge (as opposed to up against it, check), in the narrow gap between the back of the couch and the wall (the couch itself and the floor around the couch having been well-utilized, check and check) and under the glass-top coffee table (the delicate and frankly reckless task of christening the top having been accomplished, check, though you'd never guess it but for the traitorous redolence of Windex). Deirdre didn't bother asking about the memory-foam bed, because she suspected its memory wouldn't be short enough for her.

Wishing she could take the last fifteen-odd minutes of her life back, Deirdre resigned herself to letting things with Kamal happen naturally, and trying to purge her mind of the knowing, variable-intensity smiles that accompanied her pointing to each object in the apartment.

And really…that was it. Hyun-Woo didn't have

to do much more than make his place available and himself scarce. Perhaps he was just an attentive host unable to shake old habits, or perhaps his discomfort surrounding the entire topic at hand manifested in a sudden fit of anxious micro-management, but either way he seemed highly disinclined to get out of Deirdre's damn business.

Not that anybody phrased it so harshly. Paragons of tact and discretion, were the De Dernberg sisters. Deirdre gave Nur *a look*, and Nur nodded in acknowledgment. She gave Hyun-Woo a wry, tolerant but nonetheless impatient 'time to go' pat on the shoulder with an effortless technique that more commonly develops around the silver anniversary.

It was, all of a sudden, The Night In Question. Nur had a curiously maternal *they grow up so fast* sensation, while Hyun-Woo did his best to show Deirdre where he kept the condoms without swallowing his own tongue and exploding. Her all-growed-up sister had arranged a lovely little dinner at a lovely little Mexican restaurant around the corner (how hard it was to shake the slightly dismissive 'little' qualifier; Deirdre was past the age where she had little dinners at little restaurants), after which she would ask Kamal if he wanted to watch TV. This absolutely baffled Nur, because she and Kamal had already discussed sex (she being Deirdre - *key distinction, that*). There was no need to be coy anymore. Deirdre was very firm on this, though. The offer would be for television, even if the subtext of the offer was readily apparent to the both of them. She might even extend the invitation with a suggestive wiggle of the eyebrows. *A long night of American television, perhaps with reruns.* Wink wiggle blink wink.

As Nur shuffled Hyun-Woo out the door, he once again pointed out where the condoms were, stretched his hand out like a mother shouting *wait let me take my baby* as she's being dragged by bad people away from a baby she wants the bad people to wait and let her take. It was a really weird moment for everybody and thankfully it passed quickly.

Out in the bracing twilight, the dying day fled westward with a swoosh of its crimson cape, making an overdramatic exit that served as the perfect foil for the rising moon's deadpan straight-to-camera shrug.

And then Nur was all like, "well *now* what?"

And Hyun-Woo was all like, "that's a good question."

And they both understood what the other was all like with a precision they could never achieve when they thought hard about it.

So monomaniacally fixated on Deirdre had they been, they'd not stopped to ask themselves what *they* would do to pass the time while Deirdre was passing the time with Kamal.

This was the part, in a movie, where Nur would say something flirty to Hyun-Woo, like "oh, I can think of a few things." Cut to: them flopping down next to each other in a bed, or if this was a classy picture, maybe one of them hugging the other from behind, except they're both in bath towels because they had to take a shower to wash off the sweat they had accumulated from flopping around on top of each other in a bed.

What a wonderful transition that would have been, largely because it cuts out the moments after "oh, I can think of a few things," when Hyun-Woo replies "like what," because he seemed pretty slow on the uptake with these things, and then Nur would have to respond with "like sex things," and Hyun-Woo would say "oh," and then they would have to find somewhere to have sex, which they didn't have, so they'd have to go find a motel that charged by the hour, which they probably didn't have to have in Cambridge, so they'd have to get on the T and go to one of the sketchier neighborhoods and ask somebody excuse me where can we find the nearest hotel that charges by the hour, and then the somebody would give them *a look* and Hyun-Woo would swallow his tongue and explode.

Unless they wanted to have sex in an alley. Which they didn't.

So they took a walk, and they held hands, and if Nur knew enough about English to use the word 'swell' unironically, she'd have said the night was just that.

CHAPTER 30

Apparently, nobody had told Deirdre that there would be blood. And apparently, that same nobody hadn't told Hyun-Woo. Nur felt a measure of responsibility, then, for her sister's embarrassment and her lover's sheet set. But how was she supposed to know what these two did or didn't know?

This was the question she put to Deirdre, who was trying to crinkle her nose up to her forehead as she balled up the 600 thread count nightmare. "It couldn't have hurt to mention it in passing, just to be safe," she mumbled through pursed lips. Nur couldn't recall being so disgusted at the sight of her own blood when she'd been in this position, but then again, she'd been prepared for it. "Like, 'hey, it's gonna sting a bit, and maybe lay out some newspaper.'"

Hyun-Woo stood in the doorway, clutching a bundle of downy white towels with a hook-fingered intensity that invited Nur to pry them from his cold, dead hands. Hope alighted on his wan face. "Would newspaper soak it up better, you think?"

Standing motionless between them, Nur shook her head from side to side. She didn't understand *everything* Hyun-Woo had just said, but context and tone supplied what language didn't. Without really looking at either, Nur instructed Deirdre to instruct Hyun-Woo to go ahead and put the towels down, unless he was hoping to disguise the bloodletting by surprising his parents with a set of matching pink linens. This was the first time Nur had something so baldly sarcastic to say to Hyun-Woo, and in a less sensational situation, they all three might have taken a moment to appreciate this. Instead, Deirdre conveyed the message without thinking about it (she had more than enough on her plate), and Hyun-Woo received the message without hearing it (his plate was similarly weighted), instead parlaying it directly into another loss of virginity: he thought of his first English-language pun, based on a popular idiom he had heard.

"When life gives you lettings, make linen-ade," he chirped to himself. The De Dernberg sisters looked at him as though he'd gone insane. It probably didn't help that he was giggling at his own joke, and making a poor attempt at concealing it by burying his face in the towels. He had always marked fluency in a language by the ease with which he could play with words. That particular witticism was rough. He knew that, and couldn't afford to go easy on himself, as none of the present company understood enough to groan and throw small objects and appliances at him. But he'd made his first pun, and it made a kind of sense, and it sort of worked.

So he had a number of reasons to be chortling into his doilies, none of which were apparent to Deirdre or Nur, who were smeared to their elbows in their own blood and watching, respectively.

Here was the fourth first of the night, then. Nur had never seen Hyun-Woo so uncomposed, so undignified, so…exposed. The idea that his delicate tittering was *humanizing* was strange, because it implied that Hyun-Woo was in some way inhuman, or at least had room to be made more human-ish, but *humanizing* was all she could think as the hee-hawing ran itself down into tee-heeing on the way to a volatile silence that could, at any moment, reignite into shrieking peals of circular mirth.

She wanted to take Hyun-Woo, right then and there. Kick Deirdre out, bloody blankets and all, and have at it on the naked mattress. His smile, his smile, his smile had always been radiant. But that shrill, staccato laugh that dipped and drooped as each breath left him, like a roulette wheel on helium…that was a supernova, and she was a nearby planet, inhabited by a highly evolved, responsible and enlightened civilization, there one moment and gone the next, wiped suddenly from existence by the sweeping laughter at a cosmic punchline, for which they would never hear the set-up.

Which, alright, perhaps a slightly more tragic metaphor than was called for. But sometimes you look at the one you love and feel so much, so deeply, that the only way to make sense of it is to compare it to intergalactic genocide.

And it was then, with Hyun-Woo cradling a bundle of towels and trying not to start chuckling again, with Deirdre grimacing as she snapped open a trash bag to force feed it sheets blushing with her vitality, that Nur felt she finally understood the only thing she'd ever really need to know about love: it didn't make any goddamned sense. She'd been trying to parse her feelings for this entire trip, *why am I feeling why does this make me why in this moment,* and she'd finally found the answer to all of these questions and more.

Why, as we're standing around here, all feeling embarrassed for various reasons, do I feel such overwhelming love for these people? 'These people' plural because these feelings extended to Deirdre too: *humanizing,* that was how she looked at her sister's struggles with the sheets, though she felt significantly less uncomfortable with the implied inhumanity that ascribed to Deirdre. *Why now, more so than at other times?*

Because it doesn't make any goddamned sense. This is the whole of Love, Nur decided. The rest is commentary.

"Oh, fuck!" Nur exclaimed apropos of nothing two days later. The curse came in English, and Deirdre rolled her eyes at the obvious affectation. She knew her big sister wasn't yet at the point of effortless profanity, because she herself still wasn't there yet, much to her chagrin.

"What?" Deirdre inquired, more for form's sake than genuine interest. The inquiry came in Seychellois Creole, the subtext being *just speak your language, don't be an asshole.* Interesting fact: the only three universal languages are mathematics, industrial sounds and subtextual swearwords.

"What ever happened to Kamal? How did he take the, um, what happened?"

An awkward silence would have descended just then, had they not been in the heavily-trampled winter wonderland of the Boston Common, sipping steaming cups of coffee. Nur had gone to Dunkin Donuts, while Deirdre had gone to Starbucks, and each thought the other had done so simply to be difficult, but in point of fact the two establishments were caddycorner from each other, and the two sisters had differing tastes, and it was really not a big deal and bespoke nothing more profound than said differing tastes. But, anyway, since they *were* sitting in the Boston Common sipping coffee, awkward silence was shouldered out of the way by laughing children and barking dogs and tweeting birds and the open-mouthed hum of an urban area smothered by snow.

So Nur repeated "What," the subtext being *ever happened to Kamal? How did he take the, um, what happened?*

"He, ah…" Deirdre took a long, stalling sip. "You can't tell anybody I told you this."

"Unless you can find me somebody else who speaks Creole, I don't think you have to worry about that for quite a while."

"Mhm. Right. Well, he…when he saw the blood, and it looked like there was a lot of it, more than there was, because I don't think *either* of us were expecting it, because it was his first time too, and he wasn't expecting it to hurt me so much, which, neither was I, but, so, when there was blood, which is to s-"

"He fainted?"

"Straight away." Another long, artificially drawn-out sip. She pulled the cup away from her mouth, revealing the slightest arc of a smile. "He was still inside me," she said in a voice so quiet it was nearly lost amongst the hushed cacophony of the Common.

Nur's shoulders tensed as she saw the Talking About Family and Talking About Sex circles drift towards one another. Two avenues of effort lay before her: make an effort to keep the circles apart, or make an effort to loosen her shoulders and roll with it.

She chose to defer the moment of decision for at least a few moments. The sip lasted at least as long as both of Deirdre's combined. And then it all went wrong.

196 | Jud Widing

The plan backfired.

Deirdre continued, "I was trying to get him off of me, but then he…he was unconscious when he ca-," and Nur spat her coffee out into the morning in a fine mist, which was picked up by the wind and carried across the path, where it splattered onto the face of a young boy who had just knocked over his friend's snowman and so had it coming, because sometimes there is justice in the universe.

Then Nur spotted a dog, at which she pointed as she shouted "look, a dog," leapt up, and ran towards it – which was, not accidentally, away from Deirdre and this dialogue she into which she had unwittingly inserted (*pick a different word! Insinuated? Sure!*) herself. She hadn't gotten a straight answer about what ended up happening with Kamal, but at that moment all she wanted was to pet a fuzzy puppy and forget Kamal and all his works.

The puppy was a corgi, and it was very fuzzy, and she gave it a little rub behind the ears and the world was set aright for a time.

CHAPTER 31

The time for which the world was set aright kept on rolling, even after Nur had stopped petting the fuzzy puppy. A happy equilibrium had obtained between Nur and Deirdre, and between Nur and Hyun-Woo, and to a lesser extent between Deirdre and Hyun-Woo. The younger De Dernberg sister was still recruited for her translational capacities from time to time, but Nur felt her to be increasingly unnecessary. Not because she was making such dramatic leaps and bounds in language acquisition – the need for absolute comprehension simply felt less and less pressing. When one is resigned to things not making any goddamned sense, well, one is less frustrated when that's precisely how much sense things make.

One bad thing happened in the "time" in question, and it wasn't even bad. Just concerning. Hyun-Woo ascended to the very highest class offered by the Crabshoe School For The Language Of English. Riding high on pun-inspired confidence (he tried to make something along the lines of 'punfidence' work in is mind, largely because he hadn't yet developed the groaning twins of decency and shame by which even the most reckless wordsmith plies their disreputable trade), he once again approached Tuppence Crabshoe, fixing to once again retake the placement exam. She relented, and he took it again, and scored near the top. The top, of course, being the point at which Tuppence would sit a student down and explain that they probably didn't need to be enrolled in a language school at all anymore.

And then where would Hyun-Woo go?

That was a bridge still in the distance, but one that was approaching with greater haste than Nur would have liked. Except the bridge wasn't the one doing the approaching – Hyun-Woo was. It annoyed Nur, ever so slightly, than Hyun-Woo was forcing his way up the pedagogical ladder prematurely. She had no right to feel that way, and she knew it. Rich as he seemed to be, attending this school was costing him money, and if the money stopped being well-spent, it wouldn't make any goddamned sense for him to stick around just for Nur.

Not any goddamned sense at all.

Which was what annoyed her. More than ever so slightly, if she was being honest. *If he loved me, wouldn't he try to stay here with me, rather than trying to matriculate?*

It wasn't fair to frame things so simplistically.

Clearly.

She knew that.

Obviously.

But still.

Anyway, it only bothered her for a day or so. She knew it was unreasonable, and her anxieties about the future had a way of evaporating when she was spending the present with Hyun-Woo. It would continue to niggle away at the back of her mind, but the joke was on It, because she'd never be able to hear It back there. The niggledome was already quite crowded.

The hours turned to days turned to weeks, time rushed forward and all things changed, yet they remained "time", the time when the world was aright. Nur and Hyun-Woo went on dates, and had sex, and often those two things followed one another, but sometimes they existed independently, and it was great fun and 'aright'. Nur and Deirdre made concerted efforts to hang out, talking walks and going sledding and even engaging in some of the touristy stuff they'd neglected, like riding to the top of the Prudential center or hopping on one of the amphibious duck boats for a ride around the harbor (this in the blistering winds of mid-March, which turned out to be one of the worst ideas either of them had ever had, made an itsy bit better by the fact that both had had it). They didn't exactly grow closer, because in Nur's opinion they were already a little bit *too* close - the Boston Common was nearly ruined for her, so vivid were the flashbacks to the mental image of Deirdre and Kamal covered in *ohgodpuppiesthinkofpuppies* – but they found the Goldilocks distance at which to hold one another and strengthened the slightly elastic bonds to just that length. Room to maneuver, a bit closer or a bit further as the situation dictated, but always springing back to a happy medium. That was reassuring and 'aright'.

Aright things were as the snow piled high on the corners and aright they stayed as the mercury rose in its place, aright was the washing away the stupor of winter to make way for the timid lustiness of spring, first in the rivulets of snowmelt that raced through the streets, and then in the showers that promised flowers, now that March had peeled back for April's sake, it was all aright and Nur was aright with the world, and none of it warrants particular attention because it's a wonderful thing when all is aright, but it's not the most *interesting* thing. That would be when things go awrong, which is what started to happen in late April.

Unfortunately, Nur's time in America would never again be as aright as it had been for those three-almost-four months. But times like that never last, because there isn't *actually* justice in the universe. Things just happen, and sometimes the things that just happen to people are the things those people deserve, like a little snowman-demolishing turd getting a face full of second-hand coffee. But most times good things happen to bad people and bad things happen to good people and there's no rhyme or reason because, as Nur would come to realize in the twilight of her American trip, love wasn't unique in not making any goddamned sense.

CHAPTER 32

Two things happened in rapid succession. The first was Nur's birthday, which fell on a Thursday. Hyun-Woo had a lot of pun-fun with that one, and everyone else was very patient with him.

The shindig thrown for the occasion was small, just snacks and soft drinks at Uncle Bernard's. It was, much like the preceding several months, generally pleasant and devoid of conflict, and therefore not especially interesting. It was noteworthy for marking the introduction between Hyun-Woo and Nur's extended family, an introduction about which she would soon enough have mixed feelings.

"This is Hyun-Woo…" she mumbled quietly, after realizing that she had never learned his last name. Or his first name? She knew enough about Korean names to know that she didn't know enough about Korean names. She didn't know one of his names. Nor did she know the English words to explain their relationship with the nuance she felt it deserved, so venturing that her Uncle's fear of her parents would ensure discretion, she concluded her introduction with "I'm seeing him."

Uncle Bernard made the face of a man who awakens on the subway to find a rat on his chest, while Aunt Amy made the face of a woman who films a man awakening on the subway to find a rat on his chest, knowing that she'll be able to monetize this video on the internet. In a stunning display of marital synchrony that did more to answer Nur's background inquiry of *how did these two end up together* than anything else over the last eight months, Bernard and Amy's faces slid towards a mutual neutral and arrived at the same time, a feat Nur and Hyun-Woo had yet to manage, though for not lack of trying.

"Hi there," Uncle Bernard grumbled with exaggerated good humor. Behind that carnival barker's smile and the proffered used car salesman's hand, Nur saw that she and Bernard were on the same page: her parents would never hear of this from him. She grinned as Hyun-Woo took her Uncle's hand and gave it a little shake. Not the most forceful handshake, as demonstrated by Bernard's enthusiastic double-pump prior to disengagement.

Why forcing her Uncle to keep her secret should bring her such pleasure, she couldn't begin to imagine. Well, she *could* begin to imagine. Her concern was more in not being able to stop imagining. There were *so many* plausible explanations.

A few other stray friends from the school were invited, though they were more acquaintances than friends. This was the first time Nur had spent time with many of them outside of class.

She'd also encouraged Deirdre to invite Kamal. Deirdre felt quite certain that Kamal would decline the invitation, and so declined to invite him, just to be safe.

That was the first thing that happened in rapid

succession, though it hardly would have made sense to say it happened 'in succession' without the second thing that happened.

The second thing that happened was that, while having sex, the sweaty torsos of Nur and Hyun-Woo slapped together in just the right way to make a comical little fart sound. As the snowflake leads to the avalanche, as the straw breaks the camel's back, as the butterfly flaps up the hurricane, so too did the comical little fart sound lead to catastrophe.

It wasn't even a big one. Just a delicate, tooting *pplbt* noise. And at first, the noise passed without comment, because both Nur and Hyun-Woo were preoccupied with the activity that gave rise to the noise to begin with.

But then Nur started laughing. She couldn't help it. There were a few things that would always and forever make her laugh. Young children falling down, you couldn't go wrong with that one. People's voices cracking in public speaking scenarios, those moments were small treasures to be savored. And farts. Farts were hilarious, and Nur fundamentally distrusted anyone who held otherwise. They were either liars or clinically humorless, and it was a toss-up as to which type of person was worse.

The laugh started softly, a subtle hitching of the chest that she tried to disguise by timing with Hyun-Woo's less-subtle motions. And for a time, it seemed as though she had it under control. All that was left was to hope he didn't notice her pursed, upturned lips.

But he must have, because he brought his head down for a kiss, and dropped it lower still to the nape of her neck. His chest couldn't help but come along for the ride, slapping into hers and announcing the connection with an *alto voce* refrain.

PPLBT.

And then, explosive decompression.

"HA!" Nur shouted. She added, "hahahaha."

She knew there would be problems when Hyun-Woo asked her what was funny. He had stopped moving to phrase the question, and Nur became acutely aware of how silent the room was. Would it have killed them to put some music on? The *mood* had been sustained by their exertions, and she could feel the *mood* packing up with an eye towards the door, now that they'd fallen into a false-flatulence lull. Music might have carried them through, or at least put something in their ears beside the echoing remains of a chesty cheese-cutting.

But they didn't have any music. And so the *mood* seeped away, and as Nur's laughter stepped up to fill the void, it encountered a chilly resistance from Hyun-Woo. He didn't find this funny, and so the void remained unfilled for him.

This qualified as "a problem", and the fact that "a problem" arose because of a fart noise made the entire situation even funnier to Nur. She tried to stop laughing, therefore she laughed even harder. She couldn't stop. This was "a problem", and her giggles, now rushing headlong into gasping hysterics, were only making it worse. Her heart was shouting *cut that shit out!* But her head, always at a step's remove, couldn't get over how funny this all was. Hyun-Woo was tensing up, rolling off of her and slapping a palm over his eyes. She'd never seen him like this before. Was he taking the laughter personally? Did he truly not understand why she was laughing? The tender moment they had been sharing not fifteen seconds ago had vanished – it hadn't popped, or evaporated, or disintegrated, it *vanished*, all at once and in an instant – and her heart was crying out, seeing the looming danger but finding itself unable to outrun it, because the head just wanted to sit back and watch. This was an objectively funny situation. There was a thickness in the atmosphere that demanded discharge. Things were about to be said, she intuited, and all because their naked bodies had clapped together and made a fart noise.

"Sorry," she sputtered through the relentless tides of merriment. "It's not you…it's just funny."

He didn't say anything to that, just lay there with his hand over his eyes. Was he crying? Was this even worse than she'd expected? *HOW*? What the hell was happening?

And how can I make it stop *happening?*

The worse the situation grew for her heart, the funnier it became to her head. She felt their relationship to be further out on the rocks than it had ever been… because of *pplbt*. Not having the slightest clue why *pplbt* had set Hyun-Woo off if this way, she was left to imagine scenarios. All of them involved traumatic fart incidents for a young Hyun-Woo, and consequently all of them were funny, because farts are always funny, even when they're doing inexplicable damage to your relationships.

Had Hyun-Woo *always* been this humorless? She'd just seen him laugh, really truly *laugh*, and it was beautiful! Granted, it was also noteworthy for having been one of the first times she'd ever seen it…

Uh oh. Does Hyun-Woo not have a sense of humor? That couldn't be right. Hyun-Woo had said that working out humor in another language was his mark of fluency. It was simply that they didn't understand each other's sense of humor, due to the language barrier. That was it.

Except that wasn't quite it. That wasn't what Hyun-Woo had said. *Wordplay* was his mark of fluency. And as anyone who's had to listen to a group of would-be wits trying to out-pun each other at a party can attest, wordplay and comedy have a casual relationship.

The laughter grew so forceful that it started to hurt. She coughed and wheezed through it, though, because this was so *rich*. Hyun-Woo didn't have a sense of humor. It had just taken until this moment to realize it, with something as simple and ludicrous and insignificant as *pplbt*.

When she finally felt up to speaking, it wasn't that the laughter had stopped. It had simply tapered off enough for her to shape the formless outbursts into recognizable words. "What's wrong?" she inquired.

Without removing his hand from his eyes, Hyun-Woo replied "everything". And Nur wanted desperately to laugh again, because wasn't *that* such a dramatic thing to say after a little tummy-fuck-fart, but she didn't. Her heart had finally caught up to her head, and said *you fucking idiot*, and her head hung itself and replied *you may have a point there*. And they consulted one another on how best to figure out what the fuck just happened, and why Hyun-Woo was so upset. But that would be a separate thing.

The *pplbt*, that was the second thing that happened in rapid succession.

CHAPTER 33

For somebody who spoke eighteen thousand languages, Hyun-Woo was doing a very poor job of expressing himself. He lay on the bed, hand draped over his eyes, making periodic whimpering sounds, for what felt like hours. Nur just watched him, her laughter finally subsiding, and occasionally attempting to prime a conversation with things like "what's wrong?" or "what are you thinking?"

A handful of times, Hyun-Woo would take a deep breath and lift his arms skyward, like a baby reaching out to be picked up by its mother (and perhaps the mother is shouting *wait let me take my baby*). "It's just," he would begin, or once it was "*I* just," but what was just remained the primary concern, and the terminus, of these abortive preambles.

To begin with, Nur was concerned. Hyun-Woo seemed genuinely anguished over something, and it couldn't have been the fart noise by itself. Was it because she was laughing? Could he have misinterpreted that? Surely not – they'd had a great deal of sex unsullied by laughter. She quickly downgraded that to *probably* not, because dudes could be quite touchy about their sexual prowess.

And then time, as is its wont, passed. And contrary to their wont, things stayed the same. Hyun-Woo laying on his back, hand reposed on his brow like a dizzy socialite whose corset was too tight. Nur laying next to him, propped up on one elbow, waiting for him to say something, and periodically saying something herself. She couldn't help what came next – concern cracked and hatched impatience.

The words didn't change, but the tone did. The smooth, honeyed "what's wrong?" turned bitter and went pointy at the edges. "What's wrong?"

Hyun-Woo said something in Korean. Later, it would occur to Nur that he probably didn't realize he was saying said something out loud.

In the moment, this only exacerbated her impatience. "I can't understand." Were she standing, she'd have starting tapping her foot just then.

He slid his hand down his face, as though trying to wipe it off. His eyes were squeezed shut, a thin layer of dew caught in his lashes. "I wanted this to work," he blubbered.

Neither of them said anything for several minutes. Nur hadn't even begun trying to formulate a reply; she was busy parsing that sentence, attempting to sort out alternative meanings to what she *thought* it meant. *Did he seriously just say this isn't working? Because of a fucking FART NOISE?* This was coming from absolutely nowhere, as far(t) as she could tell. And the backhanded nature of it was galling. He hadn't even said something like 'I don't think this is working'. He phrased it in the past tense, as though it were a foregone conclusion that it *hadn't* worked!

She should have been devastated just then, but the impatience evolved into anger, so devastation would have to wait its goddamned turn. Her words failed her, save the one that was burning a hole in her heart, demanding to be loosed. "Explain!" she snapped.

And he did.

And she understood maybe thirty percent of it.

Is this an actual reason, or is he just using words he knows I won't understand in order to make it seem like a reason? There was a troublingly paranoid thought, followed up by a troublingly vindictive one: *I don't know that he's smart enough to pull that off.*

That was all the hurt doing the talking, but she hadn't allowed herself to feel that hurt yet.

"Speak more easily," she demanded. At this point, she was fairly certain she didn't want to hear whatever it was he had to say. Who cared what he thought? Dude didn't have a sense of humor.

*Gulp*ing cartoonishly, brow knit in concentration, Hyun-Woo silently rehearsed his words, moving his mouth without speaking. Without the words they were shaping, his lips made nearly imperceptible slurping and smacking sounds. But Nur was feeling quite perceptive just then, so they registered as moist reports from a Cronenberg cannon.

When the swamp noises finally summoned up some words from the gassy depths, they sounded as though they belonged to a strange, ancient language. The meaning came only after he'd finished talking.

"We both knew there was no future in this," he had said.

Oh, God. She had a million and one things to say, but how could she say them? Even in Seychellois Creole, she'd have struggled. In English? This was going be nearly impossible, and she wasn't about the put

Deirdre in the middle just to make it easier. "We both *knew?*" was where she ultimately landed.

"We're from different countries."

Well, that was a fair point. She couldn't really argue with that. But people had overcome worse for love, hadn't they?

But those people had usually told each other that they were in love, hadn't they? They had.

She replied to Hyun-Woo's geographical concerns by saying "I love you" for the first time. *Whoops* was her follow-up thought, as well as the next thing she said out loud. But hey, the night had been going strangely enough as it was. Why not add some emotional intensity to it, right? *Idiot.*

Hyun-Woo grimaced and nodded. "I love you too," he croaked through a tightened throat, "I wanted this to work."

The past tense again. She wanted to slap him. "So why not?"

"Why not what?"

If he was going to start critiquing her grammar, maybe she *would* slap him. "Why's not working?"

"We're friends."

"Yes."

"We're from different cou-"

"Yes?"

"We knew this was, um 'friends with benefits."

"I don't know what that means."

Hyun-Woo explained. Nur did *not* slap him, because that would have been too obvious. Instead she got dressed and left without saying another word. Not because she didn't want to, she just didn't know the words she wanted to say.

We knew this was friends with benefits. How could

he say that *immediately after telling her that he loved her?*

And why had things come to a head tonight? Had this been on his mind, and the shattering of the mood back there finally brought these issues up to the surface? She had so many questions she wanted to ask him, but suspected she'd never get the chance.

He knew he was leaving. They both did. Neither was staying in America when their time at Crabshoe was up, and Nur had thought about this from practically the first day she had felt something for Hyun-Woo. But she had ignored it, in favor of savoring each moment with him as it came. His approach, she was now discovering, was keeping his eyes fixed on the horizon. The distance she felt between them tonight – had that always been there? Had she conveniently ignored it, for as long as it had failed to be an obstacle? Or was he lying, to both of them, by insisting that it had always been there, that they had always been just 'friends with benefits', palling around for the sex and nothing more, to make himself feel better?

It hadn't been that to her. It had never been that to her. And that he should insist they had *both* always known it was the most hurtful part of this whole thing. Being demoted to fuck-buddy made her feel devalued. Being told that she had actually never held a higher position in his heart from which to be demoted, and being told that she should have known that from the beginning, made her feel *stupid*.

She got back to Uncle Bernard's and slipped into a dreamless, tear-streaked sleep. In the morning she awoke with an operating theory as to what catalyzed the previous night's crisis. The *pplbt* shattered the illusion they'd built for themselves, but what lay behind that fragile veneer was something else entirely.

Recently, very recently, Nur had introduced Hyun-Woo to her Aunt and Uncle. "I'm seeing him," she'd said. Had she told Hyun-Woo ahead of time that he'd be meeting her relatives? No, come to think of it. Would he have been less freaked out if he'd known ahead of time? Or would he not have come at all?

Meeting her Uncle Bernard as 'the guy your niece is seeing' must have freaked Hyun-Woo out. Bernard's firm handshake made things formal. Aunt Amy's capacious hug felt like a welcome to the family. If it was true that this had all been a relationship – not even a relationship, an *exchange* – without a future to him, then that day must have been something close to traumatizing. Maybe he was hesitant to get overly involved with Nur for 'guy reasons', whatever the hell reasons guys had for being distant. But that wouldn't explain his red-rimmed eyes that night, would it?

Hyun-Woo was probably hesitant to get involved because he *did* love her. And he knew that the closer he got to her, the more it would hurt to leave her.

Because, ultimately, that's what was going to happen. They would leave each other, and return to the normal trajectory of their lives.

She'd entertained fantasies from the beginning, fantasies in which one or the other (or both of them) would be willing to abandon their plans, or at least restructure them, so as to allow the two of them to stay together. But that was always pure imagination, in which she could indulge herself when departure was one year away. Now it was just over four months away.

It was late in the day for such fantasies.

If these were his actual reasons for behaving as he had (and who knew), why hadn't they discussed this earlier? They were both reasonable, rational adults. Why allow themselves to be hurt, why hurt each other, why let things go as far as they had? He could try to retcon their relationship to have included the "we're just friends with benefits" conversation if he wanted, but that didn't change the fact that it never happened.

Unless it did, and Nur just hadn't been able to understand it yet.

Because for a long while, she'd fancied that getting the gist of what he was saying was the same as understanding what he was saying.

Well, if she forgot everything else she'd learned at the Crabshoe School For The Language Of English, there's one lesson she would never forget. 'Getting' somebody isn't the same as 'understanding' them. And, if she was being honest with herself (and why not be, this late in the game, *not that it was a game*), she suspected neither was actually possible at all, on account of certain things not making any goddamned sense.

If only the world made sense. Then she could ask him questions, and he could give her answers, and nobody would be confused or hurt and all would be sensible, comprehensible love throughout all ages, world without end, amen.

But it was late in the day for such fantasies.

CHAPTER 34

After she had stopped crying, she was mostly angry.

At Hyun-Woo, obviously. And at herself. At the fact that humanity still hadn't quit flirting with globalization and just gotten a universal language sorted out already. At this country for being such a dumbass melting pot. At the dog she saw tied to a NO PARKING ANYTIME sign on the curb, because what the hell did that dog know about parking or about *anything*. At the NO PARKING ANYTIME sign, because what gave one human the right to tell another human where they could not park and when. At people walking too slowly down the street, obstructing her path and making her weave around them. At people walking too quickly down the street, weaving around her and making her stagger to one side or the other. At a tree. No reason there. Just, you know, fuck that tree.

She was angry, and anger didn't need a 'why'. Just a 'what', as in *the fuck*.

Had her anger needed a 'why', it might well have

listened to her 'why not'. Because she had a good reason why she *shouldn't* be angry, didn't she? Hadn't she already drummed up a plausible psychological portrait of Hyun-Woo and his defensive fear of emotional entanglement so near to his time of departure?

Another 'what', as in *so fucking*. That was no excuse for the way he had treated her last night. And that was no excuse for not communicating his feelings to her. Granted, the lack of a common language was a more convincing excuse, but there were workarounds. Deirdre being the most obvious, but the more delicate particulars could be delivered via semaphore and charade.

No, she had a right to be angry. Anger was justified here. Anger was fine and good and very nice.

She had so much anger, in fact, she could bottle most of it up and save it for later without losing a step in the moment.

What steps was she not losing? Why, the steps away from Hyun-Woo, of course. They began avoiding each other, which wasn't especially difficult given their different classes. At least, Nur began avoiding Hyun-Woo. Part of that avoidance meant not seeing him, to know whether or not he was avoiding her. Like she cared. Let him do what he wanted. Wasn't that what he'd been doing already? Oh, indeed it was.

Deirdre picked up on Nur's studied disdain, though 'picked up on' makes it sound as though this was some great feat of sisterly intuition. This was how Nur read it, of course, because she had a very poor concept of how she was presenting herself. To Deirdre, her elder sibling might as well have clipped a button to her lapel that said ASK ME ABOUT MY HEARTBREAK.

So Deirdre did just that, and Nur refused to answer. "Nothing's wrong," she huffed.

Deirdre sighed. "You might be able to fool everyone else," she said carefully and without conviction, "but I can see through your, um…" she had nowhere else to go with that, and so waited for Nur to pick up the slack.

Which she eventually did, through more sullen puffing. "Everything's *great*."

Another sigh from Deirdre, but this time no words followed the exhalation. Instead the sisters just sat around, sighing and huffing and puffing and heaving and making a serious go at increasing the room's carbon dioxide quotient to fatal extremes.

In time, as is always the case, the reason for the initial spate of anger shrank in importance, until it was downright insignificant. But much like a space shuttle only needs its boosters to break orbit, and happily tosses them back down to Earth once they've served their purpose, so anger only needs propulsion for so long before it can keep on flying by inertia.

Besides, she had all that anger bottled up in her whine cellar. No sense letting it spoil.

She spent the entirety of April angry at Hyun-Woo, avoiding him when possible and glaring at him when not. The catalyst for her anger was such a trifle as to be nearly forgotten, so why was she still angry with him? Well, because she'd been angry with him yesterday, and nothing had changed from yesterday to today. So anger remained the word of the day, the week, the month.

As each mention of Hyun-Woo's name resulted in a slight uptick in atmospheric pressure, Deirdre learned to stop poking at the sore subject. The no-go zone firmly established, she and Nur continued to deepen their relationship, partially by brushing up the thin, glossy bits on top. They'd staked out a few firmly off-topic zones, like Hyun-Woo and Kamal and sex in general, which increasingly left them with just the superficial bits. But they worked the hell out of these, and the felt themselves growing closer as a result. Not that they had many alternatives, if socialization was their aim. They each had casual acquaintances in their classes, but they'd regrettably put most of their time and energy into their respective dudes. And it turned out, for various reasons, those dudes were less than stellar investments of time. So now they had each other. Which was actually quite alright with the both of them.

April showers bring May flowers, that was a little saying Deirdre's teacher had taught them on the first day of the second month in question. It held true enough for them, though the flowers hadn't gotten the message and pre-empted the merry month of May by a few weeks. Either way, in the first weeks of May the city was colorful and vibrant and fragrant, if one's focus was drawn narrowly enough. Boston remained a city, and cities can only go in particular directions with color and vitality (fragrance knows no bounds, though). Nur and Deirdre took the air, breaking out the warm weather wear and strolling around the city, free and leisurely, in a way they hadn't since just after their arrival.

More accurate to say that it was in a way they never had before, actually. Because when they first landed, theirs was a contentious relationship. Whereas now, it was...better. There was still a riptide of antipathy lurking below the smiling surface, though what teenaged siblings *don't* struggle with that, huh?

By the middle of May, they'd become close enough to want to get drunk together for the first time. *Together* being the operative term, *get* the chief secondary. They'd both been drunk before, and they'd both *seen* each other drunk, when one or the other would come staggering back to the hotel after a wild night out. But they'd never *gotten* drunk *together* before, actually sat down and consumed alcohol in one another's presence.

But walking around Boston and taking paddle

boats out on the pond in the gardens and going to free concerts at the Hatch Shell and playing the chimes at the Kendall Red Line stop, all that gets old after a while. It's all fun and wonderful and Boston is a delightful city and what a privilege to be here and all that, but there exists a terminus at which the romp room runs out, and the only way to burst through is with a bit of lubrication. Besides, they had troubles and woes to be drunk away, didn't they? Of course they did. And what better way to slip off their troubles like an old skin than the very same liquid lubrication?

First order of business: acquiring said lubrication.

BEEBOO BEEBOO DANGER DANGER DANGER cried the TAF/TAS alarm.

The lubrication was metaphorical. Alcohol. They wanted to get drunk.

BEEBOO BEEBOOooooooooo ALL CLEAR

Neither of them being twenty-one, Uncle Bernard almost certainly being the sort of guy who would notice a lightness of his liquor cabinet, Uncle Bernard *definitely* certainly being the sort of guy who wouldn't supply alcohol to minors…where could they get some booze?

The hated face of Hyun-Woo, man of age, flashed like dry lightning in her mind. It vanished as quickly as it had appeared, and good riddance to bad rubbish.

Though why so angry

Nur turned the dilemma over in her head for a while, until she finally had an idea. She and Deirdre agreed that it was a terrible idea, and that they would give the problem another day or two of thought. If neither had any better ideas, they would try the terrible idea.

Neither had any better ideas.

CHAPTER 35

A great deal of maturity had been attained at great emotional expense since last August. Nur may not have considered herself an *adult* just yet, but she did think of herself as having made atypically large strides towards that inevitable classification, and with atypical enthusiasm.

So her idea, which was most definitely a terrible one, hinged upon this fundamental distinction: sneaking is for children. Rational, clear-headed discourse founded upon the points at which seemingly contradictory objectives overlap is the way mature souls conduct their business.

Just the facts, then: Nur and Deirdre intended to get drunk in the very near future. Being underaged, the only means by which they would be able to acquire the dreaded beverages capable of facilitating this state were illicit. As they had no clearly defined avenues by which to avail themselves of said means, they would be forced to reach out to some of their classmates who struck them as the 'illicit means' type. This would open them up to unknown dangers, or perhaps act as a gateway to even starker outrages to family and country. Phrased less ornately, maybe the dude who scored them booze would come back next week with weed – anything for his two newest and somehow best customers. And in a fit of boredom, maybe they would accept?

(This fantasy had little grounding in reality, but it served its purpose as thinly-veiled blackmail.)

Besides, where would they go to do their drinking? They couldn't do it out in public for everyone to see, and there were no safe spaces indoors to be found. So they'd have to retire to places of concealment, in the dark of moist, smoke-filled alleys or deep in the black throat of a culvert or in the shadow of a railroad trestle, and nevermind where they'd find those latter two in an urban environment.

View the facts with a clear head, assess their implications rationally, filter all of this through the prism of individual objectives and bring the results to an honest discourse…do all of this, and the conclusions were clear.

"You should buy us alcohol and let us drink it here," Nur concluded in Seychellois Creole, trembling like the atrophied legs of a woman just off a year-long bedrest.

Though it wasn't *just* disuse that set her native tongue aquiver. The crashing brows of Uncle Bernard and Aunt Amy had a whole lot to do with that as well. If the rest of their heads were anything like their foreheads, clarity had been buried alive beneath six feet of wrinkles.

Nur had known it was a terrible plan to begin with. But she'd also entertained the idea that it was so crazy it just…might…*work*.

Now? Not…so…*much*.

"Go to your room," Uncle Bernard suggested with

thoughtful equilibrium. Nobody is more focused on not leaning one way or another than the tightrope walker without a net, after all.

Aunt Amy nodded in assent. "Your Uncle and I need to discuss a few things." That seemed needlessly euphemistic to Nur – they all knew perfectly well what the few things that needed discussing were.

We're all adults here, she intoned to herself desperately. She needed to be an adult now more than ever, because her Uncle had just told her to go to her room as though she were a child, and goddamnitalltohell if she wasn't about to follow his order. Sorry, his *suggestion*.

Upstairs, Deirdre was wondering how it was going. She heard Nur tromp up the stairs, watched her slink through the door and flop onto her bed, and then she started wondering how poorly it had gone.

"I may have misjudged their maturity levels" was how Nur represented the exchange to both her sister and herself. Neither of them was convinced.

After an endless two and a half minutes, a less sullen set of footsteps made their way up the stairs and knocked on the bedroom door. The person to whom the footsteps belonged was technically the one to knock on the door, but now was hardly the time to be picking nits. Besides, Nur had a sinking sensation that said *the whole wide world outside this bedroom has melted into a singularity of* off-limits. She had misjudged something alright, and it hadn't been her relatives' maturity. How could she have believed her Uncle's fear of her parents would keep him from passing word of her limp ultimatum along? Hubris, that's what this was. Plain and simple. She didn't need alcohol to be making poor choices.

So whether these sounds were attached to a

person or were possessed of their own independent existences made little difference to her now. Two and a half minutes was plenty of time to place a quick call to Seychelles, and receive a parental decree most familiar to the Billy Batts' of the world: *keep them there.*

"Come in," Deirdre called to the disembodied knock.

The door opened part way, and Aunt Amy slowly poked her head in.

"We'll go in for beer, but no hard liquor," said Aunt Amy's head. "And you *have to stay here* while you drink it."

Keep them there.

Nur tried very, very hard not to laugh out loud, and she was successful for as long as it took Aunt Amy's sullen, defeated footsteps tromp back down the stairs.

The mature, adult response to this situation would be a detached acknowledgment of a negotiation well executed. But, upon further reflection, Nur was happy to put off being an adult for just a few minutes longer.

CHAPTER 36

Dr. Bernard De Dernberg, never one to admit defeat in face of the facts, apparently decided that there remained a way to spin this humiliating twisting-of-the-arm into an educational moment: the beer he got them was Sam Adams, and he gave it to them on the condition that they listen to him lecture briefly about the little historical figure on the label. That on top of the other conditions about staying put and promising to drink lots of water before they went to sleep, to keep hangovers at bay. As if Nur needed to be told that last bit. She learned from experience.

Perhaps hoping for a maximum of comprehensibility, more probably not wanting to give the girls any excuse to not listen to him, Uncle Bernard gave his little disquisition in Seychellois Creole. And, despite her best efforts, Nur found herself interested. Old Sammy Adams was far more instrumental in American history than she'd realized. He also apparently had owned a slave named Surry, but released her almost immediately after receiving title to her, like she was a used car. So that was only *sort of* shitty of him.

Deirdre was far less interested in the historical context for her beverage. Beer was beer, the smiling white guy on the label was dead, let's pour one out to his memory, and if the pouring happens to be down one's own throat, then so much more honor attends the gesture.

Bernard didn't really conclude speaking; he just stopped talking. It took Nur a few moments of his silence to realize the talking was over and done with, and she'd been *listening*. After said few moments, he shrugged and pointed towards the fridge. "You can have two each," he informed them in English. "No more. Understood?"

They nodded dutifully, extracted four chilled bottles from inside the refrigerator and a magnetic bottle opener from on it, and made their way upstairs. Bernard raised a hand to stop their glass-clacking ascent, but Aunt Amy stayed him with a shake of the head. He had convinced himself that they would do their drinking under his immediate supervision, and was stunned to discover that nobody else wanted in on his self-deception.

But all it took to throttle him back was a nod. Because despite feeling emasculated at having been played in this way (how could she have *known* he wouldn't immediately tell their parents?), he was flattered that the girls had come to him with this, and proud of them as well. What he was doing now was kind of cool. It was a cool Uncle thing to do. It was also an illegal Uncle thing to do, but Bernard could think of significantly *worse* illegal Uncle things he'd read about in the paper before, so all in all this was really not that bad.

And it was kind of cool. He hoped they thought

of it that way. It had been such a very long time since anyone had mistaken him for cool.

"I sort of feel bad for Uncle Bernard," Deirdre said sort of sincerely as she levered the top off of her beer without breaking eye contact with Nur, like a pro.

"Why?"

"What does he do?" She passed the bottle opener to Nur.

With some embarrassment, she found that she had to look at the bottle to guide the opener under the lip of the cap. "He's a doctor."

"No, I mean, like, what does he *do*? With his life. Does he have friends? I feel like he's only ever at work or here."

Nur shrugged and took a sip. "He's got Aunt Amy."

"And what does *she* do?"

This was a very good question. She sometimes rushed out of the house, like she had their first day here, but most often she was…at home. Where did she go on these outings? What did she do?

They pondered this in sipping silence.

For a while.

About halfway through their first bottles, they were relatively well into it. Their tolerances were normal for young women of their ages, and they had further stacked the decks by making this a day of fasting. A little alcohol, therefore, went a long way. And they had only had just a little alcohol so far.

"Do they need to *do* anything?" Nur wondered aloud.

"To do what?"

"Anything. We keep asking what Uncle Bernard and Aunt Amy *do*, but do they need to *do* anything? They've got each other."

Deirdre gave this serious thought. "That sounds…"

That serious thought trailed off into oblivion, but Nur had a plethora of conclusions in her back pocket. They were all variations on the theme of *unfulfilling*.

She imagined *having someone*, and *being had by someone*, such that they could each be said to *have each other*. There was beauty in that. Getting to the point in a relationship when you can be with someone and not having to be *doing* with them, reading a book in the living room while he's cooking in the kitchen, folding laundry in front of the TV while he naps on the couch, simply sharing the same space without needing to be entertaining each other constantly…that was the ideal state of romance, to her. The point at which you loved someone so completely, and were loved by them in turn, that you were secure enough in *having each other* that you could just *be* with them, and feel a rolling moment as full of romance as the grandest of jukebox gestures. The point at which the roaring cyclone of love finally passed overhead and wrapped you in the tranquility of its eye, you and your love, finally enveloped in an oasis of calm cleft from a pillar of bruise-black insanity, finally able to look them square in the eye and say *we have each other*, and feel the discharge of that ecstatic truth split the pocket of tension once and for all.

Uncle Bernard and Aunt Amy had each other, by all accounts. Nur had seen their wordless shorthand communications, she'd walked in on them doing the whole being-without-doing thing (so they weren't really *doing* it when she walked in, but anyway), and she felt the warmth between them, devoid of any dramatic gestures or professions. They *had each other*. And all she could think in response to that was, *so what?*

Once you had somebody and they had you and you had each other, how could you not still have your dreams and ambitions and passions? Surely the other person was a bonus, someone with whom you could share the good times and lean on in the bad…but they couldn't be a substitute for living your own life. A sidecar was no good without the motorcycle, right? A frame's just a piece of garbage without a picture. A…a fungus is nothing without its toe? Boy, maybe downing a whole bottle of Sam on an empty stomach wasn't such a great idea after all. She had a whole second on deck…

"How you doing?" she asked Deirdre.

Her sister shook her bottle. "Just about empty."

They both laughed, even though there was nothing funny about that.

Halfway into their second bottles, the De Dernberg sisters were still talking about their Aunt and Uncle. By this point, they were both at least flirting with the fact that they were just tracing their own abortive relationships by underlining the insufficiency of a successful one. They still believed what they were saying, and would do so even after the sun came up and their blood alcohol content went down, but the force of their professions was incommensurate to the intensity of their conviction.

So *what* if things hadn't worked out with Hyun-Woo/Kamal? Who needed them, right? Absolute best cast scenario, like, *absolute* best case, lifelong commitment and marriage and a house and a dog or a kid or whatever, and they all *had each other…SO WHAT*? They would still have ambitions and be no closer to achieving them. Maybe even FURTHER from achieving them! A family would be great, right, but what was so great about a family? That was just some stupid, atavistic imperative. The world was overpopulated anyway! More families? What Earth needed was fewer families! Love without families! What?

"I said 'love without families'!" Nur repeated.

"But why not 'love with*in* families'?"

"Ooooh, that's good."

Deirdre shrugged. "I know."

There comes a point in every person's life when pure, molten emotions overflow the lead chalice of reason and motivate him or her to say or do something completely unexpected. And that unexpected thing turns out to be so trite, cliché and played out that it seems completely devoid of the unstoppable sincerity that gave rise to it.

Nur arrived at such a point when she drunkenly leaned over to her sister and said "I love you, Deirdre." Because that's what funny drunks always do in the movies. They get sappy and say *I love you man* and everybody in the audience goes *aaawww* and then chuckles approvingly. It sounded insincere because it was something she'd heard a million times from the mouths of highly paid actors reciting poorly written scripts, but it *was* sincere, goddamnit. She felt more love for her sister in that moment than she knew what to do with. So she repeated herself, but prefaced the refrain with "no, but *seriously*." And through the strange alchemy of human communication, that time it sounded real to her. As real as it felt. Which was very real indeed.

In that moment, Nur and Deirdre De Dernberg knew they *had each other*, and at the same time, they knew that this wasn't enough. They would still have to focus on themselves, still have to strive to accomplish their individual goals. But they could help each other too, because having individual goals didn't preclude one from becoming invested in someone else's too.

And what were their goals right now?

This they wondered, having traded empty stomachs and full bottles for the inverse.

Nur thought about all things trite, cliché and played out. That was too much for a single human mind to consider, so she narrowed the parameters to 'trite, cliché and played out things in dumb romantic comedies'. This was also too much for a single human mind to consider, so she outsourced some of the burden to her sister, because that was one of the benefits of *having each other*.

If their stomachs hadn't been empty, and the bottles had remained full, they would have dismissed their conclusions out of hand. These were not the goals of intelligent young women. And they were nothing if not intelligent young women.

But unfortunately, that night they were most definitely something instead of nothing, in addition to intelligent and young and women (well, almost). They were also drunk and heartbroken. So they waited until their Aunt and Uncle had gone to sleep (they could be confident about this: Uncle Bernard snored, and Aunt Amy couldn't stay in the same room as those oinky snores unless she were just as zonked out), tiptoed down the stairs, and crept out into the balmy midnight.

CHAPTER 37

The first, and very nearly final, challenge they faced that night was where to find pebbles in Boston. Light, aerodynamic pebbles. Oh, they could find rocks. Whichever landscapers had made Brookline beautiful were no strangers to pools of heavy avocado-sized stones. And it was hardly any more challenging to hunt down some lighter alternatives, like mulch. But mulch didn't have much to offer them at present, because Hyun-Woo lived on the second floor and those stupid brown flakes had no sense of urgency when thrown.

Trite, cliché, played out. What fit that bill more perfectly than standing outside the home of your lover and summoning them to the window with the *tap... tap...tap* of well-hurled pebbles?

Nur and Deirdre each had things they wanted to say to their respective gents, but Deirdre had never learned Kamal's address. So, by default, they trekked to Hyun-Woo's, hoping to find more promising pellets in Cambridge than they'd found in Brookline.

They took the familiar route, green line to the red

line, heedless of the fact that they were catching the last trains of the evening. When they finally became heedful of the fact, they shrugged it off. Easy enough to call a cab. Not a problem.

Cambridge seemed to have little more to offer by way of pebbles. It did, however, seem slightly sketchier now than they had remembered it being in the day. Boston grew lethargic once the T shut down, but it kept on moving. This place seemed far more dramatically narcoleptic: at 12:30, Cambridge simply collapsed, toppling headfirst into a glass-doored china cabinet. Oh well. They knew where they were going, and they *had each other*. Buddy system. Not a problem.

Still no pebbles though. Slight problem. Deirdre found a few promising stones, but Nur had to take a pass on them. The cliché was the *tap tap tap*, but the subversion, by which the rock is thrown through the window, ha ha ha, had become just as trite. Perhaps even worse, because a subversion becoming the new norm was just the sort of tragic irony that inexplicably put Nur in a brooding, fatalistic mindset.

They spend forty-five minutes patrolling the area for pebbles, during which time they kept their heads swiveling defensively from homeless person to homeless person. It was a vain neck exercise, as they quickly discovered that the itinerant population of Cambridge was not lying in wait to spring upon them and steal their fifteen bucks or however much they had. With the exception of one guy, who did little more than shout "RAN ROUND IT ON THE WEST SIDE" at them as they passed, they were simply ignored. This too kicked up some of the gloomy silt lining the bottom of Nur's heart.

Even in her state of inebriation, she recognized that her headspace and heartspace were far from ideal, given what she hoped to achieve tonight. What did she hope to achieve tonight? That was a good question.

Reconciliation would be best. Their time together was limited. Sure, she'd learned some life lessons tonight or whatever, but…that was the end of that thought, really. There were no follow-up clauses.

Barring a rapprochement from their pointless belligerence (and what had it been *about*, anyway? Who could even remember) she'd settle for…what word did she want here…vindication? She wanted to hear him say that he was wrong.

Wrong about what?

Oh, nothing in particular. Just everything. Wrong. Wrong to have said what he said to her, wrong to have done what he did to her, wrong to have hurt her.

What, exactly, did he say again? How did he hurt you?

Look, there was no point getting bogged down in the specifics right now. She needed to find a pebble, and that was all there was to it.

Forty-five minutes after their search had begun, they arrived back at Hyun-Woo's. They were empty-handed, and worse, they were beginning to Sober Up. As is always the case in these situations, deep in the booze-addled brain remained a little straight-edge homunculus who vainly screamed reason into the aether.

This Is A Bad Idea, You Will Not Have A Productive Conversation In Your Current State, the homunculus cried.

What? Nur's conscious mind replied

She got as far as spinning in a half-hearted circle, as though the stones she'd seen were just behind her - as opposed to several blocks to the east – when Deirdre had a brainstorm. It was the sort of drizzly thought that could only qualify as a brainstorm when the intellectual landscape looked like the set of a Mad Max film.

"Hey," Deirdre barked with a jerk of the head, "doesn't Hyun-Woo have an intercom?"

"...yes. Yes he does." Nur stopped spinning only after she'd completed the thought.

'Blarb! Blarb blarb? Blaaaaarb!' ranted the homunculus.

Yes, an excellent point, Nur concurred. She hadn't even bothered imagining those four blarbs meant anything. They were nonsense syllables, and as the topic of conversation was love, that felt about right to her. Maybe, at long last, that was the secret to having a productive conversation about thing that didn't make any goddamned sense.

There came a flurry of 'blarbs' at that, but the time for blarb-parsing had passed.

Hyun-Woo had one of those boring intercoms. The kind that had loud buttons, but offers no auditory feedback once you've punched your numbers. Some intercoms will making a little *bbbblll bbbblll* noise, imitative of a ringing telephone. Nur once encountered an intercom that actually played a tune, as though she were on hold with her bank. Hyun-Woo's gave you the clunking buttons, and then nothing until the person being raised got their ass over to the speaker and started speaking.

Which didn't happen, and then continued to not happen.

And that was the other frustration with this kind of intercom; it allowed the buzzer to wonder if the buzzee was even being buzzed. Was the damned contraption even working? No way to know, without a reassuring tinkle or ding-dong noise. One had to simply take it on faith that the landlords and electricians had all done their jobs.

Faith, Nur had always found, was an exhaustible resource. That was the trouble with only having as much faith in something as was allowed by the evidence.

She'd never heard the intercom from inside Hyun-Woo's apartment, and so had no idea how loud it was. Or did it go straight to his phone? She'd heard of some of the more advanced systems working that way, and this *was* a pretty ritzy part of town. Would it even wake him up? Either hello he was asleep, or the intercom was broken. He couldn't be ignoring hello her, at least he couldn't be ignoring *her* specifically, because he didn't is know anybody that there it was her. Unless he had a camer-

Nur turned to her sister. "What?"

Deirdre nodded towards the intercom. "I didn't say anything."

Nur turned to the intercom. "What?"

"Hellooooo?" The intercom asked a third time.

"You have to push the button," Deirdre advised.

Nur pushed the button. "What?"

"Hello?" The intercom repeated.

"Hello!"

"What?"

Nur realized she had still been speaking Seychellois Creole. She slipped into English as gracefully as a bodybuilder slipping in to her childhood onesie. "Hello!"

"Um, hi!"

"Uh-huh."

The intercom thought about this for a moment. "Is that Nur?"

"Uh-huh!"

"…what time is it?"

"Late."

"…why are you here?"

"I want to talk to you." Nur looked to her sister, who nodded approvingly. She'd come to translate, but so far hadn't been needed. Deirdre was proud of her big sis.

"…can it wait until morning?"

Yes was the correct answer, because there was nothing technically time-sensitive about this. Except that tomorrow, the homunculus would regain relative control of the Good Ship De Dernberg. Her liquid courage was fleeting, and she had words and thoughts and feeling burning a hole in the roof of her mouth. If she didn't say them tonight, she'd probably never say them, unless she could contrive to once again get drunk before she and Hyun-Woo parted ways.

That was depressing twice over; their time in America was winding down, and she didn't have the courage to speak her mind without a bit of spirited lubrication. Obstacles to face for another day; she already had one right in front of her for today.

Or she would do, once she'd been let in.

"No, it can't wait," Nur replied.

The intercom said nothing for four agonizing seconds. And then, at long last, it provided some auditory feedback. It said "buzzzzzzzzzzzz".

CHAPTER 38

"I've got a lot of things I want to say to you," Nur said to Deirdre so she could say that to Hyun-Woo.

"Ok," Hyun-Woo replied, which rather took the wind out of Nur's sails. She was hoping for something more in line with 'good, because I have a lot I wan-' and then she would cut him off with 'no, me first!', except not as childish.

But no, he'd gone with 'ok', so she replied with 'good'. And then, for a time, nothing at all.

A lot of things to say, now unsayable at the time of the saying. Because this would be their first real conversation about a relationship, wouldn't it? Must be, because if they'd had one earlier maybe she wouldn't have labored under the misapprehension that what they'd had *was* a relationship.

This was always bizarre ground to break, she'd found. Why that should be the case remained a mystery, but the tightening of her chest that always accompanied the condensation of aeriform emotions into chunky, clunky language was impossible to deny. Feeling for and with another person was confusing, and it could hurt, but in a way it was the easiest thing in the world. Emotions come so naturally.

Talking about it was harder, even though it was just words. But 'just words' could cut deep, and if Nur had heard the little children's rhyme about sticks and stones just then, she would have tracked down the living descendants of its author and spat in their eyes. Sure, it would have been better if she cowed them with words, thus contradicting the hateful theory, but her time was precious to her and she figured they'd get the gist.

"You hurt me, very badly," she whispered in Seychellois Creole. Deirdre passed it along in a more aurally accessible English.

Hyun-Woo took a deep breath, in and out, through his nose. His mouth was a ballpoint slash across his face, underlining an expression she couldn't read. She gave him a second or two to start responding, but he gave no indication of having anything to say. So Nur continued.

"I've thought about it a lot…maybe too much, but I keep thinking about it. And I'm not mad at you." As she waited for Deirdre to translate that much, her conscience got the better of her. "Well, I'm a little mad at you. But this was your first relationship, so I can't exactly blame you for not knowing how to conduct yourself."

As Deirdre ground those words into intermediate English, Nur couldn't help but savor the look on Hyun-Woo's face, just a little bit. He was a child of privilege, well-traveled, well-heeled, well-endowed (financially, but also *wink wink* but also maybe just one *wink* to be honest), and well-educated to the point of fluency in probably north of a dozen languages. He was almost certainly accustomed to being the one speaking with authority on things. He was almost certainly unaccustomed to being spoken down to by a girl several years his junior.

She could only hope Deirdre had managed to retain some of her casual condescension through the process of interpretation. Hyun-Woo's face made it seem as though she had. Good girl.

"I wish you had told me that you only thought of us as friends with benefits. But I also wish I had told you that it was more to me than that. I wish I'd said 'I love you' sooner." Without the buzz of the beer, she probably wouldn't have allowed Deirdre to see her being this candidly emotional. But then again, it had been a while since they'd had those, and they'd done a fair amount of walking. She didn't really *feel* drunk anymore...

"We both made mistakes," Nur mumbled. Deirdre translated this, but with an eyebrow cocked hard towards the ceiling. Her face implied the next words that Nur presented for translation: "What are you thinking?"

Hyun-Woo, taking the arrival of his turn to speak as one might a particularly juicy static shock, cleared his throat and blinked nervously. "Ah..." he began, which Deirdre dutifully repeated. That struck Nur as needlessly cruel, as well as funny. Or maybe not 'as well as', but rather 'therefore'.

"Hm...well, eh...it's...I don't really..." gurgled Hyun-Woo, who was actually fluent in ten languages, eleven if one were to count English, which at the present moment one would be forgiven for not doing. "Ah-huh, um...." And then he hiccupped.

Deirdre turned to Nur, reverting to Seychellois Creole. "Do you need me to translate any of that?"

Nur shook her head, hoping to disguise her smile

with movement.

Hyun-Woo extended his fingers and chopped his hand once through the air, as if to signify that he was ready to cut the shit and get down to business. Which he did, after an unfortunately timed backup hiccup.

Deirdre listened to him speak, nodded, and translated for Nur, with an unhealthy sprinkling of editorial embellishment: "He says he didn't mean to hurt you [*rolling of the eyes*], and that he believed you were always on the same page [*subtle, single-finger 'gag me' gesture*] and he's sorry he didn't realize you were taking it so seriously, and then he just sort of rambled [*not-so-subtle jerking off gesture*] about how you're from different countries and it could never work or whatever."

Nur nodded twice in recognition, then promptly cut out the middle woman and spoke directly to Hyun-Woo in English. "I still love you."

"Oh, *Jesus*," Deirdre accidentally shouted. Nur couldn't blame her – back in their room, they'd charted out a much different course for this conversation. It was all terrifically empowered and independent and modern and who needs to *have somebody* what good does it even do you how would that make you happy what is happiness who am I where am I oh god maybe we should have eaten something before drinking this much.

Those were words. They were words that Nur believed, even now. But she couldn't fight the way she was feeling (and how Deirdre would roll her eyes at *that*). What Hyun-Woo had done wasn't unforgivable. It was shitty, but she couldn't pretend to be an innocent party in the whole thing. Communication cut both ways, and she'd harbored intense feelings for the poor dope without ever telling him. Wouldn't that be a stressful role in which to thrust somebody? Yes, she supposed it would be.

They wouldn't work together, for the long-term. That was a stubborn illusion with which Nur had finally parted company. Hyun-Woo was very likely going to be graduating in the next few weeks, and then he would go to wherever the hell he was going next, to do whatever the hell it was he was going to do. And come August, Nur and Deirdre would return to Seychelles, where they would very likely live until they died. She and Hyun-Woo were on different trajectories, and it was going to be painful to part ways with him, but that didn't help her love him any less.

So…

Why not spend these woefully fleeting days they had left together? It seemed a remarkably simple bit of emotional calculus: would she rather suffer the heartbreak of parting with this guy she loved, and had spent the remainder of her trip with…*or* would she rather suffer a lifetime of regret for having had the opportunity to spend time with the guy she loved, and forgone it in an attempt to save herself the parting heartbreak, which would surely pass in time?

And there it was again, the disparity between feelings as *felt* and feelings as *articulated*. In her heart, she knew her decision to be the right one. When she considered how best to phrase it, it sounded like the sort of thing a cost-benefit analysis CupidTron 4000 might spit out.

But robotics have gotten so advanced, Nur considered, *CupidTron would probably swallow.*

Nur couldn't help but grin at this, because she was the sort of person to grin at her own juvenile jokes, and *not* the sort of person to be ashamed about it.

She was, however, the sort of person to rewind

the thing she'd just done and be ashamed about *that*. To wit: She had said "I still love you" to Hyun-Woo in English, and then fallen silent for what she *hoped* was a number of seconds that could be counted on one hand, and then grinned as though at a juvenile joke.

Equally mortifying was that Hyun-Woo had not filled those indeterminate seconds of silence with effusive reciprocations. He just stared at her as though she were speaking a language that he didn't understand.

And with an eldritch shiver, she realized that she probably was.

CHAPTER 39

Nur had more to say – she and Deirdre really had prepared material before they staggered out the door – but she no longer felt it would find a receptive set of ears in Hyun-Woo. So she tabled it for now, because even if he'd get nothing out of hearing it, she'd still get something out of saying it. Just not right now. Now they really ought to be getting home.

There was no graceful way to make a forceful exit when one had invited oneself over in the first place, which was about as forceful an entrance as one could make under the good graces of the law. So Nur just nodded to Deirdre and said "alright let's get out of here," and thankfully Deirdre nodded back and said "yeah good idea." And then they left.

They got halfway to the T station before Deirdre remembered that it wouldn't be running, so they trekked back to Hyun-Woo's apartment, hoping to glom onto the Wi-Fi from outside. Their hopes were in vain. So Nur gathered up her pride, then followed the CupidTron 4000's lead and swallowed. The intercom buttons made satisfying clunk clunk noises and then there was no further auditory feedback which was very annoying, yes yes sure whatever, just won't this moment please end.

It didn't. The moment kept on rocking and rolling.

And rocking.

And rolling.

Nur punched the right buttons once again, and once again got nothing for her trouble.

. . .

Trouble, that was a word.

Nur had one of those ridesharing apps on her phone. As soon as they got Wi-Fi, they could call it up and some friendly stranger would come pick them up. Except it wasn't as shady as that, except it probably was.

As soon as they got Wi-Fi.

She did the clunkity clunk clunk thing again. The intercom did the nothing again.

They could also have looked up the number for a traditional cab company.

Or walking directions back home. Boston was such a small city, after all.

But they had no data plans here.

They needed the motherloving Wi-Fi to get home.

From Cambridge.

Cambridge, where they had spent hardly any time. If they were back in Brookline, or Boston proper, they could walk up to the locked doors of any number of businesses and utilize their network. Literally every establishment they walked in to, restaurant or retail or public restroom, the first thing they did was inquire about Wi-Fi. On some of the smaller, more commercially populated avenues, they'd racked up so many network passwords they could walk up and down either side of the street and enjoy a nearly unbroken connection.

But they had never come up here, and when they *had*, it was always to see Hyun-Woo. And nothing else. They never wandered.

No! That wasn't true!

"Hey!" Nur shouted at Deirdre, who was standing right next to her and didn't appreciate being shouted at. "Sorry. But that night Hyun-Woo and I, um, well, you were just sort of floating around Cambridge, right?"

"…yeah? Are you asking if I got onto any Wi-Fi networks?"

"Yeah!"

"I didn't."

"Why not?!"

Deirdre's mouth formed a word but no sound came out, which was the most effective way of conveying how bizarre a question that was. Her mouth formed more words, this time with sound behind them. "Because I wanted to see Cambridge, not my friend's selfies?"

"That is a very fair point."

"I was trying to live in the present, you know?"

"I do. I'm proud of you, with the caveat that a more…*generic* girl of your generation would have been much more helpful right now."

Deirdre snorted. "*My* generation."

"Alright, *our* generation."

"Our problem is we aren't generic enough, is what you're saying."

Nur gave an exaggerated sigh. "Pretty much."

They smiled at each other.

Deirdre's smile broke first. "So what do we do?"

"I guess…find a 24 hour store? That maybe has Wi-Fi? Or that could at least help us call a cab?"

"Alright."

Remaining calm, they calmly descended the steps

of Hyun-Woo's apartment and walked calmly down the street, heads on a calm swivel for a 24 hour store that maybe had Wi-Fi or could at least help them call a cab. They didn't talk because they were so calm as they listened to the calmness of the calm night while they calmed their way down the calmy calmy calm calm.

Nur kept her mouth shut tightly against the eternal whimper that had hollowed her out and was already tired of its shell.

This was very, very, very, exceptionally super very much bad. They had essentially blackmailed their relatives into giving them alcohol, promised they wouldn't sneak out, only to do just that, and now they were stuck on the wrong side of the Charles and it was tomorrow.

We wouldn't have done this if we hadn't been drunk, Nur reaffirmed to herself for the umpteenth time. The thought was far less affirming than she'd hoped it would be, and fared worse and worse with each re-.

On their journey they would sometimes stop to try the network of some random restaurant or store. In their run of legitimate network password acquisitions, they had been frequently amused to find that some stores made their password the same name as the network itself, or the name of the store. With calm calmocity they tried this trick on some particularly dull-looking stores' networks, and eventually found that luck was on their side.

Unfortunately, it was *bad* luck.

After what felt like hours, because it was in fact hours, they came upon a gas station with an attendant in the square fluorescent heaven. Holding hands, because at some point they had been so calm that they grabbed each others' hand without realizing it, the De Dernberg sisters slouched through the door and up to the counter.

"Excuse me," Deirdre began, "but do you have Wi-Fi here?"

"No."

"Oh." She looked around her immediate surroundings for the cheapest item. She grabbed a pack of gum. The same brand of gum, Nur couldn't help but notice, that Deirdre had stolen as her first act on American soil.

Deirdre shook the gum at the attendant. "If I buy this, can I use the Wi-Fi?"

"No."

"…do you actually not have Wi-Fi, or is the Wi-Fi only for employees?"

"Both. Are you gonna buy the gum or not?"

Nur put a hand on Deirdre's shoulder, and the shoulder shrugged it off immediately. "Look, my sister and I are in a little bit of trouble, and we need to call a cab home. Can you help us?"

The attendant, who looked old enough to have kids himself, sighed as dramatically as he could. "Sure, give me a minute." They gave him sixteen, which he used to futz around behind the counter doing…*something*, whatever it was he had to be doing at…oh *Christ*, 2:14 AM now. Finally, the attendant mustered up his courage and heroically called a taxi cab. "It'll be here in a minute," he told them, but they wouldn't be fooled. Time was relative, never more so than it was for this guy.

"Thank you," the De Dernberg sisters replied in unison. And then they waited.

One minute later, at 3:27 AM, the cab arrived to pick them up. Delirious from exhaustion, headachy from the empty-tummy drinking she'd done, and still amused by the brand of gum to which Deirdre seemed drawn in any context, Nur half expected to be picked up by the same cabbie as drove them from the airport to Uncle Bernard's on that first day. Boy, wouldn't *that* have been something.

But it wasn't anything, so it was nothing. It was a different cabbie she'd never seen before. What would it have meant if they had gotten the same cabbie? Nothing. Wouldn't have been something, come to think of it. It'd have been funny, but it would have meant nothing.

These were the thoughts massaging Nur's skull from the inside, as the gentle rocking and humming of the cab lulled her from the outside. Public transportation always made her sleepy. Well, all transportation did. She just liked to say 'public' because that made it sound like she didn't get sleepy when she was the one driving. Which she did. But which she wasn't now. So she could sleep.

Deirdre crashed just as hard, and the cabbie had to wake them both up when they pulled up outside Uncle Bernard's. "We're here," he cooed to them, as though they had adopted him as one of their own. Weirdo.

Nur looked up the house and died.

Because the lights were in the living room.

Because the lights *hadn't* been on in the living room when they left. Nur was absolutely, positively certain about that.

The cabbie said how much the ride was, and Nur put her credit card through the thing. He could charge a million dollars for all she cared; it wasn't as though it would matter. She was a dead person, after all.

The dead woman turned to elbow her sister, to draw her attention to those awful incandescent bulbs burning behind the wretched curtains of despair, but there was no need. Deirdre had already seen, and she too was a dead person now.

United in death as they never were in life, the Departed De Dernbergs shuffled up the walk, tried the door, and found it unlocked.

As though it mattered, the late Nur pushed the door open slowly slowly slowly. The door scolded her with a flatulent creak she couldn't recall it ever having made before. Nur closed her eyes against the oak's reproach, and nuzzled the rest of the way into the overly lit room.

After exactly one of the gas station attendant's minutes, Nur opened her eyes.

She saw Uncle Bernard and Aunt Amy sitting on the couch, stiff as statues. On the floor before them were two very familiar bags, fully packed, with plastic drag-handles extended.

"Your flight leaves at 11:30, so we should leave in a few hours. Your parents will pick you up from the airport."

The corpses wept.

CHAPTER 40

Plenty obvious in hindsight, sure. When they snuck out, Uncle Bernard had been snoring, and Aunt Amy had been in the room with him. And everybody knew Aunt Amy couldn't be in the same room as those oinky snores unless she was just as zonked out as he clearly was.

Flawless logic, save one rather obvious wrinkle: human beings take anywhere from fifteen to twenty minutes to fall asleep. Aunt Amy was in the room with Uncle Bernard, well on her way to slumber, but *not yet there*. She was awake, and sufficiently well-attuned to her house's nocturnal complaints to recognize an atypical, descending creaking on the stairs. Even Bernard's thunderous snores couldn't smother the furtive foreign fanfare.

She flipped the covers back, padded over to the window, and watched with a heavy heart as Nur and Deirdre staggered down the street. Could she sprint down the stairs, whip open the door and summon them back? Probably not. Her knees ached in anticipation of such a high-impact course of action. The ostensibly obvious choice would be to rack the window open and call to them, but that would awaken Bernard. Which she didn't want to do.

Not because he would be angry, as Nur and Deirdre might have suspected. Oh, he certainly would be angry, but not as angry as Amy. It would have surprised the girls to no end to discover which of their homestay relatives was possessed of the more volatile temper. No, Amy didn't want to awaken Bernard for his own sake; because he would be *hurt*. Nur and Deirdre were his blood relatives, and he wanted desperately to have a good relationship with them. He wanted to have a good relationship with *everyone* in his family. He had chosen a life on the other side of the world, and he rarely if ever had cause to regret his decision. But Amy knew that there were times when he longed to feel closer to his kin. Contrary to what Nur and Deirdre suspected, Uncle Bernard wasn't afraid of their parents. There was no monetary reason for his desire to remain in their good graces, or for changing his surname. Bernard De Dernberg was, quite simply, desperate to feel a part of his own family.

He made a deal with his nieces because he assumed a.) it would never get back to his brother in Seychelles, and b.) that it would encourage his nieces to feel closer to him. A shared secret and all that good stuff. Amy knew how much it meant to Bernard, that he was able to see eye to eye with the girls.

And there they went, betraying his trust. She was mad about it, you bet she was. She wanted nothing more than to punch through the window and shriek at the girls until they came scrambling back inside. But that would break Bernard's heart, and despite outward appearances, his was a large heart easily broken.

Amy went downstairs and paced a bit, wondering what she could do. She didn't know where they were going, and she couldn't call them to find out. Which way had they gone? They stepped out of the house and turned right, but quickly hit an intersection. Had she been thinking, she would have rushed downstairs as quietly as possible, to try to see whether they'd gone left, right, or straight at the intersection. But she hadn't been thinking, not about that at least, and so she didn't. So she could hop in the car and have a 1/3 chance of driving in the right direction. Except by now they'd almost certainly hit another intersection, hadn't they? So her chances further diminished. And so on, with each passing moment.

So she paced some more, because that was something she could do. Unfortunately, she wasn't the only one on familiar terms with the house's usual moans and groans.

Uncle Bernard came tromping down the stairs, wondering what was wrong. And Aunt Amy, not sure how to cover for the girls and not feeling particularly inclined to, told him. Deep in those flinty poker-player's eyes, she watched his heart break in real time. Nobody else would have seen it, because nobody else knew Bernard the way she did. And how lucky they all were, to be spared a spectacle of such restrained agony.

Against her better judgment, she resented those girls. They were young, and drunk, and they didn't know any better. But still. They should have.

And they would. Because this was what they called a 'teachable moment'.

Bernard took some convincing. At first he was worried, as was Amy, beneath the simmering rage. But they were big girls, and Boston was a pretty safe city, and rage and concern could coexist quite easily. So they sat tight, confident that the girls would return, planning for that eventuality. Because that was something they could do.

Calling Bernard's brother was a big step. Bringing him up to speed on the whole scenario would damage Bernard's relationship with him, *and* with his nieces. He'd spent the better part of a year trying (and, Amy couldn't bring herself to tell him, mostly failing) to strike the balance between what would endear him to his brother and what would endear him to his nieces. There was precious little overlap between those two categories, so it was a perilous high wire he was walking. Now here he was, pondering a deliberate leap into the yawning chasm below him, just to…teach the girls a lesson? Why should he suffer for their mistakes?

Well, Amy pointed out, they would be paying for their mistakes, far more than he would. His brother would very likely thank him for having brought this to his attention. The whole 'giving the girls beer' thing wouldn't be received with a great deal of gratitude, and no Bernard, you can't just gloss over that fact, yes it would be their word against yours and yours would almost certainly win the day, but it was important to have integrity in moments such as these.

So Bernard dialed his brother at an unreasonable hour, and his brother picked up at a reasonable hour, and they spoke across the geographical gulf of temporal reason.

Bernard's brother very tersely announced his intention to call the airline, and hung up, presumably to do just that. As per his instructions, Bernard and Amy gathered up the girls' belongings, folded them, packed them up as neatly as they could, and dragged the suitcases down the stairs. With eerily punctuality, the phone rang just as they finished bringing the luggage into the living room. It was Bernard's brother, calling back with the updated flight information. Nur and Deirdre were no longer leaving in August. They were leaving later that day.

Once again, Amy looked into Bernard's eyes and saw the things he would never – *could* never – put into words. But they were things he would never have to. They *had each other,* and part of the beauty of *having* someone is *getting* them. Not in the sense of 'comprehension', that one suddenly understands one's partner perfectly well. Quite the opposite, really. This *getting* is meant in the same sense that one *gets* exposed to an airborne disease. *Getting* somebody means you get *all* of them. The contradictions and the mysteries and the absurdities, you get all of the things that don't make any goddamned sense and you say *ah, right*, because that's the person you love and you'll never fully understand them, you'll never come *close* to understanding them, and the more one *gets* of someone the further away the mere concept of 'understanding' vanishes, because people don't make any goddamned sense no matter how hard you try to bend them into a comprehensible set of drives and instincts and psychoses and interests, they'll always surprise you if you let them.

Bernard, hard-edged, tough-as-nails Bernard, looked like he could cry right then. If he had, it would have been the first time Amy had ever seen him do it – outwardly, at least. She's seen such sadness in him before, but it had never leaked out. Tears would have surprised her, and she'd have held him and comforted him without a second thought, because she loved him, and what was the odd surprise or two in the face of that wonderful fact?

But he didn't surprise her. He just flopped down on the couch, shoulders slumped, saying nothing. And that was alright too – she flopped down next to him and held him just the same.

They waited like that for a long while, until the door opened and the girls walked in on a great big surprise of their own.

CHAPTER 41

What was the last thing I said to him?

Nur wracked her brains as she and Deirdre tumbled into backseat of Uncle Bernard's mid-sized crossover. She continued wracking them as they weaved their way back through Boston. The streets that seemed so familiar from the sidewalk looked absolutely foreign to her now that she was on them, being driven along them with relentless attention to the speed limit, out towards Logan International. The ride was long and silent, which gave plenty of time for wracking.

What was *it?*

Probably something like, 'ah, anyway, we'll be going'. Had she said it to *him*, or to Deirdre to be passed along? She couldn't even remember that. This was enraging.

She imagined all of the Hollywood endings. This was the part where the heroine seemingly passes beyond the point of no return, because that's where the tension always is. Now how would she get out of this? Maybe they'd pull up to a red light and she would see Hyun-

Woo on the street corner. What a coincidence! She'd leap out and they'd have one final, poignant moment together. And then, because she wasn't a fucking idiot, they'd exchange contact information.

Then again, maybe she *was*, because they *hadn't*. She didn't even know his last name. What a glaring oversight!

The romantic in her made reassuring noises. *No no, it's so much better this way. You two had a wonderful thing, made all the more beautiful for its isolation in your lives.*

Bullshit. They had a semi-wonderful thing that got sort of fucked up at the end, and she'd still have wanted Hyun-Woo as a pen pal. Maybe, given the width and breadth of his travel, they'd even find themselves in the same city one day, and reconnect.

A long shot, made long enough to wrap around the known universe and tie itself into a bow by the fact that they had no way to let each other know if they were in the same city. What, were they going to bump into each other at a café in Victoria? Smart money was on Hyun-Woo coming to stay at the De Dernberg Towers, if his business brought him into Seychelles for whatever reason…but did he *know* that's where she worked? Did he even know *her* last name?

They had each others' phone numbers, but Hyun-Woo's was what the Americans on TV shows called a "burner". It was disposable. So he had her phone number. That's what it all came down to. He could reach out to her, and if he didn't, or didn't think to get her number off of his phone before he "burned" it, then that was that.

Still, there was some hope to be found there.

Nur sighed and leaned her head against the window. The fact that she was being taken to the airport to be taken to Seychelles hadn't sunk in yet. Everything had happened so quickly, so abruptly, it had a dreamlike surrealism to it. Of all the increasingly improbable intercessions she imagined (a taxi cab screeches to a halt in front of Uncle Bernard's car, and who gets out of the driver's seat but HYUN-WOO!), she hadn't yet gotten to "this is all just a dream", but she would. Right around the time she started seeing planes taking off and landing in the distance, she'd start to wonder if this wasn't maybe a nightmare.

None of this tracked to her understanding of relationships. Granted, she'd never been in a real one, and wondered if she could say what she'd had with Hyun-Woo fit the bill, but she had firm expectations. Those expectations included second chances and romantic gestures and tearful apologies and beautiful reconciliations and giddy recollections of the time when things almost fell apart but they didn't let it, they couldn't let it and so they didn't. Mostly her expectations were about time, having it and spending it and looking forward to doing more of both.

But this? This was garbage. Where was the closure? Where was the grand summation of what they had meant to each other? Hyun-Woo had meant a lot to her, in ways she found nearly impossible to articulate in any language. He was the first man she had ever loved, probably. The first man? Why stop there? She wasn't especially close with her family, which meant Hyun-Woo was the first *person* to whom she had ever said "I love you", and absolutely meant it (it would be a few minutes before Nur realized that this was tough luck for Deirdre and the rest of her family).

It was impossible, she felt, to love someone without changing yourself. "Without being changed" might better describe it, but it made love sound like some alien parasite that gutted you like a pumpkin and carved you a new face. No, it was more self-sufficient than that. She'd like to think feeling such an overwhelming connection to another human being made her a better person, as she certainly wished she could be. But that might be overly optimistic. It made her different, and she could feel it. She looked forward to discovering just how different over the next few years of her life.

He'd also, in an indirect way, brought her closer to her sister. That was something she would get to take with her forever. Particularly now that they were heading off to apocalyptic punishments that would likely follow them for years to come, it was a gift to know she and her sister would face the reckoning hand in hand. They *had each other* now; *having* wasn't just for lovers. Deirdre wasn't through with puberty (or perhaps that would be best phrased the other way around), so Nur fully anticipated plenty of strife in their future. But they had a positive bedrock now, which was more than they had on the car ride in to the city last August.

Nur reached out and placed her hand on Deirdre's. Without turning her eyes from the window, Deirdre flipped her hand over and wrapped her fingers gently around Nur's. They sat that way for the rest of the ride.

It was the soft squeeze of her sister's hand that dispelled the final illusions for Nur. This wasn't the moment where something suddenly happened, or someone suddenly had a change of heart. She was leaving. Not just the relationship, but also her time in America (and, dear god, it was only now that she realized how much she had fallen for this strange, slightly gross country!) was over in an instant. No prelude, no fanfare, not even a thank you ma'am, just wham bam. And that was a lesson right there. Sometimes that's how things ended. With neither a bang nor a whimper, but an

The Year of Uh | 259

(absence)

If Nur and Deirdre hadn't been straining to fight back tears, they might have noticed that Bernard was struggling against his own ocular waterworks. These girls never seemed to have taken to him in the way he would have hoped, but he was going to miss them just the same.

Aunt Amy sniffled for a bit from the passenger seat, but limited her outward grief to her presence in the car. She didn't have to come, but she did, because she wanted to see the girls off. That said something. She just hoped the girls were listening to it.

They pulled up to the departures curb. Uncle Bernard clicked his hazards on and unlocked the back. Being in the backseats, Nur and Deirdre got out and made to pull their own luggage onto the curb, but Uncle Bernard insisted on doing it himself.

And that was it. They said their goodbyes, made slightly awkward by the circumstances, and went their separate ways. Nur led Deirdre into the terminal, passports at the ready.

Oh, hell, she realized too late. If she'd left her passport at Uncle Bernard's, that would be one of those romcom things that could happen to bring her back from beyond the point of no return. Too bad she hadn't.

She sniffed and stepped through the door, feeling a fresh sense of perspective hit her as hard as the air conditioning.

What she'd had with Hyun-Woo *was* beautiful, partially for its brevity. She conceded this to her latent romanticism. He had helped her become a better person, or at least different, but on reflection yes, perhaps better, and she could only hope she had reciprocated in some small way. Or not so small. She had been his first, hadn't she?

Despite the punitive darkness in front of her, she smiled. There was so much light and warmth behind her, and if it was, well, behind her, she felt privileged that she'd gotten to pass through it.

Besides, she mulled on the threshold of laughter, *he's got my phone number!* Looking ahead, perhaps those were slanting rays of light cutting through the stormclouds. And who knew what was on the other side of those thunderheads? *There's only one way to find out,* she thought in a jaunty voice not quite her own. *Perhaps we'll turn out to be Seoul Mates after all!* Boosted by the joy of emergent fluency, evinced by her first English-language pun, Nur trekked to the terminal with a hopeful spring in her step.

She and Hyun-Woo never saw each other again.

EPILOGUE
DEPARTURE

There was and remains a saying in America that Nur and Deirdre never learned. They probably would have, had they gotten to stick around for their full year. It wasn't anything especially difficult to parse; just something to the effect of how every cloud has a silver lining. And in case there was any lingering confusion over the symbolism, their own situation would have clarified. There was valuable metal to be found limning those metaphorical, frostbitten thunderheads looming in their immediate future, and in time it would be found. But there were more immediate clouds of a more literal persuasion, that yielded results in kind.

Immediate and literal, that is.

Somewhere in the world, there was a storm. It was an actual storm, featuring actual atmospheric disturbances and actual drops of rain the size of cherries that had a way of falling directly into one's eyeball. It was the sort of storm that's almost always happening somewhere around the globe without your knowledge, because if the storm isn't happening to you, it might as well not be happening at all.

The storm wasn't happening to Nur and Deirdre. The sky over Logan International was, by now, a pillowed azure, like the ocean reflected in a pearl. But, in a sense, the storm was happening to them. Because it was happening in the path of their flight. Or maybe one of their *three* connections? They weren't entirely clear, nor did they need to be. The voice garbling out of the loudspeaker gave them a great deal of extraneous information, when it could (and should) have announced *your flight has been delayed* and then returned from whence it came.

And so Nur and Deirdre's American adventure was extended by three whole hours. They spent a large portion of this time trying to coax a bag of chips from a selfish vending machine. In went their coins – coins they wouldn't be needing back in Seychelles, coins they might as well be rid of – F7 went the buttons, *whrrrrrr* went the lazy spiral ring holding back the colorful bag of the flavored favor…and that was the end of it. The bag didn't fall. It just hung in there.

Deirdre slapped the machine. Nur laughed and put more coins in, because there was no point in saving them. When could they ever expect to come back here? She punched in F7 once again. The ring *whrrrrrr*ed some more, and the first bag fell…and caught on a sleeve of cookies, leaning out over its own silver spiral railing. The second bag from F7 caught on the ring just as the first one had.

At this point, Nur's laughter had escalated to something near mania, and it was catching. Deirdre shook her head and fished some more coins out of her pocket. This time they hit the keys for H7, the slot of the hated cookie sleeve. The machine *whrrrrrr*ed, but that was it. The ring didn't spin, the cookies didn't tumble, the chips didn't fall, all things stayed the same.

The De Dernberg sisters were doubling over with hilarity. They scavenged their pockets and purses for more coins, and came up empty. This struck them as a spectacular punchline, though they could never have articulated the setup. It was all just funny, and that was that.

Beyond those coins, they didn't have much cash on them. They'd set up their bankcards to handle foreign transactions, and considered relying on these safer than carrying cash. What a bummer! If they'd loaded up on greenbacks, and now had fistfuls of currency that would be no good to them just a few hours from now, they'd have an excuse to go on a bit of an airport bender, spending up a storm without zero guilt, because what else were they going to do with that money?

Granted, they should have been glad they'd have that money to spend on things more substantive than neck pillows and Panda Express, but the cheap thrill of going on a last-minute tear in the airport would have been well worth the actual expense. Independently, they considered saying 'fuck it' and doing it anyway, making it rain plastic and foreign transaction fees. Each independently decided against it, though several years later they would reminisce about their final moments in America, and learn just how similar were their wavelengths in that moment.

Even then, they were planting the seeds of sisterhood that would bear so much fruit throughout the rest of their lives.

They milled around the airport, not spending any more money together but spending plenty more time, until whatever it was that had caused their plane's delay resolved itself (as these things sometimes do), and the 767 that would take them to Paris, their first and most glamorous layover, came whining up to the gate.

The last-minute seats their parents somehow secured for them were way in the back of the plane. No surprise there. This meant they were the last to board, and would be the last to debark. Joke's on mom and dad though – that was just more time for them to spend with one another. And, more importantly, to not spend with mom and dad. Oof, that was going to be rough, but there was no sense dwelling on it. Pain was coming their way, so why not savor the small pleasures to be found in these preceding moments?

Like how they had laughed at the vending machine, or like how they could lift the armrest between them for a little extra shoulder space, or like how the view from their window was unobstructed by those pesky wings one gets in the more centrally located seats, or like how they were right next to the bathroom, which was a wonderful convenience and would remain so as long as nobody went in after, say, going on a last-minute tear at Panda Express. Surely the crew had air fresheners though, so that was alright.

They settled into their seats, falling silent as the flight attendants attended to their duties, slamming overhead compartments shut and politely suggesting certain people bring their chairs to the full upright position. Deirdre leaned her head on Nur's shoulder and almost immediately began to doze. They hadn't gotten very much sleep the night before, after all. Being in the window seat, Deirdre could just as easily have leaned up against the Plexiglas. Nur supposed she was a softer cushion, because she wasn't aware of how sharp her shoulders were. Other factors had gone into Deirdre's choice of headrest.

The plane made its various noises, humming and dinging and thwunking and finally roaring, and then they were airborne. Nur's ears popped, as they always did. She'd forgotten to get gum. Drats! Perhaps it was nonsense, but she'd been told that chewing gum helped with the pressure of takeoff and landing. Something to do with keeping your jaw moving. Or something.

Carefully, so as not to wake her, Nur reached past Deirdre, to the purse she'd stuffed under the seat in front of her. Delicately, because mustn't wake her now, Nur pawed through Deirdre's bag in search of gum.

She found none, which figures. Would it have killed Deirdre to steal a pack, ha ha ha, just this once?

Amused by her own wry irony, Nur returned Deirdre's bag to its proper place with slightly less elegance than she'd brought to the extraction.

She settled for pinching her nostrils shut, clamping her lips together and blowing. This…forced the air to her ears, or something? It was another method of relieving the pressure, and she was pleased to find that it worked. Who had told her about this one? Deirdre, wasn't it? Deirdre who didn't need to know it after all; she remained fast asleep. If the pressure was bothering her at all, it wasn't enough to wake her up. Lucky.

Anyway, Nur knew from last August's journey that the descent was always much worse.

As the plane reached its cruising altitude, Nur took a deep breath and rested her head atop her sister's, eyes lolling heavily towards the window. They were above the clouds now, and the sun turned them golden - an endless field of perfectly roasted-marshmallows, i.e. Nur's conception of heaven.

Oh, sure, somewhere out there the marshmallows burned and wept acid tears for the celestial s'mores that could have been. Even if Nur couldn't see them, the belated departure of their plane attested to their presence. Somewhere. But that was fine, because the world was round, and in both principle and practice (though the practice was so impractical as to be, in principle, impossible) they could just keep going, through the crackling pillars of heavenly discontent, through the raging winds and slanting rains, keep going going going until they had come all the way back around to this oasis of rolling down, comforter of the gods, where everything was as it should be, and always would be, and if not here, then somewhere else.

ABOUT THE AUTHOR

Jud hopes you enjoyed this book.

 @judwiding
judwiding.com

CPSIA information can be obtained
at www.ICGtesting.com
Printed in the USA
BVHW032228131218
535609BV00001B/1/P